T0196253

Other Works by Daniel B. Hunt

Poetry
The Modern Day Poet
North Wind Muse

Fiction
Stories of the Midnight Sun

Science Fiction
The Dark Abyss – A Dryden Universe Collection (Pending)

The Eclipsing of

SIRUS C

A Dryden Universe Novel

DANIEL B. HUNT

THE ECLIPSING OF SIRUS C
A DRYDEN UNIVERSE NOVEL

This is a work of fiction. All of the characters, names, incidents, organizations, and dialogue in this novel are either the products of the author's imagination or are used fictitiously.

iUniverse books may be ordered through booksellers or by contacting:

iUniverse
1663 Liberty Drive
Bloomington, IN 47403
www.iuniverse.com
1-800-Authors (1-800-288-4677)

The Dryden Experiment multiverse is used by permission under the Creative Commons License.

Cover Art, "The Citadel", by Gavin Revitt, Copyright 2015, used by permission from the artist, http://www.kokoroartstudio.co.uk/.

Any people depicted in stock imagery provided by Thinkstock are models, and such images are being used for illustrative purposes only. Certain stock imagery © Thinkstock.

ISBN: 978-1-4917-7154-9 (sc)
ISBN: 978-1-4917-7155-6 (hc)
ISBN: 978-1-4917-7156-3 (e)

Library of Congress Control Number: 2015910560

Print information available on the last page.

iUniverse rev. date: 09/18/2015

To my beloved daughters, Mykenzie and Lindsey

O MEGA COMPANY stopped in the dark. Quiet. Tense. But ready. Their weapons clinked, and their eyes strained as they searched for the foe. A damp morning breeze rose through a dark carpet of ash left after yesterday's raging fire. Tendrils of smoke still danced here and there like scattered will-o'-the-wisps from the matted earth, twirling and dissipating in the breeze. The first gray clouds of an approaching storm slowly gathered over the field, mixing and churning with quiet unease. In the far distance, the towering shadows of Cave Dweller's Mountain seemed to hem in the world.

Captain Jean Joyce watched the smoldering ground for an instant, letting her mind linger on thoughts of home. She adjusted the weapon in her hands and allowed her eyes to drift over the dark field to where the planet's moon seemed to kiss the edge of the horizon. Soon, Jean knew, the system's sun, Sirus C, would arch upward and intersect the sleepy moon in a spectacular eclipse. *How could the universe retain such beauty in the midst of so much suffering and pain?* she wondered.

Had her father seen such beauty too? What sights haunted him in the silence of his dreams?

Jean had followed her father's example and joined the Federation Marines. But he had not warned her of these moments. He had said almost nothing at all.

Jean watched a curious display of lightning as it swept from one corner of the dark sky to the other. *At least the rain will wash the smell away*, she thought. The musty odor of ash and the acidic smell of the dead were not completely screened by her Hadrellie and

Killitz multipurpose FAMP-BH23, high-impact battle helmet's air-purifying system. With each breath, Jean filled her lungs with the musk. Here and there, sometimes alone, but mostly in small clumps of four or five, the enemy dead were strewn like dice upon the field. Jean did her best to ignore them.

Little Paradise? Maxim? Jean chewed the thought. Whatever the name, the planet was at the center of a war that stretched back for twenty-five years. The soil had gorged on the blood of thousands of soldiers. The newly dead in Edmund's field were just the latest victims to be left rotting beneath the unforgiving, alien moon.

"Rest period is over," Jean said into her tactical radio network. "Move out."

Omega Company rose like ghosts, figurative shadows strewn in battle order against the blackened field. Jean stood up from her kneeling position. She was lean and fairly tall for a woman. She could look most men in the eye, adding to her command presence. She reached a reflective hand up to brush her short-cut, auburn hair, only to have her hand slide slickly off her battle helmet. She swiveled her head to the left and right, watching.

Yet it was almost impossible to see anything with the naked eye. Jean's commander's visor, with its enhanced graphic interface, allowed her to short-focus on a tactical display. Small blips of light represented each of her marines. The blips were overlaid on a scrolling terrain map, showing the company's formation on her heads-up display. She critically studied the display for a moment.

Jean then looked out to the unit's front. Only the occasional slope of ground, rise of dirt, or rare, smoldering tree stump offered any semblance of cover. The marines were marching through an open graveyard toward an unknown yet certainly bloody conclusion.

"Spread out," she ordered. "We're too close together."

People tended to clump together. An old survival trait hardwired into the human psyche through countless generations of evolution, it was dangerous on the modern battlefield. A single shell or automatic fire could wipe out a clump of marines in the blink of an eye.

It didn't help that this was a fool's mission, Jean thought. It was tactically stupid. But orders were orders.

Still, Jean grimaced. She knew what was coming.

The Consortium troops were there, hidden in the dirt, waiting to do battle. It was inevitable and unavoidable. Fate had brought her and Omega Company to this place. The company was being drawn inexorably deeper into the open. People were going to die. Yet all Jean could do was push forward.

Though Jean thought this tactical movement not the most sound maneuver, she was all for pushing after the enemy. Never let them rest. Push and push and push until their command structures crumbled, along with their will to fight. Only a major encounter would end the fighting on Maxim. And Jean preferred a large bloodbath to a slow bleeding. *This is it*, she thought, *the final campaign*. It lay there, ahead of them, in the distant, hulking mountains. That was where the battle for Maxim would be decided. The marines could all taste it. A Federation victory would reverberate through the systems, weakening the will of the Consortium while strengthening the Federation's resolve. It would be a true step toward ultimate victory.

Most importantly for Jean, defeating the enemy would get her and her marines off Maxim and headed for other distant shores. Though full of natural beauty, they were all through with the planet. They hated the look of it—every flowered field; every branch of every tree; and even the crisp, terra-formed air left a bad taste in their mouths. Let it end.

"Draiger," the captain said into the microphone that hung just off her lips. "You're bunching up again. Spread out."

"Acknowledged, Captain Joyce. Spread out, you dogs!" Draiger barked to his platoon.

Jean watched with satisfaction as the red blips on her faceplate display began to separate, moving out in a wedge. She pressed a stud on her wristband, and her visor turned green, activating her night vision. Jean liked the heads-up display well enough, but to get a true understanding of the platoon's maneuver required watching them with her own eyes. Making sure she avoided looking directly at the moon, she glanced right and back, watching Draiger's platoon redeploy along the company skirmish line. She pressed a second stud, and the virtual view of the battlefield widened, showing her the position of the support platoon on the far left.

She nodded to herself, satisfied, and then spoke a brief command into her microphone. "All of you, keep your distances."

She waited for a moment, watching as her troops slipped across Edmund's Field.

Captain Joyce knew that the heavy guns of the battalion were shifting invisibly as the company continued to advance. Fire Command would keep the guns trained a few hundred meters in front of the maneuvering marines, allowing for rapid artillery support. The knowledge did little to ease her fears.

Jean tried again to call in the birds to lift her troops off the ground and deposit them closer to the mountains, knowing before she did so that she would be denied flight support. She had no qualm about fighting, but an ambush here would just delay the inevitable combat later on and weaken her unit's strength. However, Jean's commanding officer, ever conscious of his supply routes, felt differently, and he was in charge. Nevertheless, Jean punched in the request. A flashing amber light instantly denied it. The beacon seemed irritated.

Well—she sighed—*I tried.*

The sun had begun to rise, a faint halo creeping over the crest of the setting moon. A rare thing on Jean's home world of Baile Mac Cathain, the eclipse was a common occurrence on Maxim. Sirus C, the large orange star dominating the system, rose every morning behind the planet's moon. It had long ceased to fascinate her, and it was dangerous right now. The eclipse effectively cut their distance vision by nearly two-thirds.

Jean flipped her visor up, letting her eyes adjust to the murky light, and her breath rose before her in a steamy cloud. Her mouth filled with the full power of the musk of death. It clung to the roof of her mouth and wrapped like film about her teeth. She almost gagged. She was about to lower her visor again when a tentative drop of rain tapped cold against her cheek. She brushed the water with her free hand and smiled. Rain would work to her advantage. She let the cool air flow against her face for a second more and then flipped her visor back down.

Omega Company swept forward, electronically enhanced eyes and ears straining in the muffled colors of Maxim's dawn. The rain began falling in lazy morning drops, splattering on the burnt ground. Then with a sudden gust, the rain came heavy and fast, quickly forming puddles. The unit sloshed through them, their chameleon-like battle suits shifting through dull colors of brown, green, and gray.

"Captain," Senior Lieutenant Kross's voice metallically hissed in her ear, "I can't cover the front much longer. My fire is masked."

"Okay, Kross." Jean directed a command to her other platoon leaders. "Draiger, Smiley, hold up here until Kross gets the support platoon on line."

The rest of Omega Company hunkered down as the support platoon moved forward. After a brief time, Kross's platoon arrived, and Jean gave the order to begin alternating bounds by platoon. During the brief wait for Kross's platoon, the clouds had become a solid blanket of black across the sky, and angry cries of thunder rang across the flat ground. The rising sun was now completely hidden by the storm, leaving the field as dark as a graveyard.

The company continued bounding for some time, the forward unit leaping up to five hundred meters in front of the main element, stopping to allow the rest of the company to pass them, and then moving forward once again. Jean remained with the forward element as often as she could, relying on her radio to maintain control of the maneuver, the silhouettes of the soldiers appearing like fuzzy shadows against a backdrop of black and gray.

Weapons fire erupted to their immediate front, showering the air with zipping tracer fire as several explosions went off all around. Something struck Jean severely, picking her off her feet and slamming her to the ground. Jean lay on her back for a second, stunned, her eyes following the deadly passage of tracer fire above her, oblivious to the anguished cries of the dying. For a moment she thought she heard her brother's voice. Rafe? He sounded lost and far, far away. Rafe?

A moment later, Jean's head cleared.

Jean swiveled around to face the direction of the enemy's fire, careful not to raise her body off the ground. Whatever had hit her had not incapacitated her. She felt no pain. Behind her, the support platoon had started with counterfire, laying a heavy barrage of small arms rounds at the enemy. The returning fire increased as the crew-fired weapons joined the fray.

Jean joined the fight too. She fired from the prone position, not bothering to aim. Instead she bounced the rounds toward the enemy, who were entrenched in holes dug through the sodden ground just a few meters to her front—a near ambush. She swore and cursed. With the enemy so close, the artillery was useless.

Jean launched a grenade from the under barrel of her weapon, arching the round high in the air so it would arm before falling back to earth. Jean felt the thud of the explosion.

"Kross, direct support fires low." Jean was grateful her most experienced platoon leader was in the best tactical position to influence the battle. "They're entrenched in spider holes just a few meters in front of us. We need to fight through. Kross, isolate the far left. Draiger," she said, firing her weapon, "on my mark, assault."

Jean watched as the fire from Kross's platoon danced across the left front, isolating the enemy positions from any Consortium troops that might be moving along that axis to assist their comrades. The volume of fire reached a crescendo.

Shooting wildly as enemy fire danced perceivably closer to her, Jean fumbled a hand grenade from her side and threw it at the nearest enemy position.

"Now!" she yelled as the grenade exploded in a brilliant flash. "Assault!"

Rushing forward, Jean fired into the nearest spider hole, jumping in on top of the remains of a Consortium soldier, the young man's body broken and bleeding, his head partly missing and pieces of his limbs gone or smashed into pulp. Jean ignored the sight; poking her head over the hole just enough to get a mushy sight picture, she fired across the ground at what she suspected was the next enemy position. Her left leg hurt where she had been hit, but the sudden flair of pain was already receding as the automatic features of her battle suit applied pressure to stop the bleeding, releasing at the same time a small amount of narcotics into her system.

"Captain." Draiger's voice, strained with adrenaline, burst into Jean's ears. "We've tak—" His voice broke off for a brief second, and a heavy volume of fire came from Jean's right, hitting the head of a figure that had appeared over the lip of a hole.

"We've taken the first few holes," Draiger continued. "I think we have four of them to my right secured. Hard to tell through the heads-up. I don't think we can move from here, but we can support."

Jean thought about Draiger's situation for a moment and agreed. "Kross, take your unit to our left flank. Assault across. We'll provide supporting fires. Draiger," she added unnecessarily, "maximum fire. Look out for friendlies as they come across."

"Smiley," she added to her reserve force that was moving about five hundred meters behind the main unit, "move up. After Kross clears to the south, bring your platoon straight through our positions and"—she fired at a shadowy shape that disappeared back into a curvature of the terrain—"take a defensive line in the east. Half of Kross's platoon will then sweep back to the north for our 360. We'll reconsolidate and then decide what to do."

"Yes, ma'am," Lieutenant Smiley's bass voice replied. Jean could hear him breathing hard as he led his platoon at a quick jog toward the battle.

Jean watched the situation as it developed, her life no longer directly threatened, and fired only enough to keep people away from the hole she shared with the mutilated corpse. Jean nodded appreciatively as the fire from Kross's platoon dwindled but did not die. Kross was leaving a portion of his platoon on his far left to help with covering fire. She could see the rest of his platoon move out on line, bounding forward in squads toward the impromptu objective.

The noise of the battlefield held a type of silence that Jean now relished. The roar of fire and clash of explosions muffled the air like a thick mist. It wrapped her in a cocoon of noise, reminding her of a large symphony orchestra, the kettledrums pounding, the frenzied whining of violins, and the occasional clash of cymbals dancing through the spellbound air. Though it wasn't unlike the simulations she had been through, the battle was somehow different. It was alive with an elasticity and rhythm of its own. Jean's heart beat in conjunction with the noise, and her ears ached with the whimsical sounds, harshly alluring.

"Shift fires!" Kross barked the command through the radio.

Draiger's platoon dutifully shifted their fires to the far south to isolate the southern part of the battlefield.

Jean watched as the Federation troops slashed in a jagged line across the enemy positions. Here and there to her front, she occasionally saw a marine fall to the ground. The remaining marines continued onward, moving through the smoke and rain across the muddy field, leaving death in their wake.

In a few minutes, it was all over. The only things moving in the dark registered on her heads-up display as friendly. Jean noted that several clumps of the marine's electronic signatures sat unmoving. They were either dead or wounded.

"Eagle Five, this is Eagle One. Over," Jean said as the radio automatically switched to a higher radio net.

"This is Five. Go ahead."

"We've had contact. I'm downloading the coordinates to you now. I have several down and need some evac. Punching vitals to you now." The computer in her battle suit short-burst the encoded data stream back to the command post. "I don't think we're going any further tonight. Evac ETA?" she asked.

"Fifteen minutes," the voice answered, clear and concise.

"Copy, Eagle Five. Eagle One, out."

"Conducting a secondary sweep," Smiley said as he motioned his platoon forward.

Jean joined Smiley's platoon as they moved through Draiger's and conducted the sweep across the enemy position. She stepped over several bodies and began thinking about a possible counterattack. Her left leg was starting to throb again, and she took a brief moment to look down at it. It was too dark to see clearly. At least it was holding her weight, she thought. That was something.

Jean broke off from the platoon and made her way toward the approximate center of the enemy positions, her hand reflexively clasping her leg. Suddenly, she slipped and fell. Lying on the wet ground for a surprised moment, Jean was suddenly confused. It took her a moment of struggling before she could get to a sitting position.

A shadowy figure bound toward her, leaping across the intervening space between what she had assumed was just another corpse and her position. Time seemed to slow as the man fired a single shot from a handgun. The sound rippled through the relaxed battlefield like a klaxon in a very small room. The sharp report stretched out, lengthening and ringing through Jean's ears. Jean fell back, bringing her weapon to bear and squeezing the trigger. At close range, her assault rifle tore through the man's body armor, blowing a gaping hole through her attacker's chest and back. Jean tried to roll out of the way of the falling corpse but found herself pinned beneath the dead man, struggling for breath.

The world grew dull, and Jean heard her mother crying and her brother's sardonic laugh. A haze settled over Jean's mind. She found she had lost control of her arms and hands. Fascinated, she tried to move them, but they lay unresponsive. And then time became a blur, and the world shifted.

"Ma'am," a voice floated through the void that was Jean's mind. "Ma'am, don't worry. You'll be all right."

Jean tried to answer, but her throat was full of something warm. It choked her as she struggled for air. She opened her eyes and tried to focus them on the form that knelt over her. Lightning flashed silently in the rainy sky, silhouetting the marine in brief flashes of light and shadow. *I should know him*, she thought. But she could not pull the name out of her muddled mind. His lips moved, and Jean wondered if it could be her father.

Her father had been destroyed by Rafe's desertion. Rafe had fled. Fled. A coward! Jean thought her mother had been relieved. But her father had raged.

No, she thought. The man kneeling over her was covered in mud—mud and shadow. Her father would never play in the mud. He was always impeccably dressed in his colonel's uniform. This man, with the gruff echo of a five-day beard, dark eyes, and dark skin, was not her father. Her father's eyes were bright blue, crisp like the sky.

Jean tried to breathe. It hurt so. There was no air. She tried to think. *Where am I? Who is this? Is this what death is like?*

And then suddenly, she could breathe.

Cool, wet, refreshing air poured into her aching lungs. Jean nearly wept from the taste of it. The world came into sharp focus, and her ability to think rushed over her. She remembered now. And there was pain. Such pain! She tried to cry out but found herself unable, and for a brief moment, panic threatened. She realized that she had taken a direct shot to her neck.

My God! I'm going to die! I have to get up. Get up! If I can stand up, the frantic thought drummed, *then I will survive. I have to get up! I have to get up. Get up!*

She struggled.

"Take it easy, Captain," a voice said. Rough hands pinned her down. The dead man was pulled off her and dumped unceremoniously into a puddle.

For a moment, Jean ignored the pain that wracked her body and concentrated on feeling her toes, her fingers, afraid that she had broken her neck. To her immense relief, she could wiggle her toes. And no longer pinned under the corpse, Jean could lift her arms. The marine kneeling above her pushed her arms back down.

"We've got you, Captain. Lie still."

Kross, Jean thought. It must be Kross. And was that Doc Stephens with the medical kit? She couldn't see clearly.

Jean tried to speak again but found she could not. Instead, Jean slid her right arm over to her left forearm and depressed a command key located on her battle suit. Instantly, a change-of-command signal was sent to her unit, to Kross, and to her commanding officer.

"I'll take care of them," a voice said. Then Jean knew the marine who had been hovering over her was indeed Kross. "Just you lie still for a minute. Try not to move."

Kross gave some short orders to the unit to find defensive positions and prepare for a counterattack.

Jean listened to his orders, proud of how Kross had transitioned to command with soldiery pragmatism. She slowly swiveled her head to the left, testing, and found herself staring into the opened eyes of the man she had just killed. Blue eyes, like her father's, looked hollowly at her, dull and unseeing. A drop of water was beading on the dead man's nose, a rich blob that sparkled once before it dribbled down across the waxy face, over lips pulled back to expose the teeth and tongue. A bedraggled shock of hair stuck out from the man's helmet, like a puff of cotton or the tail of a rodent. And Jean was glad he was dead. Glad she had pulled the trigger. Glad she had been true to her mark. She looked at the man an instant more, and then she turned her attention to Doc Stephens, the medic, who was preparing her for transport.

Jean was aware of being lifted onto the stretcher. She berated herself for having lost touch with Kross, whose voice was fading away. She was vaguely aware of the evac ship, felt the gentle vibrations of the twin engines that kept it hovering above the ground. She mysteriously had an IV in her arm, though she did not remember having it inserted. Her eyes focused on it as it swayed to the movement of the evac. Someone inserted a needle in the IV, and in a short span of time, Jean slipped into irresistible darkness.

Nine months later, Jean looked up from her desk. She unconsciously reached toward the wound on her throat, half expecting to feel the bandage there. She had been luckier than she'd thought. Not only had she not been paralyzed, the injuries to Jean's voice box had been repairable. Her voice still sounded strained and probably always would, but that was a small price to pay.

She had learned that the Federation had pressed the battle of Edmund's Field to their advantage and had swept the Consortium from the mountains. Jean wished she had been in the final battles. Consortium forces had chaotically fled to their last bastions on Maxim, before being completely destroyed. The victory in the Sirus C system marked, as everyone said, the ending phase of the war. But what would happen after the war? Jean wondered. The war had started when she was young, and her father had gone off into the thick of it. The whole of her life had centered on the war. Who was she without it?

For her small part in the victory, Jean was given a citation and a comfortable desk job in the Isa System as a combat instructor for new recruits as they rotated through advanced individual combat training before heading to the front. It was a good job, interesting and even informative, but she felt a certain restlessness and guilt about leaving her unit behind.

Her leg wound had healed too. Jean had been hit by a small piece of shrapnel. It had taken some surgery and stitches, but the prognosis was good. The doctors expected that, given time, Jean's leg would return to 100 percent. It was still stiff from time to time, particularly in the morning or after sitting behind her desk for a long period of time. The rehabilitation had been painful too. Her muscles had atrophied, and stretching the tendons and building her strength back up had been one of the biggest challenges she had faced over her recovery period.

"Ma'am," said the orderly who had disturbed her, shuffling uncomfortably in the silence. The white garrison uniform, clean, pressed, and polished, made the young man look like something straight off of a recruiting poster.

"Yes, Corporal?" Jean asked. She let the papers lie on the desk and smiled disarmingly at the man. "What is it?"

"Package for you, ma'am," he answered, his voice stiff and official.

Jean noticed the brown, wrapped parcel in the corporal's left hand and extended her hand toward him. "I'll take it," she said. "Is there anything else?"

"No, ma'am." The corporal handed the package to Jean and stepped back away from the desk, turned, and walked toward her open office door.

Jean raised her hand and called, "Corporal, please close the door behind you. I don't want to be disturbed for the next two hours. I have to finish these student reports."

The corporal paused. "Yes, Major," he replied before stepping out of her office and closing the door behind him.

Major. The title sounded strange to Jean. She had been promoted after Edmund's Field. It meant a small raise and slightly larger quarters. But it also meant she had been promoted out of her job as a company commander and was destined for staff work. She was not thrilled. While she had wanted the promotion, she had never really considered what it would mean for her. She was supposed to lead troops, not draft reams of orders. But majors were staff officers, she knew. Jean wouldn't lead on the battlefield again until she was a colonel. That would take forever. The thought left a hollow feeling in her heart.

A staff position, she told herself for the hundredth time, was a necessary evil.

Jean was just tracking time in the training unit as she waited for a staff job at a battle group headquarters. If things went well for her, it was possible she could make light colonel before she was thirty-five. Maybe she would get another combat command then—if there was still a war to fight.

Well, she mused, she would focus on positioning herself for another command. She would just have to be patient.

Fingering the package left by the corporal, Jean dropped it on her desk and studied the markings. It was a rare thing to get an official package. Most official messages were digital. Jean looked at the sending address. It was from the Federation's Bureau of Intelligence and Insurgency. That was doubly rare.

Suddenly, Jean felt very uncomfortable.

Hell, she thought. Nobody she had ever met had received a package from the BII.

The Bureau of Intelligence and Insurgency was a civilian branch of the Federation government with primary responsibility for gathering information on everything from the movement of enemy troops to technology theft and assassination. Jean was not sure why the BII would be sending her a package. She wasn't even sure she wanted to find out. So she sat for a few minutes staring at the little unassuming-looking box.

Eventually, her curiosity overcame caution, and she tore it open. Inside the otherwise nondescript box were a palm-sized digital reader and two small discs. There was nothing more. No note. Nothing.

Jean hesitated. *What is this?* she wondered. Why had the BII sent her these data discs? It would be foolish for her to ignore them, Jean knew. The BII had its ways. The agency could ruin her career. Damn.

Jean stared at the discs for a moment more and sighed. She stretched back in her chair, ran her hand through her hair, and then popped one of the discs into the reader. The screen blinked to life, and an error message appeared.

"What the hell," she muttered at the error message. It was rather unique.

It said, "Major Joyce, put in the other disc."

Jean smiled and pushed the eject button, sliding the other disc into the machine. The BII logo swooshed across the screen with a little fanfare music. Jean rolled her eyes and sighed. *The cool guys,* she thought. When the logo faded, a middle-aged man appeared in the center of the screen. He wore a gray suit and a white shirt, and he held a photo of Jean's brother, Rafe, in his left hand.

The man smiled. "Major Joyce, or can I call you Jean?" he asked with a familiar smile. "I am the station chief here in the Isa System. My name is Paul Temple, and I have"—he paused for a moment, considering his next words—"an offer for you.

"Your brother," he continued, walking toward and sitting at a desk, "Rafe, Lieutenant Rafe Joyce, lately of the Federation Marines (well, to get technically accurate, still a member of the Federation Marines) has been on a rather long … personal holiday, shall we say? I have been reading your file," he added as his hand wrapped around a cup of coffee, "and you've managed to make quite a name for yourself, almost erasing the stain that your brother's desertion brought to your family—a real battlefield hero."

Jean tensed as the man spoke. His voice was too smooth, too friendly, and too familiar with her private affairs.

"What do you want?" she snapped aloud, feeling foolish a second later at having talked to a recording.

"On the other disc," Paul continued, "are the coordinates of an asteroid mining field on the edges of the known universe. Your brother is there, Major Joyce. And though he doesn't know it yet, he needs help. No, he is not working for the BII. He is not working for anyone, but he is a gifted young man." The BII station chief smiled again, his lips pressed tightly against the surface of his teeth. He gave a short, sarcastic laugh. "Rafe likes data systems, doesn't he?" Paul asked rhetorically. "He has made some powerful people very angry. Major, Rafe crossed a line, and now the Federation is about to send the authorities to recover him. And I think you know what that means."

Jean did. The Federation shot deserters.

"But you can put an end to that mission," Paul continued. "All you have to do is bring that disc to my office, and you'll be given the opportunity to redeem your brother's life. A full pardon. Maybe some glory." He shrugged. "If you agree, well, let's leave that for our interview. Come when you have the time. My office is in the sublevel. Ask the receptionist. She'll see you in."

The message ended. The disc self-ejected, falling and landing on Jean's desk. There it began to blacken, until its once silver surface was as dark as midnight, and a strong metallic odor filled the air.

Theatrics.

Jean pushed the disc off her desk into the trash.

Jean looked at the other disc and popped it back into the reader. The same message appeared: "Major Joyce, put in the other disc." She tried putting it in her desk reader, but the reader would not even recognize the disc. *Obviously encoded*, she thought. *Stupid*.

She stared at the unfinished reports on her desk, and suddenly anger swelled within her. *How dare he?* Jean thought. How dare Paul play with her life, with her brother's? If the BII knew where Rafe was, then the agency should go and arrest him. Rafe had known the risks when he'd deserted. He knew the penalty. Why bring Jean into it at all? Why jerk her around? Rafe had accepted the risk. Rafe had abandoned her and their mother and father. Why should she interject herself in his life?

Jean was a marine. Honor, sacrifice, comradeship, and the steely taste of command—she yearned for those things. If she were lucky, like her father, Jean would live long enough to retire and return home. That was the life she wanted. She did not want to skulk in the shadows. That was the life Rafe had chosen. He had run. He had surrounded himself in dishonor and covered Jean's family in shame. This was Rafe's problem—let Rafe deal with it!

But Rafe was her brother. She softened. *Damn*. She had thought she had put all of these thoughts and feelings behind her.

Well, she thought fiercely, if Paul Temple wanted to interview her about Rafe, then he could damn well do it now!

Jean stood abruptly, took the disc and the palm reader, and slipped them in her pants pocket. She picked up her hat and strode out of her office, moved down the hall to the elevators, and made her way to the sublevels, where she soon stood before a glass door inscribed with "The Bureau of Intelligence and Insurgency" in sleek, black letters. *Not very sneaky*, she thought.

Stepping inside, Jean confronted the receptionist with the palm reader in one hand and the disc in the other.

"I just got this!" she snapped. "Paul Temple?" She glared at the woman.

"He is expecting you," the woman replied curtly and motioned toward a door in the back center of the suite.

The door opened, and Jean walked determinedly through it and into a spacious office. The same middle-aged man from the disc, with a touch of gray at his temples, looked up from his desk and stood. The scowl he had been wearing vanished; his features relaxed; and his frown morphed into a wide, welcoming smile.

Jean felt like kicking his ass.

The door closed. Paul Temple motioned with his hands, ushering Jean toward the blue couch that sat before his desk. "That was fast," he said, bemused. His voice was as smooth in person as it had been on the disc. He reminded Jean of a TV news anchorman—clean to the point of extreme, well spoken, dark hair, and dark eyes that sparkled upon command.

"Thank you for coming so soon, Major Joyce. Can I get you anything? No? Please, have a seat."

Jean sat stiffly on the couch as Paul poured himself a cup of coffee from a decanter that stood on the coffee table between them.

"What is this all about, sir?" Jean asked seriously. Jean did not try to hide the anger in her voice. She already didn't like the man.

"Straight to the point; very much the soldier, aren't you?" Paul replied. Instead of sitting back behind the desk, he sat effortlessly down in an armchair to Jean's left.

"Marine," she responded.

"Oh, yes, of course," Paul replied, "marine."

"That is what I am, sir," Jean retorted. "Or was that *not* in my file?"

Paul considered her for a moment. "I gather you are angry, Major. But that is no reason to be impolite. Can I assume by your tone that you are not interested in the offer I have to make? I am sure we both have other things to do."

Paul took a sip of coffee, holding a fine bone-china cup to his lips. He took a cube of raw cane sugar from a glass container on the coffee table and slowly mixed it into the drink, letting the silence hang. Placing the tiny silver spoon on the waiting saucer, he waited patiently.

Jean sighed. In spite of herself, she was interested. "I'm listening."

"Good," Paul continued. "Your brother was miscast, Major Joyce." He shifted a little in his chair. "Let's be honest for a moment. I know that Rafe should have been anything but a combat marine. I suspect your father knew it, and," he added with a smile, "you must have known it too."

"What is your point?"

"Direct, aren't you? Well," Paul took another sip of his coffee and looked at Jean, "we have a job for you. The catch is that I will not tell you what it is without your prior agreement to the terms."

"Sir, how can I agree to something when I do not know what it is?" Jean asked.

"Major, sometimes, in a war, you have to do certain things without knowing all of the reasons. You take commands on faith," Paul replied. "I am giving you the opportunity to redeem your brother and help the Federation win the war and the peace. There has been a lot of killing, Jean," he paused. "Can I call you, Jean? Major Joyce is so formal. Good.

"Jean, there are more ways to fight a war than with a gun. I have read your file and you are a good soldier—I mean marine. You are smart, a quick study, and tactically sound, and you have a leadership style that even the roughest enlisted person respects and follows."

"Don't—"

"Please," Paul interrupted her. "I'm not prone to flattery. There are any number of officers who meet that description. You have talent, to be sure, but you are not so unique as all that."

"Then why me?" Jean asked. At least Paul could be honest when he wanted. "Why come to me? What makes me special?"

"You're not, frankly." The station chief leaned back in his chair and crossed his legs. He took another sip of coffee. The cup rattled as he placed it back on its saucer. "It is your brother, Jean. Rafe has fallen in with some very interesting people—like souls, let's say. He is a member of a group that calls itself The Miscreants. Have you heard of them?"

"No."

"Not surprising, Jean. They are a loosely affiliated gang of thieves."

"You're saying Rafe is a thief?" Jean asked.

"Oh, yes. He is that. And your brother has been busy for the last five years. Very." The station chief took another drink and searched Jean's face for any reaction.

But Jean remained calm, refusing to rise to the bait.

"Rafe has studied and become quite proficient at hacking into data systems," the man continued. "He has caused the authorities some moments of concern, but not only Federation authorities, those from the Consortium as well. He is an equal-opportunity computer hacker. He likes to play with other people's money and has become very good—very, very good at his job. Some might call him a genius."

"And you want Rafe to do something for you?" Now he was getting to his point, Jean thought.

"Yes. But I am curious. Why did you think we wanted him to

perform a little job for us? Why didn't you assume we were going to ask him to simply stop his activities?"

"You could do that yourself. You apparently know where he is. If you wanted to stop him, you'd just go and arrest him. But here I am. You need me to ask him. You need someone he trusts. If you, or the heavies, go talk to him, he'll run or refuse; either way, you don't get what you want," Jean replied, adding, "but he will not listen to me."

"Perhaps not. But I think he will."

"Why? Why Rafe?" Jean questioned. "You must have computer geniuses falling out of the sky."

"I cannot tell you that, yet."

"What makes you think Rafe will agree to work for you?"

"Because"—Paul Temple leaned forward and his voice dropped to a hush so that Jean had to strain to hear him—"because it's the chance of a lifetime." He sat back. "He'll do it."

Jean watched the man for a moment, wondering just what the game really was and how much she was going to regret her next words. "What's the mission?" she asked.

"Good. Do you agree to the conditions then?"

Jean held a retort in check and nodded her head. Rafe was, after all, her brother.

"Yes."

"That's great. The hard emotional part is now over." the BII station chief was all confident as if Jean's answer had been preordained. "To start, your mission is simple. You will be transferred. You will be hardwired to fly a ship, and you will do whatever you are told. In return, you will have the opportunity to redeem your brother and help defeat the Consortium."

"Vague," Jean commented. "Is that all?"

"No," Paul added with a smile. "There is one more thing."

"What is that?"

"You'll call me, Paul."

The ship transitioned to sub-light speeds. Jean stretched her back in the acceleration couch, feeling the tug of the wires jacked into her skull. It had been a strange couple of months. She had agreed to Paul Temple's terms, and the next day she was having surgery to install the computer jacks under her ears. They were small implants, not the gangly things she had always imagined. When her hair was down, they were barely noticeable at all. Then it was off to flight school, where the newly installed hardware allowed her to interface directly with the navigation computer. It had all happened very quickly.

Flying an interstellar ship was not what Jean had expected. She had always held the belief that pilots managed everything with their uplinks. What she had discovered was that piloting an interstellar was a combination of physical and mental control. And it was more difficult than she had imagined. But what surprised Jean the most was that she could actually "feel" the inner workings of the ship when she was jacked into the navigational computer. Wherever there was a sensor to monitor doors, lights, air support systems, fuel, engine thrust, Jean could feel them as if they were all extensions of her body. Nobody had warned her about that. She had never even imagined it before.

When she'd asked her instructors about the sensations, they had smiled and said the feelings were not important for what she was supposed to do. But for Jean the sensations of the ship had become something more than the electrical interaction of her brain with the computer. They were comforting. They made her not so lonely. She wondered how she had ever survived before, limited within her human frame, only half-alive. The thrill of space, the power of the ship's sensors, and the subtle creaking of its hull opened a new universe to her, and for the first time in her life, she understood why pilots were such a strange breed. When she unjacked from the ship, the universe was … bland.

"Good job, Major," Captain Mike Estury said from the copilot's chair. "I think you are officially functional."

Mike was a friendly and energetic naval officer in his late

twenties, a combat ship pilot, and Jean's flight instructor. Jean's little ship was courier class. Small and sleek, it was designed for speed rather than brawn. But it had some additional items that most courier ships did not, forward and aft lasers and a sublight torpedo tube. Its shields were also enhanced, the tactical system surging the shields' strength when it determined the ship was about to be struck. This saved energy and allowed the small craft to support the higher energy yields that a ship of this size could not normally handle. Jean's ship was designed to hit and run, and run fast.

"Boy this baby can fly," Captain Estury exclaimed. He pulled the wire links out of his ears and stood up smiling. "My God, but she can move."

Jean was pleased with herself and with the ship. She respected Mike's opinion, and it meant a lot to her that he was impressed. The ship wasn't like the trainer models Jean had first flown. They had been rough, sluggish, almost unresponsive when compared to this ship.

"What are you going to name her?" Mike asked. He stepped across and helped Jean out of her acceleration couch. "Any ideas?"

"I've been thinking," Jean stated, standing, "I'll name it the *Fallen Star*." She lifted her hands and dropped them, a little embarrassed. "For my brother," she added with a sad smile.

Captain Estury looked at Jean seriously and said, "I know about him."

"Oh?"

"It was all over the news after the fall of Maxim." His voice was tentative as if he knew he might be on shaky ground.

Jean had forgotten how the news agencies had relished juxtaposing Rafe's desertion and Jean's heroics. Of course Mike would know.

"It's a good name—for the ship, I mean." Mike brightened up and clapped Jean across the shoulders, suddenly laughing. "I'll get it registered. And congratulations, Major. You've graduated flight school. Let's go get drunk."

Jean thought that was a great idea.

It took them a few hours to dock the newly christened *Fallen Star* at William Bennet Station. The space station orbited around the fourth planet in the Bhante system, a gas giant called Luna Reach. The station, named after Captain William Bennet, who posthumously earned the Federation Golden Cluster after one of the first engagements between the Federation and Consortium fleets, was not much more than a fueling stop for long-haul freighters. It had a small naval garrison and was of little to no strategic value. The station had been deemed the perfect place for Jean's training.

"I'll get changed and meet you in the bar," Jean said, heading toward the locker room and the showers.

A little while later, refreshed, she made her way through the metallic corridors of the station to the tiny pilot's club, where she promptly began drinking herself into blissful oblivion.

Lately her dreams had become more hauntingly real. Jean's dead marines wandered in the gloaming, stalking her. She could smell their rotting corpses, and accusation flared in their lifeless eyes. The sounds of the battlefield rose around them, the sharp slap of steel on flesh, the tear of laser fire, and the concussive blasts of bombs, artillery, and mortars left her quivering in dread and fear. And the dreams always ended the same. Lying in the rain in Edmunds's Field, she would turn her head and find herself looking into the eyes of the man who had nearly killed her—his face chalky white, his eyes accusingly mocking. Jean could hear his final breath wheeze out of fluttering lungs. It was hard to breathe. Then the world would spin and slip into darkness until, caught in a vortex of remembered pain, Jean felt she was likely to vomit. She would dart awake, covered in perspiration. Her shaking hand would snake gingerly toward the old wound on her throat like some type of benediction. She would try to cry, to feel something, but her heart was empty and as silent as the tormenting dead of her dreams.

Alcohol helped, for a while. If she drank enough, she wouldn't dream at all.

Captain Estury joined her at some point. She knew he had become aware of her drinking and sleeping problems. But he did not judge her. He just kept the male sharks at bay and tried his best to curb her need.

"Have a juice, a coffee," he would offer. But Jean would just smile and order another drink.

Jean enjoyed talking to the naval captain. He deftly avoided her clumsy advances, but Jean noted that, tonight, when she leaned in toward his bar stool, setting her hand so close to his on the counter she could feel the heat, he found a reason to place his hand over hers and then kept it there.

The night wore on in a muddle until, at some unknown point, it all went blank, and the voices, smells, and sounds of battle were enshrouded in an impenetrable tomb of nothingness.

Jean was surprised and somewhat disappointed when she woke up alone. The alarm on her dressing table beeped incessantly, and her mouth felt uncomfortably dry. By the time she stumbled out of bed, showered, and dressed, Jean's head felt a little clearer. She drank several glasses of water and took some painkillers, ate a bite, and started toward the door.

Jean suddenly stopped. She realized she had nowhere to be today.

How long has it been since I have had some free time? she thought as she sat back down on the edge of her bed. She felt too awake to go back to sleep.

After tinkering around in her room for a little while, she decided to go out and check on her ship. Jean wanted to see if the maintenance team had painted its name on the hull yet, and she missed her interaction with the *Fallen Star's* navigation system. The feel of extended self gave her an almost godlike sense of power and awareness. Jean needed that right now. She felt alone and restless.

Jean found the hangar empty except for one member of the cleaning crew, a short man with a nondescript face and a shadow of a beard who was sweeping the floor. Jean ignored him and, running her left hand along the smooth hull of the *Fallen Star*, she moved toward the front of the ship, where she noticed the ship's name painted in clean script just besides the main hatch. Someone had taken the liberty of painting a blue-and-white angel into the first letter. Painting a person or symbol on a spacecraft was a tradition going back farther than Jean could remember.

She stepped away to get a better look. Jean had not chosen a mascot, but as she looked at the angel, how it blended with the rising curvature of the ship, it seemed right. She wondered if that had been Mike's—Captain Estury's—idea.

God, what was she going to do about him? She was being a fool, wasn't she? Jean was not sure whether or not Mike was attracted to her. He was a couple years younger too. *Hell*, she thought, *I'm not sure if I'm attracted to him or if it's just been too long.* She considered it for a moment and decided not to let her thoughts linger. There was too much danger in following that line of thought and, besides, with her training complete, she would be leaving on her mission to find her brother. She didn't have time for romances.

Jumping up on the *Fallen Star's* ramp, Jean walked inside and made her way to the pilot's acceleration couch. Leaning back in the artificial leather, she started the command protocols that would link her to the ship's systems. Though she knew the *Fallen Star* belonged to the Federation, Jean felt as if the ship were hers. It was sleek and powerful, and when Jean was at its commands, she felt incorporated in the universe around her. It was intimate.

Settled, she pulled the wire out of the console and slipped it into her jack.

It was as if a door opened in her mind.

Jean could feel the ship come to life as she activated the *Fallen*

Star's internal systems. There was a small leak in one of the aft hydraulic lines. Jean made a mental note to tell the mechanic about it. After mentally exploring the interior of the ship for a while, Jean activated the sensor arrays one at a time until the whole universe expanded around and within her. She floated in that way for a long time, reaching, exploring, testing the abilities of the *Fallen Star's* sensors in a way that her pilot training had not allowed. There simply had not been enough quiet time for her to do more than learn the basics, just enough to get her where she was going. Now Jean luxuriated in her newfound senses.

Jean reached through the twirling clouds of the gas planet below to its far, hidden center, the poisonous gases of the atmosphere registering like an afterthought as the sensors automatically categorized them into their constituent classifications. She pulled back from the planet and let her senses flow farther. She drifted deeper, registering the cosmic rays that radiated outward from the system's sun. She followed their ebb as they skipped across the vastness of space like a rising tide to the edge of the galaxy. It was like swimming in a deep ocean, she thought. Time slipped silently by as Jean twirled on a darkling sea.

"Major Joyce." Captain Estury's voice broke through the calm. "I thought I would find you on the *Fallen Star*. Can you come up to the station's command deck? Your orders have arrived."

It was still very strange to hear someone else's voice communicate directly to her mind. "So soon?" Jean replied, subvocalizing. She was not quite ready to leave the peacefulness of the universe just yet.

"I'm afraid so," the captain replied. Jean could hear the smirk on his lips.

"All right," she answered over the communications link. *God, he must think I'm a mess.* "Let me shut things down. I'll be right there."

Jean checked the ship's chronometer and noticed that it was well past noon. She had been floating for several hours. With a sigh, Jean shut the *Fallen Star* down and unplugged, trudging her way back through the corridors to the command deck, where she found

Captain Estury and someone else, a man she had not met before, waiting for her.

"It is nice to meet you," the stranger said. He wore civilian clothes. His hair was long, and his voice rolled, like too much sugar in a glass of tea. "My name is Danner Tomblin," he added extending his hand. "I believe you know Captain Estury."

"Please to meet you," Jean answered cautiously, shaking the man's hand. "Mike"—she paused—"Captain Estury is my flight instructor, Mr. Tomblin. How can I help you today?"

Danner Tomblin laughed softly, covering his mouth with his hand. "I was told you were direct." When Jean did not reply, he continued, "I have your orders." He pulled a data disc from his pocket and extended it to her.

"I should be going back to my work," Mike said.

"No, don't," Danner reached out and stopped the captain, placing a hand on his shoulder. "I have orders for you too."

"Oh?"

"It seems as if you will be joining the major aboard the"—he looked at the floor for a moment and then smiled—"the *Fallen Star*. The major needs some assistance, and since you have both worked well together," he said, letting the insinuation hang in the air for a moment before continuing, "it was decided that you were the perfect match."

"Excuse me? Mike asked. "I have my own ship, my own command waiting."

"It can continue to wait," Danner replied. "Oh, don't worry. You'll get it back. I can assure you of that. It is just that, though Major Joyce has completed basic pilot's training, we feel she needs someone of more experience to help her on her way. You understand, don't you?"

"We? Wait a minute," Jean interrupted.

But before she could continue, Danner Tomblin held up his hand to silence her. "Paul Temple and I, Major. I'm with the BII. And I will be joining you too."

Nobody had said anything about others going with her. "Captain Estury does not need to come along. I don't need his help. In fact—"

"It can't be avoided, Major. Time is of the essence, and it would take too long to train you with another copilot. Of course, Captain Estury will be the primary pilot and you, Major, will copilot. There is no reason to change the current arrangement. I am sure you both see the logic in that."

"A captain in the navy is not the same as a captain in the marines," Jean stated. Her voice was flat. "Captain Estury is the senior flight officer. But I thought this was my mission. Now it's *his* mission?" She looked over at the naval captain and softened her voice. "I didn't mean it that way, Mike. It's just … Really. I did not expect this. I thought I would be going alone. I …"

Danner Tomblin smiled and gestured to the empty seats at a small round conference table. "I am sure it will all be explained in a moment," Tomblin said. His voice sounded oily and slightly pleased.

"Going where?" Mike asked Jean. His voice was wary.

Danner answered. "Didn't you ever wonder why a major in the marines was being fitted and trained to fly ships?"

"The thought had crossed my mind. The major has talents. I assumed I was not the only person to recognize them. It is difficult to find people who can handle the sensory overload that pilots have to deal with. I thought, perhaps, that she had met the testing requirements. And with the shortage of pilots these days …" He trailed off with a shrug.

"Are you stealing my thunder, Tomblin?" Paul Temple stepped through the door.

A small, oriental woman with straight black hair that shimmered like silk as the light reflected off it followed behind him.

"Akemi Murakami, meet Captain Mike Estury, Major Jean Joyce, and BII operative Danner Tomblin."

"Pleasure," Akemi purred. She cocked her head slightly like a cat. It was as if she had heard something nobody else could. "Countermeasures are active, Mr. Temple."

"Paul."

"Whatever you say, Mr. Temple." Akemi slipped into one of the open chairs.

Jean thought Akemi Murakami was likely the most beautiful Asian woman she had ever seen. Jean wasn't sure she liked that.

The station chief sighed and shook his head in amusement.

Major Joyce, Captain Estury, and Danner Tomblin all took a seat.

Moving to the front of the table, Paul Temple joined the others. He interlaced his fingers together before him, resting his forearms on the table.

Paul took a moment to study the four people. They were an odd group, but the computer simulator had selected them as most likely to succeed. And everyone else seemed happy with the selection. But Paul had his doubts. He always had his doubts.

The station chief began, "Welcome, all of you. I am so glad you volunteered for this rather important mission."

Mike snorted. He did not look happy. "What exactly did I just volunteer for?"

"You and your companions have all volunteered to save a dissident soul—Major Joyce's wayward brother to be precise."

A holographic projector beamed a likeness of Rafe Joyce onto the center of the table.

Jean caught her breath. She had not seen her brother in a long time. Rafe was older. Lines of worry were etched at the edges of his eyes, and his hair was longer than Jean remembered. She reached toward the image before she noticed her reaction and quickly pulled her hand back and placed it in her lap.

He looked healthy, Jean thought. She wondered if it were a picture of Rafe or just a reconstruction. Either way, seeing his face again convinced her that she had made the right decision. She would save him—save him, her father, and her mother. She would save them all.

Jean looked up and noticed Akemi Murakami's feline-like eyes staring at her.

"You," Akemi said. "You are Major Joyce? Ah, yes. Siblings, I see."

"Yes," Paul said into the gap of silence. "This was, or is, Lieutenant Rafe Joyce. He is the major's disgraced brother." Paul held up a hand to forestall Jean's retort. "Your first task is to retrieve Lieutenant Joyce from his hiding hole and to convince him to accompany you on your mission."

"Finally," Jean exclaimed. "Wait," she added. "I thought that was the mission. Get my brother and have him hack into some computer network."

"Yes and no … Please," Paul Tomblin said, "be patient. Let me explain.

"First you will fly the *Fallen Star* to Metis Five in the Tianjin System. It is a small asteroid." Rafe's face disappeared, and an image of the *Fallen Star* flew through space to a small dwarf sun and beyond to the system's asteroid belt. "Lieutenant Rafe is a rather capable computer hacker," Paul explained, "whose projects are prolific in the Dark Web. And the major is correct. We have a job for him."

"The Dark Web?" Mike asked.

"May I?" Akemi said.

"Yes, thank you." Paul smiled pleasantly. "Do explain."

"It is easiest to understand the Dark Web as an intersystem network that runs in parallel or tandem with the normal system communication's nets," Akemi explained, her voice taking on the dull hum of a university professor. "In reality, they are one and the same, with intertwined code. It is a shadow system where criminal gangs roam, setting up false sites and preying on people. It is estimated that 5 percent of all intersystem web locations are fictitious, even those with famous and well-recognized brand names."

"And," Paul prompted.

"It is also the launching platform for attacks against computer systems—theft of customer information; pilfering of bank accounts;

manipulation of financial markets; and trafficking in stolen technologies, porn, black market items, and drugs."

"Thank you, Ms. Murakami."

Akemi smiled and fell silent.

"What good does that do Jean's brother?" Mike asked. "He's out in the middle of nowhere. How can he even talk to any of the intersystem webs? It would take a hundred relative years for his code to get to any of the nearest systems and another hundred or so to get back. What good does that do him?"

"Framing drives and courier drones," Danner Tomblin interjected. He sounded a bit bored. "Hackers load their code onto incoming drones, and when they flick back to other systems, the code is transmitted via standard message buoys into the intersystem nets. They do their dirty work," he waved a hand, "and then skip the proceeds back into the next communication drone to move tech, money, whatever back to a predesignated location. It is all done hyper fast too. Very difficult to track."

"Oh, I see."

"And Major Joyce's brother is very adept at his chosen profession," Paul added.

"And we're going to tell him to stop it? Offer him another job? Seems like a lot of trouble for just one hacker." Mike smirked. "Sorry," he added to Jean, "I didn't mean anything by that."

Jean smiled tightly, but she understood the question. She had asked it too.

"Nothing quite so simple, Captain Estury. Look at the holographic projection." The Tianjin system faded and was replaced by the image of a large planet. "That is the planet Nibiru. It lies in the Kururumany System on the edge of known space. It's an icy world orbiting around a blue-white star."

"Kururumany?" Mike tried the word out.

"Yes, Captain. As I was saying," Paul continued, "the planet Nibiru's atmospheric spectral analysis shows it is rich in oxygen and has plenty of water, mostly in the form of ice. As you can see, the planet has three moons." The image shifted as three moons zipped around in orbit over Nibiru. As each moon passed, its name was superimposed upon it—Alauda, Caleo, and Gargantuan.

"Wait a minute," Mike broke in, pointing. "What were those? Go back."

"What?" Jean hadn't seen anything.

"There, right there." Mike said. The image stopped turning, and sure enough, a tiny speck could be seen just above the planet. "And there," he pointed farther along the horizon, "another and another. They are in sequence."

"You have good eyes, Captain," Paul said. "We are not sure what those are. But they are in medium geostationary orbits and are about twenty-five kilometers apart. As you can see"—the hologram adjusted again—"they form a ring around the equator of Nibiru. But that's not all. This ring repeats itself all along the full lateral spectrum of the planet, toward its north and south poles."

"Do you mean the planet is surrounded by these objects?"

"Yes, Captain. That is one way of looking at it."

"Why do you say that? What other way is there to look at it? And what is it?"

"We have no idea what it is. It's an enigma."

"Why not send a probe and find out?" Jean chimed in. She had never seen nor heard of anything so comprehensively orbiting any of the known worlds.

"We did."

"And?"

"They didn't come back. Vanished. All of them. But that is only half the story," the station chief continued. "We are able to maintain courier and communication drones outside of the system. And what they have been picking up on subspace communications has been very interesting. It took our best people a very long time to break the code and then decipher the message. Akemi, this is your area of expertise—mostly. Maybe you should explain it."

"Yes. How to explain?" She thought about it for a moment. "We were able to extract a message of sorts."

"What type of message?" Mike asked.

"An SOS. A request for help. An emergency beacon. It says, as best as we can tell, 'Help us. We are all dying.'" Akemi shifted in her chair, leaning forward toward the holographic image. "Here"—she pointed at the largest moon, Gargantuan—"the message seems to be coming from this large moon. And we don't think … we don't think the message is human in origin. That is to say, we're nearly 90 percent certain it is not human."

"I don't get it," Jean said. "We've only found a handful of other intelligent, advanced species—the Europan, Khajuraho, a few others." One of the great mysteries of the universe was why it was so strangely devoid of sentient life.

"There is life on the planet near the equator," the station chief continued. "But mass spectrometer readings suggest it is low level, vegetation and the like. Therefore, we think this is an old message. A very old message. Ancient. It might even be prehuman. And then we found this, ladies and gentleman. Up until now, only three people in the Federation have seen what I am about to show you. There is no classification high enough to mark it, so beware, it is a death sentence to talk about this outside of this room or the *Fallen Star* once you are all safely isolated on it. No, Akemi, you have not seen it either. I am sorry; it had to be that way."

The technician seemed nonplused. But she kept silent.

"The video was subvocalized, as it were," Paul Temple continued. "A spread spectrum analysis used to discover steganographic military messages was applied to the alien communication. We discovered dithering, or a noise signal meshed with the vocalized message. This noise signal carried a hidden video stream. But it was broken in a million shards. We were able to use predictive decoding to increase the intensity of the pixels in the enmeshed signal, and using a nonlinear function, we rebuilt, or to be a bit more precise, extracted a pure version of the video. It is still a bit grainy. Here we go." Paul pushed a button on the table.

The group turned and watched as the holographic image flickered and cracked. Suddenly it cleared, and the group found themselves looking at a rectangular chamber. On the immediate right was a row of desks that looked built into the wall. Strange devices were neatly arrayed down the row. On the left, a bank of electronics, similar to a server array but larger, with lights blinking in various colors, ran from the doorway all the way to the rear of the room. In the center back of the room was an arch made of some metal. One side of the arch was simply a support pillar while the other side was a long machine with two or three video screens and a multitude of arrays. Centered below the arch was an oversized couch. It was curved in the center as if to provide support to the lower back, and the presumable head of the contraption was slightly raised. Above it was a crown of sensors and multiple black wires. Jean thought they were maybe a few inches thick, indicating the capacity for an abundance of power. The video shifted and approached the couch. Suddenly it whipped back toward the doorway where a flicker of movement darted across a dark hallway. Just as suddenly, the video died.

The group sat in silence for a moment.

"Can we see that again?" Jean asked.

Paul started the short video again. This time, the station chief stopped the video just before it ended and enhanced the sensors that hung over the couch. The image blurred a bit, but the general shape of a dangling loose end could be ascertained.

"A computer jack?" Akemi Murakami posited.

"I knew you were the right woman for the job." Paul beamed. "That is exactly what we thought. And that is why we chose you to go on this mission. Your cybernetic computer interface expertise is exactly what is needed—your technical skill and Rafe Joyce's hacking skills."

Jean's eyes grew wide, "That's it. That's it! You want my brother to hack into that alien piece of machinery!"

"Yes," the station chief replied. "That is exactly what we want him to do. Ms. Murakami will modify Rafe's computer interface to fit that connection." He pointed at the still frame of the alien wire. "And then we want him to tell us what he discovers."

"Why?" Mike inquired. "You're spending all this money and effort to plug into some random computer on some random world? That doesn't make any sense."

"Don't you see," Danner Tomblin said. He sat forward and scratched his head thoughtfully. "Alien technology. And the war with the Consortium is near ending. Peace."

"I don't see the connection," Mike managed. He looked at Jean, and she shrugged back. It was a mystery.

"Trade," Danner replied as if explaining to first-term university students. "If that is truly alien technology, then we have first dibs. We have found it. The Federation can exploit it, and then maybe we can manage on our own against Terra Corp, Lin Corp, and the other systems. Wealth and independence—that is what the Federation is looking for."

"You are a sharp little man, Danner." Paul Temple stood up and stretched. "At the end of this war, we will have to turn our attention to rebuilding the Federation. And the corporations are a threat that we cannot overcome based upon our current circumstances. Eventually, the Federation will succumb to their heedless rush for profits, and we will fall under their sway."

"Nonsense," Jean scoffed.

"Really, Major? Whose weapons do you use when you go into combat? Kuball Arms? Laymay jump ships and H&K battle suits? Our ships—the *Fallen Star*—they are from Syrch or Huritz. Our water filters and computer gear, our terraforming equipment, they all come from Terra Corp. Do you really think it is nonsense?

"We need to balance the odds. If what you have fought for—what your father fought for, what all those people have died for—is to have any lasting meaning, we need this alien technology. It could save us. It could make us truly independent. Do you want the bloodshed and pain that comes along with being a corporate-sponsored system? Do you?

"Now do you understand? Now do you see why we are willing to grant your brother immunity? He deserted. He should, by all rights, be executed. But we are offering him a pardon and redemption. This is why we brought you all here." The BII station chief stared at each of them in turn. "This is what we want you to do. This is what we need you to do. This is what you are *going* to do. Understand?" The BII station chief's voice had grown hard.

Paul Temple faced each person sitting around the table. He did not waiver in his attitude, and each person in his or her turn acknowledged the order and accepted their fate.

"Good. Thank you." His voice softened once again. "Now it is getting late, and tomorrow is a busy day. You must oversee the loading of your ship and stow your gear. We will meet again and go over the mission in more detail tomorrow. You will be departing in a two-day. Clear?"

"Clear," the group replied, though not with much force or confidence.

"Good. Don't let me down. Don't let the Federation down."

With that, Paul dismissed the gathering. The chairs scuffled the floor as the group all stood. Only Danner Tomblin looked pleased. His eyes shown, and when he walked out of the room, his step was lively. Jean and Mike ambled after him, lost in their own thoughts. Ms. Akemi Murakami was the last to leave. She lingered for a moment and exchanged a personal look with the station chief. Paul softly smiled. Akemi returned it tentatively. Then the woman slipped out of the room into the hallway, and the door sealed behind her.

Paul sat wearily back down. He picked up a small remote-control device and replayed the video. Only this time, he let the whole video run. As shadows flickered in the hall, a shape lurched into the room. It was large and metallic, but the image began to falter and it was not easy to make out the figure. It looked robotic. Suddenly, a humanoid creature dropped from the open doorway and lay at the platinum legs of the lumbering, metallic being. The alien clasped its head and opened its mouth. It looked to Paul as if the creature was screaming, but there was no sound. Abruptly it convulsed, and large wounds appeared along its body, as something seemed to eat the creature from the inside out. Paul strained to see, but what had caused the wounds remained a mystery. Then, with a flash of fire that leaped from the towering, metallic shape, the humanoid began to burn, and the video died.

In the conference room, Paul Temple sat quietly. At the best he had just saved the Federation. He could, however, have just sent five people to their deaths. And the worse-case scenario? He shuddered to think about it.

Life on William Bennet Station was a whirl. Even with the docking and loading crew helping, preparing the *Fallen Star* for its mission took all of Jean's energy. The normal provisioning and stocking of the galley and basic ship's diagnostics took several hours. But the difficult part was a total refitting of the ship's medical bay, a task claimed by Akemi Murakami. That would have been fine and dandy with Jean, except that Akemi seemed to have the organizational skills of a wet bag. Oh, Jean knew, Murakami was brilliant but in an eclectic way. She seemed to have no sense of depth or size. Jean had tried to stay out of it, but when the ground crew chief burst out of the *Fallen Star*, his feet ringing on the boarding ramp, and yelled that he was going to kill that so-and-so, Jean knew she had to step in. It took four hours that Jean would never get back. And she still had so much to do. As copilot, she had diagnostics to run, and she was acting as loadmaster as well. To make matters worse, the rest of her ill-begotten crew seemed to have difficulty recognizing what was necessary and what was, as Jean put it to Captain Estury, "nice to have." A starship, even one as luxurious as the *Fallen Star*, had limited space.

Jean was watching Danner Tomblin stow his gear when he

revealed that he had filled his equipment cabinet with crap he had snuck on board.

"And where did you plan to put your space suit, your pack, your weapon, and that contraption of yours?" she asked, pointing at a midsize, black suitcase that the BII operative handled like it held expensive crystal. She sounded a bit like a teacher pointing out the obvious. She pointed at the equipment cabinet and said, "Empty it."

She then ordered everyone in the party to "get the hell off my ship" with all of their bags and other accoutrement.

Even the normally snide Danner Tomblin obeyed, and Jean led them all in a packing exercise, throwing their personal belongings out onto the platform and meticulously going through their items, one by one. Though she felt like each of the crew had managed to get something over on her, at least all of their allowable personal gear would now fit in their storage spaces.

The mission members stacked their official equipment in a pile before them. Jean had them all put on their space suits—weird things that looked to Jean suspiciously like specialized military biological and chemical combat suits. When that was done and adjustments made, she led them through a packing exercise similar to the ones she'd held with her old marine company before they had deployed. Jean called out an item and then told them where specifically to pack it.

"I'd like to tell *her* where to pack it," Jean heard Akemi mumble. But when Jean looked at the Asian woman, Akemi just smiled.

Those tasks complete, she slipped into the copilot seat and ran through a laborious prelaunch systems check. Both she and Captain Estury spent several hours on the oddly arranged insanity crystal that powered the framing drive. One of the peculiar things about the *Fallen Star* was that it was both an air and spaceship. It had wings like most suborbital planes and was cylindrical in shape. But due to frame shearing during framing, the crystal had to be placed nearly four meters away from the spaceship's hull. To allow for this, the designers of the *Fallen Star* had created a retractable device that stowed the insanity crystal in a special compartment of the spacecraft. When the ship entered a planet's atmosphere, the crystal would be retracted and stowed to prevent the wind of reentry from tearing it off. But that created other potential problems. And they were going where nobody could help them if the crystal cracked or they suffered a particularly nasty shear that left the crystal floating in space and the crew of the *Fallen Star* floating helplessly beside it.

To top it all off, nobody so much as offered to help her load equipment for her brother! So Jean packed it herself and stored it in Rafe's empty room. When she went to stow his spacesuit, her heart caught for a moment as she noted the name inscribed above its right breast. Lieutenant Joyce. LT Joyce was also emblazed on the center front and back of the helmet so her brother would be easy to identify on a spacewalk. All of the suits had their names and titles. Tech Murakami; Mr. Tomblin; CPT Estury; and MAJ Joyce. But seeing her brother's name caused a surge of emotion that was a mix between anger, frustration, and a little sister's love. Jean took a deep breath and then, with a soft touch, she hung the space suit and tucked in its arms so as not to catch them in the sliding cabinet door. As she stepped out of the small room, like the others with a bunk against the wall, a small desk and chair, and the wall-sized storage closet, Jean paused.

Soon, she thought. Soon she would see Rafe's crooked smile and hear the boyish sound of his voice. How would she react then? Would she cry? Would she rail at him? Maybe, she thought, she would do a little of both.

Sixteen hours after their meeting with Paul Temple, Jean finally stumbled into her shower and took a moment to clear the stink of the day from her body. She then grabbed her final small bag, left her room on William Bennet Station for the last time, and headed toward her quarters on the *Fallen Star*. She was giving herself five hours of sleep aboard ship. It would be enough to get her through the last dockside hours and keep her alert during initial launch. She knew she could catch up on sleep once they were framing and the computer took over.

The alarm rang too soon, and the lights of her room rose brightly. Jean squinted, grunted, and rolled over toward the wall, pulling the pillow over her ears. She ignored the alarm for a couple more moments before collecting her energy and getting out of bed. She was dressed quickly in typical marine battledress and headed up to the cockpit, where she found Captain Mike Estury already at the helm.

"You look better," he commented dryly. "You looked like complete—"

She smiled and cut him off. "That is exactly what a woman wants to hear when she wakes up. Is everyone else aboard?" Jean knew only a couple hours remained before launch.

"Coming on now," Mike answered. "Major Joyce ... Jean ... About the mission command."

Jean tensed as she sat down in her seat. She didn't answer.

"This is as much a surprise to me as it is to you. But I've been thinking. It makes sense that I'm in charge. I am the senior officer, and I do have more piloting experience than you do. Fact," he added. "But when we are on the ground, I expect you to take the lead. My job, as I figure it, is to get us there and back again. You're the tactical ground pounder. So I'll follow your lead on the ground."

"Makes sense," Jean said a bit softly. She hadn't really expected to have anyone else on the team besides herself and Rafe. But she also knew that, looking back at it all, she'd had no idea what she was getting into in the first place. Nobody had ever told her she would be in charge. Nobody had ever told her she would not be part of a team. She had gone in blind because Paul Temple had dangled her brother's redemption before her. Jean hadn't even asked. She needed to suck this up and be professional about it, but it left her a bit frustrated regardless of the logic.

"Good," the captain replied. "Then, Major," he added, "we have a final mission briefing in about fifteen minutes. After that we'll run the standard preflight checks. And then …"

"We'll get the hell out of this puzzle palace and do some real work?" Jean offered with a hard smile.

"Come on," Mike laughed. "They're gathering in the galley."

"Let's pray they thought to have the computer brew some coffee," Jean said.

The two of them left the cockpit and followed the central hall to the galley. It was on their left and consisted of a bank of food processors and a small, rectangular table. Danner Tomblin was sitting at the table, tête-à-tête with Paul Temple. Paul's presence was a bit of a surprise.

"Captain. Major." Temple offered as the two military personnel entered the room. "Join us?"

"Of course," Jean replied. "Coffee?"

"I'll grab you a cup," Mike said as he made his way to the coffee brewer and poured two mugs. Returning, he placed a mug in front of Jean as well as two creamer packets.

The four of them managed halting small talk as they waited.

Akemi Murakami was the last to arrive. She carried a small silver box in her hands, which she placed on the table. It was about twelve by twelve inches tall and had a simple combination lock.

"Lunch?" quipped Danner.

"It is for a toast," Akemi replied, opening the box to reveal four flasks of sluggish liquid in test tubes. Each tube was capped and sealed and was embossed with Lin Corp's medical augmentation division symbol.

Jean whistled. "Juice?"

"Yep," Akemi acknowledged. She read the labels and handed everyone except Paul a different colored vial. Danner did not seem pleased to get one.

"How good?" Jean asked.

"They are just high-end maintenance doses. The nanobots

will give everyone a little physical tune-up. They are basically the same with minor adjustments for everyone's unique physiology. For example, the men don't need prolonged birth control."

Mike nearly choked on a sip of coffee.

"Did I say something wrong?"

"No, Akemi. Ms. Murakami," Mike stammered.

"Akemi is fine, Captain."

"Great."

"What else does it do?" Danner asked. He was eyeing the container like it was a contagion.

"Builds muscle tissue, reduces fat, cleans arteries—that sort of thing."

"It's non-altering then?" Danner asked.

"Of course," Akemi replied. "It is standard before going on a long assignment. It may," she added, "be a little uncomfortable. I suggest that we begin to rest within four hours of consumption and then take it easy for another sixteen hours afterward. Now, the captain's and the major's also have a mix to help clean out their implants and make sure they are at their optimal. And then the major has the standard precombat ... How did you name it? Juice?"

"Ah, juice," the major replied. Jean always felt like a million dollars after taking the juice. Those little nanos did wonders. Jean was, however, a bit disappointed it was not a more potent mix. Still, she couldn't complain. And it was high stock from Lin Corp. Lin Corp made quality stuff.

"Shall we?" Mike said, raising his opened tube. "Apple?" he asked.

"Yours, yes. Mine"—Akemi lightly sniffed her serving—"is cherry. Cheers?"

"Cheers," they all said.

"Take it like a shot," Jean suggested to Danner, who was tentatively trying to taste his. "It tastes good, but it's a goo. Better to slam it all down." To show what she meant, she upended her test tube and drank the entire contents. She made a slight face and then smiled.

Danner eyed her for a moment, and then he too, reluctantly, drank his in one shot.

"Good, now that is done, we have a little additional information for you before you depart," Paul Temple said. "The BII has been able to determine that your target, on Gargantuan, has a name."

"A name?" Mike said perplexed. "What do you mean?"

"It is a computer of sorts, right. We all know that. But what we didn't know is that it is called the Core. We were able to eek that out of some of the alien transmission that we are still decoding. We speculate that it controls the ring of orbital bodies that surround the planet. And we expect it is an artificial intelligence."

"The Core? Sounds rather dramatic," Jean said. She took a drink from her mug and smiled.

"Well, we modified the translation a bit," the station chief admitted. "Central command processing, quad capable quantum synapse, cognitive attribution apparatus," he managed. "I think that is it. It was a very long name when translated."

"The Core," Mike repeated. "It's catchy."

"I am glad you approve, Captain."

"What does that mean for us?" Jean asked.

"Two things, really," Paul replied. "First"—he took a small, stiff plastic package from his inside breast pocket and handed it over the table to Akemi Murakami—"we decided to change Lieutenant Rafe's upgrade package."

It was Akemi's turn to exclaim. "This must have cost a small fortune!" she said as she rotated the package and read the label.

"It is uploaded with our translation software and has a few terabytes of memory. It is all state of the art. We figured he might need the extra power and storage space if the Core really is the CPU for not only the moon base on Gargantuan but for the sat ring."

"This is jaz!" Akemi replied.

"Okay. If by that you mean it's half a million credits, then yes, it is Jaz. Don't drop it," he advised.

"Half a million?" Jean nearly burst.

"We get one shot at this, Major. Just one. And you can tell your brother that, if he joins us, it is all his. No refunds necessary."

"That's generous."

"No. Not really," Paul replied. "The device has a cranial mesh. Once in, it can't be removed. But it sounds better to say it's a gift." He winked.

"And what is the second thing? Mike leaned forward and looked around the table, his eyes settling on the BII station chief.

"Oh, that." Paul returned the captain's serious look. "Rafe, I mean Lieutenant Joyce, is going to have to talk to it—to the Core. After he plugs in, it won't be like a normal data stream. He will have to"—he thought about his next words carefully—"charm it. He will need to convince it that we are answering its distress call and are only there to help. And then he will have to persuade the Core to download a good share of its raw data and allow you to bring back amble samples of whatever alien technology you might find. It is more than I had hoped he would have to do. I was hoping he would have a firewall to get through and then he could just do a massive data scoop. But now?" He shrugged.

"Rafe? Convince an alien supercomputer to share its secrets?" Jean's voice was skeptical.

"Major Joyce, I assure you that your brother is quite the social engineer. He will need that skill."

"Anything else?" Mike prompted. Nothing he had heard required him to change his flight plan.

"No. Not really. The standard information and briefing materials have all been uploaded to the *Fallen Star's* computer. You will find basic schematics, coordinates, that type of thing. And of course there is some anthropological and linguistic material that you should peruse. It is all theoretical. Much of it is derived from the classic study, *Cybernetic Cognition*," Paul added.

"I chose most of that material," Akemi explained. "Have you heard of *The Cognition Conundrum*? It was another early earth essay suggesting an equivalency between biological and artificial intelligence. The essay led to the more precedent-setting study in artificial intelligence, *Cognitive Imagination*, which has defined the field for the last hundred or so years."

"There's not a test at the end of this adventure, I hope," Mike mumbled. "Did you download something good to read too?"

"Yes," Akemi admitted with a bit of a laugh. "*Cognitive Imagination* can be a bit droll—even for me. But yes, we have a full e-library on board."

"Read the briefing material," Paul instructed. "It has been simplified—put in layman's terms. And it may save your life."

"Know your enemy?" Jean suggested.

"Exactly."

"Well, then," Captain Estury said. "Is there anything else? No? Well, Mr. Temple, I have a ship to sail, and we launch in just a few hours. Should we say our good-byes?"

"Of course." Paul stood, and the rest followed his lead. "Good luck, everyone. There is much riding on this voyage of yours. And you, Major, for you particularly. Don't let me down. Don't let your family down. Don't let your mother and father down. And don't let the Federation down."

"We won't," Jean offered, though she suddenly felt a deep pit in the bottom of her stomach. She hoped the feeling of dread was just the effects of the nanobots getting adjusted.

The group shook hands. The station chief departed, and the gathering broke up. Soon, Jean and Captain Estury were back in the cockpit conducting their final preflight checks.

It all seemed a bit surreal to Jean—her brother, Rafe, a genius computer hacker; her commander a hotshot navy pilot who was a bit too cute and, she could tell, was a little resentful at having been stripped of his normal command to fly this mission; a techno-geek beauty who was more comfortable with mathematical equations, cybernetics, and computer chips than with people; and an odd little BII operative. How had she become entangled with such a diametrically dysfunctional group? And though she could understand flying off to save her stupid brother, what did that say about herself? When you mixed in an ancient, alien supercomputer and a mysterious planet that was imprisoned beneath a ring of satellites, it made Jean wonder if she was crazy to be going on this mission. Were they all crazy?

What was the alien's message? She tried to recall. Wasn't it, "We are all dying?" Dying from what?

Money. It is such an odd thing. It has no intrinsic value. You can't eat it, drink it, or build anything of real use from it. And in today's universe, money is less substantial than it had ever been in the course of human existence. Most of it is just an electronic blip in a well-protected computer financial network—a digital on-and-off sequence that said, "This is a penny unit," or, "This is a thousand credits unit." Billions of electronic sequences called money flowed over the financial networks of the worlds and fueled all the industries of humankind. But it is all an illusion, a shared mirage by trillions of people throughout the cosmos. The singular belief that these electronic blips of data held value made the financial system viable. If those beliefs were ever to falter, if faith in the financial network and its quantum calculated firewalls and layers of overlapping controls ever failed, people would once again realize that what they worked so diligently to accumulate was just a computer blip. The markets would crash, and a hundred worlds would fall into the greatest economic depression in history. That is why governments retain the exclusive right to create and define each electronic on-and-off sequence that people called money. And that, Rafe knew, was the key.

He sat in his quiet room hewn out of rough rock that was the color of sea stone and sparkled with bits of dolomite, calcite, and mica. He pushed back from his paper-thin computer screen and stretched his back. He was almost done. His masterpiece of computer programing was nearly ready. When released, it would infiltrate the financial network at a hundred different points and issue billions of instructions per second to create false invoicing trails for minor purchases and their corresponding incomes. Written in assembly language, the base language of microprocessors, the software would blend into the natural superstructure of the financial network and be nearly undetectable. And it would only remain active for a few hours in each star system before total dissolution. Years of work would vanish in the blink of an electronic microsecond. But what it would leave behind, he smiled broadly, pleased with himself, would be a wonder.

Rafe was not going to steal money. No. That was too easy. He was going to create it. He was going to create his own electronic blips of on-and-off and move them through a billion tiny routes to a centralized electronic account. It would be impossible to trace. He would create pennies, dimes, quarters, single-credit units, and twenty-credit units and move them through countless parts of the financial system until they took on a real aspect and were indistinguishable from their government-created counterparts. And then the newly coined funds would transfer to his shell computer consulting company, as if he had actually provided services. A billion small transactions over a period of three earth years of routing would all end up in Rafe's pockets. Rafe would become very, very wealthy.

And what did it matter if eventually the authorities discovered what he had done? Could they afford to admit that their financial system was flawed—that someone outside of government had created money? Would they dare risk destroying the faith that people had in those little electronic on-and-off blips that drove all human economy? No. Once faith is destroyed it takes years, perhaps generations, to rebuild it. They would have to let Rafe be. They would have to acknowledge the legitimacy of his self-created fortune to sustain the mythical, collective obsessional behavior that is the delusion of money.

Rafe Joyce stood up and walked across the small room to the dark leather couch he had lugged to the asteroid retreat a few years ago. His naked feet swept across the plush area rug that sat upon an artificial mahogany wood floor. The floor, thank goodness, was heated. He collapsed on the couch and adjusted his position until he was comfortable. He felt tired. Programing was a mentally intensive activity, and he was often exhausted after an evening of code writing. At least this newest residence was comfortable. Rafe had done as much as he could to make the apartment-sized asteroid homey. In place of windows, he had large video screens hung on the walls. Depending on his mood, he had them loop through feeds from various planets that showed either cityscapes or landscapes, which made him feel as if he were living a real life. Right now, they showed a rain-sprinkled landscape of a coniferous forest. A lake was visible in the distance, and strange birds flitted occasionally between the quiet trees as the planet's sun struggled to peak through a thick cover of cloud. He had no idea what planet it was, but it was pretty.

Ever since he had fled the Marine Corps of the Federation worlds, Rafe had lived a shadowy existence. He had to be careful. There were many extradition agreements between the various governments, and nobody, not anyone, liked a military deserter. Of course, Rafe had hidden his identity—had changed it many times over the last decade. But he had not really perfected the art until this last incarnation as Henry Janyar, a small-time life insurance agent. But in an age of retinal, bio heat, palm, and fingerprint readers, creating and maintaining an alternate identity was extremely difficult. That was why he spent most of his time here, in isolation, in his little asteroid home. Oh, he had neighbors. They shuttled back and forth between each other's residences in little in-system spacecraft and parked on personal space jetties.

Rafe lived in an avant-garde community in the Tianjin System. Many people chose to make homes in the asteroid belt. The homes ranged from small little things like his to huge mansions. The majority of people were artisans—musicians and writers, painters and composers, and the serious to the ridiculous intellectuals. A thriving yet small community of merchants and service providers supported the community. Most of them had business establishments on the larger asteroids that plied their trades near the center of Tianjin's asteroid field. It was the perfect place for Henry Janyar to blend in. Henry was an aspiring writer as well as an insurance salesman. That part of his persona allowed him to move in the little social circles of the system. And Rafe had found it the perfect place to ply his real trade and avoid the authorities. Still, it was a lonely life. He hoped that his greatest caper would provide him the economic means to buy his freedom. People with real money, god-awful hordes of it, did not obey the same rules as the rest of society. That would be his true salvation. He would buy his way back into the broader, civilized universe.

Rafe closed his eyes and tried to sleep. But as often happened, thoughts of rejoining mainstream society led his mind back to his family on Baile Mac Carhain. He had not seen his mother, father, or little sister in many years. Once or twice, Rafe had risked contacting them, but Rafe was a disgrace in his father's eyes, and those attempts always ended in frustration and pain.

He knew his sister, Jean, had joined the marines. Rafe suspected Jean had done it in some gallant attempt at family redemption. And from what he gathered from the various news outlets, she had managed fairly well. Now the war was winding down. The last gasps of effort from the Consortium were ragged things, hissing like the stagnant air in an old man's dying lungs. Rafe hoped that his mother and sister would accept him back when it was all over, but he had little hope that his father, a retired marine colonel, would ever forgive Rafe for deserting. But what else could Rafe have done? Rafe had fought in one battle. Just one. But it was enough to convince him that only fools cast away their lives on the orders of other fools. The carnage, red and searing, had been the things of nightmares. No. Rafe was no fool. Let the fools stab each other and blast each other to bits in the nowhere land between sanity and chaos. He had a life to live.

What did that, in Rafe's eyes, make of his sister, Jean? She was a damn fool too. But she had been led to stupidity for reasons of the heart, for honor and salvation. Jean had always been the dreamer. She believed, in the purest sense of belief, that some things were right and some things were wrong. What would become of Jean when she finally discovered that they all lived in a meaningless universe? He hoped that that revelation was not so destructive that Jean would falter and fade. Of course, Rafe knew, most people never made that intellectual jump and remained placid in a world as simple as dark and light. Maybe Jean would never make the intellectual leap and would continue living in that realm of ignorant bliss too.

Fine. Be that as it may ... He let the thought trail off as he settled into the couch.

"Damn it! Lights off!" he snapped. The house computer switched the lights off, and Rafe was left in the murky darkness with the ambient forest glow cast through his video screens mixing and churning.

A repetitious thought danced in his mind. *I am almost free. I am almost free. Damn it, I am almost free.*

Sleep came slowly. It crept upon him like a silent tide until he succumbed to its watery embrace. And when Rafe dreamed, he dreamed of a vast, oscillating electronic web, where his mind slipped like a quick-footed thief. And in his dream, Rafe was laughing.

The *Fallen Star* moved effortlessly through interstellar space. Having left William Bennet Station far behind, the framing drive propelled the spacecraft ever silently toward the Tianjin System. Major Jean Joyce's mind was wandering. She looked around the table at the other crew members, but she didn't hear a word they were saying. How would her brother react to the *Fallen Star's* sudden arrival in the system? Would he even notice the courier ship as it framed in a few AU beyond the asteroid belt? If he did, would he flee? And what if they were able to talk to Rafe? What would she say to him? How could she make him understand the amount of pain he had put their parents through—had put her through. Jean shifted uncomfortably in her chair and smiled benignly at a random comment thrown out by someone in her little group of unlikely heroes.

What if Rafe said no? she wondered. Would Danner Tomblin attempt to force Rafe to join their expedition? Would the capricious man simply call local authorities? And what a strange man Danner Tomblin had turned out to be. Jean's mind and eyes flicked toward Tomblin and she felt a surge of unease and dislike flow through her. Tomblin was speculative, manipulative, and spouted innuendo like volcanoes spouted lava. Why in the world had Paul Temple decided to send such an odd, little man? What was it about Danner Tomblin that made him uniquely qualified for this mission? Jean could find nothing about him that was remotely positive. That feeling had grown the more she'd had to interact with him. In the end, she had decided to just avoid Tomblin as best she could. But there were moments, like right now, sitting across the small table from him at dinner that seemed unavoidable.

"The inquisitors were educators, correcting errors in humanity's view of God," he was explaining with fervor to Captain Estury. "And yes, their methods were painful. Foundational corrections are always painful."

Mike was goading the man on a bit, Jean suspected. But in reality, Jean had stopped listening to them a while ago. Leaving her thoughts behind, she reentered the conversation with really no idea what they were talking about.

"The inquisitors were educators?" Jean asked. "Wasn't that in the Dark Ages or something, back on old earth? Didn't they torture people?" Ah, she could shoot herself! She shouldn't have encouraged the man at all.

Now Danner focused his eyes on Jean and smiled almost snidely. He ran a hand through his near shoulder-length hair and leaned forward. "Such believes the unwitting mind. The inquisitors were judges who were trying, originally, to stem an abuse of civil authoritarians with little to no judicial education—or any education for that matter. These civil authorities killed uncounted thousands due to their lack of jurisprudence. The lords of the Dark Ages, as you describe them, would execute people with little to no proof of guilt. True, the inquisitors' real purpose was polluted and warped over time. As the Dark Ages evolved into an age of mass heresy, they applied their methods to those who had succumbed to the false religious teachings of others to redirect and correct the people's belief system. They were trying to save people's souls."

"They tortured people," Jean concluded.

"You're missing the point!" Danner exclaimed. "Their approach was admittedly rudimentary, but the intent was pure."

"And you think that it was, therefore, well-meaning torture? And the end justifies the means?" Mike asked.

"I am saying," Danner huffed, "that we use many ways to curb human behavior nowadays. We indoctrinate them in schools. We bombard them with social constructs through video vision and social media. We shape and bind their actions for all their lives. And that, in turn, results in the modification of their behavior and creates the force that bind societies together. When those binding forces are threatened or cast aside, chaos abounds."

"Is he saying that mind control is okay, Mike?" Jean shot at Captain Estury.

The captain shrugged.

"All I know," offered Akemi Murakami, "is that, if social interaction is defined by video vision, then all women are whores, and all men are backstabbing assholes."

Jean laughed, "Why do you say that?"

"Have you never watched a soap opera before, Major?"

"And I thought your starting point," Mike said, "was that chaos is a constructive force in the universe. How does that jive with the apparent stabilizing goal of the inquisition?"

"Never mind!" Danner said, exasperated. "Obviously the concept is too subtle for you to comprehend."

"Obviously," Akemi agreed. Her sarcasm was not lost on anyone.

The BII operative crossed his arms and glared around the table. Jean felt like waving in an overtly friendly manner to him, but decided against it. He might think she actually meant it.

"We should arrive in the Tianjin System tomorrow," she said, changing the subject. Jean really did not have a game plan yet.

"About midway through the day cycle," Mike confirmed.

"And how long to get to the asteroid belt?"

"Last calculations had just a few hours from the nearest jump point. We can't get to near due to framing effect."

"And what do you think, Major?" The Asian woman refused to call Jean by her first name. "Will your brother readily join our expedition?"

"I don't know," Jean admitted. "I think if we can get to him before he runs off, he will listen. And if he listens, I think he will come along," Jean lied. She thought Rafe would laugh at them and disappear in a puff of smoke.

"Then we have to get him to listen," Danner Tomblin said. His voice sounded a bit too maniacal for Jean's taste.

Jean smiled tightly. "Yes. He will have to listen." *More likely I will have to beat him over the head*, she thought, but she kept that thought to herself.

"And then?" Akemi prompted. "Have you finished your plan, Major, for the next part of our mission?"

"The long jump," Mike stated flatly. "Lots of downtime to get that far out of system."

"But there will be a lot to do," Jean said. She leaned forward against the table. "We have a lot of prep work. We need to be ready for space walks, and that means getting used to our suits. I've been reading the technical manuals."

"Really?" Mike laughed and shook his head. "The technical manuals?"

"Somebody has to," Jean retorted. But she had to laugh at herself too and admit reading the technical manual for a space suit was fairly sad. "They do have some neat and unique features. They are XM Flash biohazard environmental suits. I've never worn anything like them before. Terra Corp makes them for extreme alien environments. They are armored, use high-tech heating and cooling coils that use the Peltier effect to save on energy, and apparently flash burn or freeze biologics off their exterior surfaces—self-decontaminate. But they are a bit complicated and are rigid. We're going to have to practice in the things.

"Then we have to come up with a plan of action once we get in the Kururumany System and start our approach on Gargantuan. We need approach vectors, an infiltration plan, an exit plan, and everything in between. I have the basic idea down, Akemi, but it still needs work. Paul Temple did not leave us much time in terms of planning. We'll just have to make up for it on the long jump."

Mike smirked. "And here I was hoping for a vacation."

"Or we could just wing it," Jean suggested sarcastically. "After all, its just an alien moon fortification over a super earth of ice surrounded by a net of satellites where some unknown intelligence is crying out for help because, whatever they are, they are all dying. I mean … what could go wrong, right?"

"When you say it like that," the captain quipped, "you make it sound like this might be a little dangerous."

"I think a plan is a good idea," Akemi added.

"Good," Jean said. Akemi had missed the banter and sarcasm. Jean took another sip of coffee, and for a moment, her mind returned to the problem with her brother. But she pushed it to the back of her mind. "Because you are all going to help me flesh the plan out. And we are going to rehearse until you all hate me."

"Wonderful," Danner Tomblin mumbled.

Jean ignored him.

"I'm going to get some rack time. Midway through the cycle?" She directed the last question at Captain Estury.

"Before we arrive in the Tianjin System?" he asked. He shrugged. "Yep. Give or take a few hours."

"Good." Jean stood up. She wondered if she would actually be able to sleep. She felt like her nerves were on fire. "Then I'll set the alarm for midcycle. And I suggest the rest of you get some sleep too. Who knows when we'll get another chance for a solid eight?"

"So no plan on how to approach your brother?" Mike asked.

"Plan?" Jean considered. "Why don't we try talking to him?"

"That is a detailed plan, Major," the captain replied with a short laugh.

"I aim to please."

Jean put her coffee cup on the table and left the kitchenette. As she was stepping out of the door, she noted that the BII operative was still sullen, and she wondered if they had pushed the odd man a little too hard. The last thing she needed on this trip was infighting among the team. Jean had the feeling that they would all need to be on their marks if they hoped to be successful on this mission. She had taken the job for her brother, at the height of an emotional rush, but since then, she had taken the time to study the mission and its objective. It made her uneasy. The mission was beyond anything she had experienced before, and that made her feel as if she were going in blind.

It wouldn't do her brother, her father, or her mother any good if she reconnected with Rafe only to get him and herself killed on some bizarre mission to steal alien technology. Paul Temple and his damn Bureau of Intelligence and Insurgency had really played her emotions. Well, it was a lesson learned. She just hoped she lived long enough to apply it.

The *Fallen Star* continued on its preprogramed route as Jean made her way to her cabin. The hallway was silent, and it occurred to Jean that the lack of noise must be similar to what the dead heard, buried deeply within their earthen tombs. The thought made her shudder.

There is something that lingers in the dark of a man's mind. We project upon the universe our own frailties, insecurities, and desires, and in so doing, we imagine that God's mind is our own. What folly! What dire mistake! Are we so bold to believe that the universe is our personal playground?

Fools! The universe without and the universe within are unknowable in their totality. We are but sheep under a desert sky. We dream, and our thoughts are like weeping.

Danner Tomblin typed furiously on the flat surface of his digital diary. His mind was focused as the words tumbled out of his impenetrable convictions. A golden wheel with spiked edges, like a wagon wheel with arrows pointing in all directions, tapped gently against his chest as the neck chain that held the simple pendant bounced in rhythm to his flowing hands. It was an ancient symbol of chaos and the guide stone of his heart.

The delusions that people cast!

A soul without blight, without the blind trappings of our meager selves, a soul that looks not up and around the endless space of the dark and unknowable void, but inward to the ultimate truth of our own evolution, is the soul that resides in the light of truth. God's light. As the prophet said, "A soul without denial is a soul in rapture."

Out of infinite nothing, God gave birth to infinite chaos. The chaos of creation gave birth to the soul of man. And it is in the heart of evolutionary chaos where all true men abide. The lights of the heavens are pinpricks in the endless, foul night; these are the truths of the universe. Its essence. These are the simmering bones of God.

Yet we immolate our souls to our intellect.

The air is silent. The ship moves in constant technical revolutions as we ply with the rapist's glee through the bosom of the cosmos. We travel in space toward an alien world, but what is our true destination? What path has God laid before me?

Though I wonder and doubt, I shall not fear the shades that round me ring and mock me to agitation. I shall not lose my soul to impure humanity. God has placed me here, through the chaos of selection, through chance and lonely circumstance. I shall be strong. I shall persevere. I have been cast by His hand as a servant directed toward the shadows!

Here, within the reach of my arms, is an article of pure chaos. It is a bomb. A planet killer. In it swims the lifeblood of the beginning, raw with the elemental powers that God forged in time. At the first moment. At the birth of it all.

He paused for a moment, his mind swimming. How had it all come to pass? he wondered. The cycled air was crisp, its thin breath moving across the smoothness of his face. He had never even imagined such a fate. Danner ran a hand over his chin and then bent back to his task.

By what means did the Church of Chaos discern the clue? How did my fathers and mothers discover so minute a place at the edge of man's understanding? Have they completely infiltrated the BII or have they some way of directing the bureau that is beyond my knowledge? How did they know about the alien message? How did they discover this mission? And how did they get their disciple, my humbled self, assigned to the investigative team? The amounts of seemingly random threads leave me amazed.

If I did not believe, I would feel so appallingly lost.

It has been a long and terrible road. I have, an acolyte of singularity, long shuddered under the weight of false representation. Was it for this moment that God sent me forth into the heathen world? It must be. For to deny is to dwell in terror. To deny is to wail in the dark.

"A soul without denial is a soul in rapture." It is my prayer. "A soul without denial is a soul in rapture!" I will not deny. I shall overcome and bide my time until the moment is right.

I am the harbinger of chaos. I am the cleansing soul. I am a warrior—a speck of stardust.

Danner Tomblin closed his encrypted journal and sat staring at the dark suitcase that he had gingerly carried aboard the *Fallen Star*. He brushed his hair out of his eyes and sighed. He had not asked for this mission. No. It had been thrust upon him almost in eagerness. How had the Church managed that feat? His stomach curled. Was it fear he was feeling? Was it glee? The Church of Chaos and not the Bureau of Intelligence and Insurgency was his true master. Danner had been sent by the Church to destroy the alien base. The Church desired a conflict between the Federation and the corporate worlds. Such a conflict would seed chaos, and in chaos was the means to the advancement of humanity.

Order and stability eventually led to a malaise of inactivity that bred corruption and degradation. In contrast, all conflict generated rapid technological advance and brought necessary change to societies grown rich and slovenly, comfortable in the order of things. The BII, Danner snorted, lacked the clarity of vision to see the universal whole. The alien technology would be used by the Federation to maintain stability, the status quo. The war against the Consortium was also an attempt to maintain the universe in its current state. Better to destroy the alien technology, force a conflict as the corporations encroached upon the Federation, and see that struggle renew the universe. While the BII would have the alien technology to combat the corporations, Danner and the Church of Chaos would have a war, where the social order of the Federation and the corporate worlds were recast and remolded. Chaos led to renewal, Danner knew. That had been his entire point he'd tried to convey to the naval captain, but Mike Estury didn't understand. *How could he? How could any of them?* Danner thought. *None of the others are true believers.*

He shifted uncomfortably in his small, stark cabin. The electric light sparked on the side of the suitcase, and it seemed to Danner as if it were a reflection of an elemental sun.

What was, he thought, *was.*

How was Danner to know the ways of God? He was here, and so was the device. And it was a device designed with but one purpose— to destroy a world.

The door chimed, and reflexively, Danner flipped the switch that was imbedded into his dressing table. The pocket door to his cabin automatically opened. Danner was surprised to see Major Joyce step into the doorway.

"I'm sorry if the conversation at dinner was a little harsh." The major stood silhouetted by the yellowish light from the hallway. She leaned casually against the far side of the doorframe. She brought the heel of her left boot up against the frame, raising her left knee so it formed an "A" with her right leg. The halo of light behind her accentuated her feminine curves and made Danner's lips tremble.

He looked away. "They didn't understand. But I didn't expect them to." Danner put his closed electronic journal on the bed behind him, hiding it from view.

"I don't think I understood you either, Danner," Jean admitted. "But I was distracted. I am sorry I was not listening more closely."

Danner smiled though inside he sneered. "It was just a theological discussion, a vague point."

"Theological?"

"Social theology, if you will," Danner corrected. "You know," he added with a shy voice, "people say I think too much."

Jean looked at him silently for a moment. She didn't trust him or his overly innocent tone.

"I don't want you to believe we don't appreciate your role in our team, Danner." Jean sighed and smiled sincerely. Had they pushed the BII operative too far? "We have not had a proper integration period, and that will make this transition tougher to bear—for all of us. And I recognize I didn't help matters with my snide comment."

"I'm a big boy, Major."

Jean considered Danner. He was impeccably groomed. The bureau's man had a naturally open expression, and his voice was soothing. Was she being played? Or did he mean what he said?

"I know," she replied. "They are good people." She gestured behind her indicating the rest of the ship and its crew. "They are doing something that I am not."

"And what is that, Major?"

"They are doing this mission because they were ordered to do it. You—you were ordered to do it. You are all honoring your oaths." She paused for a moment, and her eyes became unfocused, as if she were looking far away.

"And what are you doing, Major?"

"That is just it, Danner. I'm not doing this mission for country or creed. I'm just trying to save my brother. And that bothers me."

"It bothers you?"

"My world is a simple one, Danner. The mission, the unit, and the marines—that is the motto that I have lived by since forever. It has been a very long time since I did anything for myself. And that is what this whole crazy mission is about for me. And I am afraid I am doing it for all the wrong reasons and that those reasons might get some people killed."

"Why tell me all of this, Major? What is your point?"

Major Joyce's eyes focused sharply. She was trying so hard to like the man, but Danner was making it difficult. "We have brawn, brains, and technical skills on our team. I could tell this to any of them, but I don't think they would understand. And I think that is why I am telling you. Because you do understand. You are a deep thinker, and I believe we will need your nuanced thought before this mission is through. So don't let the banter turn you off of the group. We need you. I am not sure how or when, but this is not your average mission. Do you know what I mean?"

"Yes," Danner conceded. *She is good*, Danner thought. Charismatic. A strong leader. He had underestimated her ability to manipulate just because of his own stereotypical view of marines. He would have to revise his estimates. "I think I understand you, Major."

Jean nodded and stepped out of the doorway and back into the hall. "I'll see you later, Danner. I am glad we had this little talk. But right now, I have a bit of work to do, and then I really need to catch that sleep."

"Later, then," Danner said.

The door swooshed closed, and Danner Tomblin sat in the renewed silence of his cabin. His eyes were drawn back toward the dark suitcase sitting forlornly on the floor of the room. Major Joyce would not have so openly invited him into the group if she knew, he thought.

Danner wasn't on the mission to help the major decide how best to tackle the problem and save her brother. No. He wasn't there to serve the ends of the bureau either. Danner Tomblin was a servant of the Church of Chaos. He was an acolyte. And the Church had its own mission for him. Danner was here to decide when it would be the best time to destroy them all.

Destroy them all.

A soul without denial is a soul in rapture, he thought. *And I am not in denial.*

The midcycle came quickly as the ship bounded into the Tianjin System a few AU from the system's asteroid belt. The navigation display rolled the names of various asteroids across the screen as Captain Mike Estury navigated the *Fallen Star* toward the belt's main travel corridor. The system's space traffic control center queried the ship for its name and purpose in system.

Fallen Star. Private Yacht. Space tourism.

The response raised no concerns, and the traffic controller gave the captain the vectors required to enter the asteroid belt.

Major Joyce, acting as copilot and navigator, stretched her electronic sensors out into the twirling mass of rocks and ice, feeling her way toward Metis Five, the asteroid her brother had made into his home. Jean's heart was pounding, and it took all of her will to steady her hands and her mind as the ship slipped ever closer to the brother she had not seen in years. Jean heard a noise behind her and turned to see Akemi Murakami calmly peering over Jean's shoulder at the navigation screen. It was distracting, but Jean smiled at the

Asian woman and turned her full attention back to her remote scanning.

Jean's interface with the ship's computer had grown stronger as the major had become more familiar with the ship. Now, when Jean connected to the CPU and extended her senses through the various external sensors or allowed her mind to play across the ship's internal components, she could feel the ship, just as if it were an extension of her physical form. She wondered what would happen when she returned to the marine fleet. Would she miss the sensation like an amputee misses the feelings in an amputated arm or leg? Would ghost images and sensations run through her mind to torment her with what she had lost? It was a disturbing idea. Jean had not really studied the effects of such long-term interfacing with spacecraft. But she had heard experienced pilots refer to it as "junking in." Was that because it had a narcotic effect? Was Jean becoming addicted to her ship-enhanced senses? The way this made her feel, with her mind now floating through the vastness of space, left little doubt that such an experience could become addictive. She would have to remember to ask Mike about it when there was time.

The *Fallen Star's* in-system drives pulsed as they pushed the spaceship through real space. Captain Estury had retracted the framing drive and its crystal into the ship's rear fuselage, where it was now ensconced in a special protective chamber. The in-system drives sent a trill of reverberations throughout the hull. Jean could feel the vibration in the heart of her bones. She wondered if anyone else could feel it.

Despite the *Fallen Star's* unique ability to be both spaceship and airship, the craft still had a small shuttlecraft that could be used to ferry people and supplies. She was grateful for that. Her scans had begun to pick out small docking platforms along the sides of the asteroid homes. These docks were too small for the *Fallen Star* to use. But the *Fallen Star's* crew could access them with the shuttlecraft. Jean suspected her brother's home would have a similar-sized dock.

Farther into the belt, she noticed, were larger asteroids that the navigation system identified as commercial hubs and shopping centers. Jean found that the docks to those facilities were large enough to handle several ships the size of the *Fallen Star*. A few could hold larger, interstellar passenger and transport ships. Small ships flitted through the intervening space between the asteroids like little rowboats making their way between islands. The flare of the small spaceships' engines danced in the darkness. Some of the asteroids seemed not to rotate at all, and some spun and churned. All of the asteroids caught the faint, gray light of the distant sun. The overall effect was a peaceful canvas of light, shadow, and movement. Jean understood why her brother Rafe had taken up residence in such a place.

"So what is your plan?" Akemi Murakami's feline voice interrupted the routine of the cockpit.

Jean sighed. "Well …" She looked back at the Asian woman, who was hovering over Jean's shoulder and staring out the cockpit window. "I thought about it long and hard."

"And what did you come up with?"

"I thought you and I would just go and knock on his door."

"That's your plan?" Akemi asked. "Knock on his door?"

"It seems pretty straightforward to me," Jean responded. "What else are we going to do? Blast a hole in the side of his house and kidnap him? Sometimes the obvious and mundane make the best plans. You know, KISS."

Akemi looked at Jean, confusion registering across her sculptured face. Everything about the technician screamed femininity, Jean thought. Symmetrical cheekbones and dainty eyelashes fluttered over stunningly dark eyes that Akemi perfectly offset and emphasized with just a blush of makeup.

"Keep it simple stupid," Mike interjected.

"Excuse me." Akemi turned toward the captain.

Jean could see that even the captain was not immune to the sudden spotlight of Akemi's bewitching eyes. He smiled uncomfortably yet remained transfixed.

"It is an ancient principle of planning," Jean replied.

Akemi turned back to the marine major. When her eyes broke contact with the captain, the man seemed to be physically released from a spell.

Jean sighed.

The captain made eye contact with Jean, smiled weakly, shrugged, and thought it best he return to piloting the spacecraft.

"People tend to overplan—to make complicated plans that are so clever that they are bound to fail."

"Oh," Akemi said, thinking for a moment, "like wasting time using a reduction algorithm to show that one mathematical problem is as difficult to solve as another, when you can just look at the second problem and figure out that it's a bitch too. Who cares about the degrees of unsolvability?"

"Yes." Jean had no idea what Akemi was talking about. "Exactly. Or something like that."

"Why me?"

"What?"

"You said you and I were going to go and knock on his door."

"Oh, computer nerd to computer nerd and you are …"—Jean tried to think of a delicate way of saying it—"my brother's type. My brother is just going to love you."

Akemi looked at Jean for a moment before her eyes shifted back to the asteroids and its menagerie of houses, shops, and growing space traffic.

Jean took Akemi's silence as acceptance and glanced quickly at the accelerometer, noting that the *Fallen Star* was slowing as it approached the inner space lanes.

"Let's find a place to park this thing," Mike suggested. "Then you and Akemi take the shuttle and find your brother."

"What will *you* be doing?" Jean asked the captain. "You know, while the women are both working?"

"Oh, I don't know." Mike laughed. "Go shopping? Day spa? Find a nice restaurant?" The captain brought up a schematic of the asteroid community and virtually overlaid it on the main cockpit window. He brought up the visual for Akemi's benefit, as he had also pushed it through the ship's computer directly to Jean's interface. "We'll park here on Skyway Wharf. They have large bays that can handle the *Fallen Star*. Then we will do what we told the control tower. Danner and I will go all tourist while you and Akemi go speak with your brother."

"Ah, the *plan* comes together," Akemi sarcastically noted. She looked at the captain and major and announced, "I shall go get ready. If I am to seduce your brother"—she directed her comment at the major—"I had better look the part."

Akemi walked out of the cockpit. Mike watched her go.

Jean reached over and gave the captain a slap on the arm. Mike grinned back at her.

"Look the part?" He was amazed. He noticed that Jean was giving him a sharp look. "Shall we?" he said.

Major Joyce quickly calculated the approach vectors, and she and Captain Estury guided the *Fallen Star* in among the inner space lanes and their teeming shuttlecraft. Jean was concentrating so hard on not ramming one of the flighty little spacecraft that she barely noticed when the computer navigator highlighted Metis Five. The asteroid was smack-dab in the middle of a residential zone, an easy jaunt from where the *Fallen Star* was now beginning to dock. Jean punched the auto docking sequence, and the ship began firing small bursts of propulsion as the *Fallen Star* jockeyed up to an empty stall and eased to a stop. With a loud metallic clang, the gangway moved from the wharf to marry against the *Fallen Star's* air lock. An alarm sounded, warning the crew that the ship was about to match the gravitational field of the dock. This was followed by an audible hissing sound.

"We're uplinked and settled," the captain said, unhooking his safety harness and standing. He stretched. Then he removed the computer cable from his skull jack and helped Jean from her acceleration couch.

Jean braced herself for the expected sensory loss caused by unhooking from the ship's CPU. Holding her breath, she disconnected from the circuit. Jean stumbled a little with the loss of sensory input from the ship's systems but quickly righted herself. She was getting better at handling the transition, she thought.

"Okay," she managed as she stepped toward the main compartment of the ship. "I guess I'll change, and then I'll go see my brother."

Mike placed a soft hand on her shoulder and stopped her for a moment.

She looked back at him.

"Are you all right?"

"I'm fine."

"Do you think he will come along?"

Jean considered it for a moment, smiled sadly, and then the features of her face hardened. "He'll come, or I'll kill him."

Mike grinned. "I can see how, given those options, he'll come along."

"Let's get moving," Jean replied.

Mike and Jean walked out of the cockpit and into the hallway beyond.

The ship's computer automatically dimmed the cockpit's lights and continued its protocol handshakes with the dockside computer. Beyond the *Fallen Star*, along the edge of the Skyway Wharf, people in lively clothing with brilliant colors enjoyed their dinners from their vantage point at the Last Chance restaurant and bar. The protected space of the observation deck allowed the diners to enjoy the many lights and sights of the community from behind para-glass windows. The ultrahardened glass carbonate kept instantaneous death from the vacuum of space just a few inches away.

Each in their own rooms, Danner Tomblin muttered, Akemi Murakami primped, Captain Mike Estury slipped a small handgun into a concealed pocket, and Major Jean Joyce fretted. What was she going to say to her brother? More importantly, how was she going to stop herself from hitting Rafe squarely in the jaw?

The doorbell rang.

The doorbell rang? Rafe Joyce froze. His doorbell almost never rang. The few times it had rung had been on account of a small dinner party he was throwing. And then there was the time he had requested a technician to fix a leaky faucet. He was fairly isolated. Rafe liked it that way.

Closing his eyes and using his implant, Rafe tapped quickly into his residential security system. How had he not noticed the approach of that small shuttlecraft? And there were two people, in weird, copper-colored space suits, standing in the air lock just outside his door.

Rafe looked at the air lock status. It had cycled and was safe to stand in and breathe. Why had the two figures not removed their helmets? What were they hiding?

Rafe's mind raced through the possibilities. Perhaps the local authorities had managed to get their facial recognition software to identify Rafe from one of his many trips into the commercial sector—though Rafe had taken some precautions.

Rafe adjusted the camera again to get a close-up of the two visitors; they did not appear armed. Shifting to infrared, Rafe saw that both figures presented the heat signature of women. That was a bit odd too. But their gender made the uninvited guests only a little less threatening. He scanned the most recent air lock activation sequence and saw nothing unusual in the air that had been pumped into the lock; nor was any trace explosive detected. Rafe had augmented his home air lock with a molecule sniffer that could identify most major types of explosives and drugs, and a few other things.

The doorbell rang again. It sounded insistent.

What was he going to do?

Rafe stood up quickly and started his escape protocol. His own shuttle would be warming engines, and his home computer began overwriting his searches and shredding the important information that it stored. The computer could destroy everything, Rafe knew, and it would not matter. He always kept a full backup in the computer link in his head.

It rang again.

"Who is it?" he chimed back with a subvocalization through the computer system to the door speaker. *Damn it! Now they know I'm home. Why did I do that?*

A wave of panic hit Rafe, and he quickly dashed to his bedroom and started packing a few of his necessities.

"Rafe? Rafe!" a familiar voice answered. The second iteration was angry. "It's me. Jean. Open the damn door!"

Stopping cold, Rafe turned and poked his head out of his bedroom door and looked at the main entrance. He closed his eyes and used his uplink to look through the security cameras again. It sounded like Jean. But that didn't mean anything, he said to himself.

"Jean who?" he answered.

"Jean—your sister. God, you moron! Open the door!"

"Jean-Jean?"

"No. Not Jean-Jean," Jean retorted forcefully. "Just Jean. Now are you going to open the door, or am I going to have to kick it in?"

It sounded like Jean. Hotheaded and demanding.

Rafe slipped over to his nightstand and pulled a laser pistol from the drawer. He tucked it behind the small of his back. "Oh, *sure* you're Jean. Couldn't you have come up with some more believable stunt?" Rafe taunted. He moved back to his living room, a small suitcase in one hand. He'd installed a small escape chute behind a display case. He activated the escape door through his computer link, and the case dutifully slid to one side. "And who is your partner there? Mom? Mom? Is that you?" he snorted.

"Damn it, Rafe!" Jean shouted.

That sound caught in Rafe's ear, and he stopped halfway into the escape chute. How often had he heard his sister yell that when they were younger?

"Why do you have your gear on?" he asked suspiciously.

"So you don't freakin' blow us into space by opening the air lock on us before I have a chance to talk to you, moron!"

Rafe paused. "Well, take the helmet off now. I promise, if you are Jean, I won't void the air lock."

"You better damn well not," Jean muttered.

Rafe watched as the first person reached up and disconnected the helmet of the space suit and pulled it off. He nearly choked. It was Jean.

"Satisfied?"

"Now the other one," Rafe ordered.

He watched as the second figure removed its helmet and found himself looking at one of the most beautiful women he had ever seen. She shook her head, and her hair cascaded like dark silk. She was breathtaking.

"This," Jean punched, "is my friend Akemi. Now can we come in?"

"Are you robots? You can do amazing things with robots nowadays."

"What? What? You idiot! No. We are *not* robots. Are you? No. I forgot. You're a moron!"

Rafe smiled and closed his escape hatch. He could still feel the weight of the handgun in the small of his back. He was pretty sure that it was his sister standing outside of his door. But how? Why? There was only one way to find out.

Rafe clumsily shoved his small suitcase by the side of the couch. He then crept to the door and took a moment to look at his sister and the stranger for a few seconds. Then, with a resigned sigh, he keyed the lock open, and the door slid to his left.

Jean stalked in, brushing by him.

"Hi?" Rafe offered. "And you are?" he directed toward the sparkling Asian woman.

"Akemi," the woman purred. Her voice was soft and lithe and hinted at vulnerability. Her voice evoked an instant masculine response in Rafe.

"Quit blathering," Jean demanded from behind him. "And nice pistol. Careful you don't shoot yourself in the ass with it."

Rafe rolled his eyes toward the ceiling and then put on an overly friendly smile and spun around to confront his younger sibling.

"Jean!" he held out his arms as if he was going to hug her, but she stared back as if he were a bothersome child, stopping his motion in an instant. "Jean?" he rumbled, laying on the charm. Then his manner changed again, and he strode by her toward the living room. As he went past her, he tapped her on the shoulder like he would do when they were younger and said, "Good to see you, kid. How goes the war? Maybe you should close the door." This he directed at the Asian woman. "You're letting all the heat … out. Come on over and sit on the couch for a bit while I get some drinks; I think I am going to need one or two of them."

The women followed Rafe into the living room with its video scenes, leather couch and armchair, and glass-top coffee table. The room was fairly bare but impeccably clean. Rafe's place contained none of the clutter that Jean had expected. Jean and Akemi sat down on the couch, Jean tapping her left foot angrily while Akemi took it all in. In a moment, Rafe returned with a decanter of red wine and three wine glasses. The stems of the glasses where intertwined ropes of red and blue crystal that cupped the bowl with a diffusion of color.

Rafe poured the wine, all the time peeking at Jean, his face a mask of curiosity. He handed Akemi a full glass. She swirled it and breathed in its aroma. The wine was a light rose. It smelled sweet with hints of black cherry and spice. Rafe gave a glass to Jean and then poured for himself. Relaxing in the armchair, Rafe kept the bottle, raised his glass high, and said, "Cheers!"

The three of them sat silently, stewing in their own thoughts.

When she finally spoke, Jean's voice was soft and resonated with a deep pain. "How could you, Rafe?"

The question hung before them, wounded and woeful.

Rafe sighed. "How is Mom?"

"Fine."

"She's healthy and all?"

"Yes."

"And, uh, Dad?"

"Good, I suppose."

"Ah, well, that's good. And you?"

"Can't complain too much."

They were awkwardly silent, each not sure how to broach the distance, how to connect to each other once again.

"Jean." Rafe was sullen and subdued. "I just couldn't do it anymore. I couldn't."

"It killed him," she accused. "He was devastated."

Rafe's head sunk toward his chest. "I know."

"And Mom—she went nearly out of her mind."

"I think she understands," Rafe countered, though his voice remained solemn. "You … you look older."

"Oh, thanks." Jean smiled slightly and shook her head incredulously.

"You're not a kid anymore, Jean. You grew up."

"I had to grow up. Somebody had to do something. We can't all just run away like spoiled brats. Someone had to be responsible. Someone had to save Dad, Rafe. After you left … someone had to …" Her voice trailed off, and she took a drink. Jean promised herself she would not cry. Oh, she could just strangle him!

"Well, isn't this pleasant." Rafe's boyish charm struggled to rise through the weight he was feeling. Better to put it all aside. Suddenly his smile broadened, and he turned to face Jean's friend.

"I don't think we have formally met. I'm Rafe Joyce. Of course, you know that. And you are?"

Akemi lowered her chin a bit and looked up at Rafe through long eyelashes. "Akemi Murakami. It is nice to meet you, Lieutenant Joyce."

The use of his military rank drew the smile right off of Rafe's face. He leaned back in the chair and sipped his wine, contemplating.

"Rafe, I've come to take you back," Jean blurted out. "Moron," she mumbled for emphasis.

"Oh, back, right," Rafe stammered. "Just like that? And while they are standing me in front of the firing squad, you and Dad'll have the pleasure of knowing I finally did the right thing? Is that it? What a loving reunion that will be."

"Don't be stupid," Jean snapped.

"Stupid? Stupid!" Anger flashed in Rafe's voice. It took an effort to retain control. "You know what is stupid, little sister? Stupid is lying in a ditch with your friend's guts all over your faceplate while your lets-get-everyone-killed commander screams at you to stand up and take one for the team! And for what? What! So some damn businessmen somewhere and their as-damned politicians can pat themselves on the back and come in afterward to take all the wealth bought by our blood? That type of stupid? Is it that type of stupid, *Major*"—he stressed Jean's rank—"that good little soldiers display when they walk cheerfully off to their deaths for someone else's gain?"

"God, do you even listen to yourself?" Jean exploded. "Poor little Rafe. You're special. Let some other jerk do all the heavy work, while you lounge around and reap the rewards from a thousand AU away! The rule of law—a system of laws—loyalty and honor! That is what matters, Rafe! Not you. Not me. The universe doesn't revolve around you. Did you learn nothing from our father? Where the hell is your honor, Rafe?"

Rafe stared back. "I left it in some muddy hole on that damn, fucking planet! I left it with the marines who died next to me calling for their mothers and for God. What good is honor when you are dead?"

"Oh gods! Listen to yourself."

"I am. I started listening to myself years ago. I stopped believing all the claptrap they—Dad—sold us. I saw through the illusion of honor and found out it was a euphemism for horror and pain."

"There is that." Jean's voice was suddenly soft, and her eyes looked far away.

They all sat in silence again.

The energy that had infused Rafe dissipated. "I don't want to fight with you, Jean. You caught me way, way off guard. It's good to see you. Really. It is really, really good to see you. But why? How? How the hell did you find me?"

Jean looked across the space between them and wiped a stubborn tear from the corner of her eye.

"You tell him," she quietly demanded of Akemi.

Akemi looked at the two siblings for a moment. She put her wineglass on the coffee table and took a small, plastic bag out of a leather carrying case and put it next to her glass. Rafe looked at it suspiciously.

"We have a job for you, Lieutenant Joyce."

"Please don't call me that," Rafe insisted.

"What should I call you then?"

"How about Rafe?" Rafe replied. "And who is we?"

"Of course, Lieutenant Joyce. As I was saying, I work for the Federation's Bureau of Intelligence and Insurgency."

"Nebulas, Jean!" Rafe lurched to his feet and nearly dashed from the room. But there was nowhere to go. If the BII knew he was here, and this woman worked for the agency, he was already lost. Instead, he stood there staring accusations at Jean. Jean turned her head away.

"Please, sit down, Lieutenant. I am not here to incarcerate or kill you." Akemi smiled pleasantly. "Those are not my specialties. Please. Please sit down."

Rafe sat down and took a gulp of wine. "What do you want?" All the pleasantness had left his voice.

"It's a job, Lieutenant. Nothing more." Akemi pointed at the still shrink-wrapped item sitting on the coffee table. "And that little device is part of the bargain."

"What is it?"

"It's an implant. A Syndicate implant with a cranial mesh."

Rafe leaned forward and looked at the package like a deer scenting fresh food but skittish.

"Syndicate …" he slowly said. "What model?"

Akemi smiled. The man was hooked but didn't know it yet. The tension faded from Akemi's face and shoulders, and she leaned back, confident and enjoying a bit of the wine. "There is none. No model number."

"What do you mean, no model number? That doesn't make sense. Unless …"

"You guessed it, Lieutenant. It's not on the market yet. Four commercial generations out, that little beasty. The mesh is slow grow—no known adverse side effects from the weaving. And it's 100 percent organic. It builds using your own blood chemistry—a little at a time. Smooth. Almost human. Only two other people in the known universe have this tech."

Rafe shuffled to the edge of his chair and picked the device up, cradling it like a newborn child. "Three gen out?"

"Four."

"Four." Rafe studied the device through its protective wrapping.

"Half a million credits, Rafe," Jean added. Her voice was a bit raw, but this was what she had come for—to save him. And she knew he was falling under the spell of this little piece of tech. She could see it in his eyes and in the way he held it, like a caress. "So I'm told."

"Four gen? Whew!" he looked steadily at Akemi, and his face suddenly morphed into a warm, beguiling smile. "What's the catch, Akemi?" He said her name softly, seductively.

Akemi did not flinch.

"What's the job? And the terms?" he asked.

"Hack into a computer," Akemi replied. "Download everything you find. You get the Syndicate implant, a pardon, and a cover story about going under deep for the BII, which will clear up your little … personal issue."

"It's not one of the three corps, is it? I prefer living."

"Terra? Syrch? Lin? No. Nothing so mundane as that."

"Mundane?"

Akemi Murakami leaned forward, allowing her blouse to push forward, giving Rafe a small glimpse of her neckline, its smooth skin, and a hint of her bosom. "It's a big grab—a once-in-a-lifetime opportunity. So far, you have just been playing around in the Dark Web," she added, her voice teasing. "We think you're better than that. I think you're better than that. The real question, Lieutenant, is how good do you think you truly are? Are you the real deal or just another box job?"

"They want you to hack into an alien computer system and steal all the aliens' technology," Jean interjected.

"You're joking, right?"

Akemi pursed her lips and ran a fingertip over them. "Alien system—never, ever been touched by a man. New language. New structures and architecture. A virgin system. Just there"—she pointed, and Rafe's eyes automatically followed—"sitting there on a newly discovered alien moon base. Waiting for the right person. The question I have, Lieutenant, is, are you the right person? Or are we just spinning our time here?"

Rafe looked at his sister.

Jean shrugged and looked down at her hands.

"Jean?"

She looked at him, and for a moment, Rafe saw hope flare in her eyes, hope and anguish. But she quickly smothered it.

"Alien system? A torqued implant? Redemption? And for pay?" he added.

"You are a lieutenant. We'll throw in your lieutenant's pay. What do you say?"

"What if I said no?"

It was Akemi's turn to shrug.

The room was still as Rafe considered. If what Akemi had said was true, breaking into an alien computer was a challenge, a true test of his abilities. It was tempting. And there wasn't really a choice. The BII knew where he was.

"Bear?" he asked Jean. Bear was a nickname he had given her when she was just a little kid. It was familiar, and its usage gave no room for deception.

"You can come home, Rafe," Jean answered. "Mom. Dad. Everything else doesn't matter."

Rafe fingered the Syndicate implant device and decided. "On one condition," he said.

"What is that?" Akemi replied.

"You have dinner with me."

"Oh gods, Rafe," Jean said, exasperated.

Rafe smiled, sat back, and stared unforgivingly at the lovely Akemi Murakami. "That's the deal."

"Then pack your bags, Lieutenant Joyce." Akemi's voice was warm and welcoming. "We have a long way to go."

The moon Gargantuan hovered above the frozen planet of Nibiru like a wayward son. Rafe studied the probe data, hoping he would catch a clue from its crater-pocked valleys and plains. A mountain range rumbled like a giant scar along the moon's polar axis, a long twisting maze that started deeply in the south, carved its way northward, and then split into three points of a trident. It was a barren, dark rock.

The distant sun, Kururumany, spun, blue and cold yet brighter than earth's sun. The planet Nibiru, which Gargantuan orbited, was outside of the system's habitable zone. It was at least three times the size of earth and had an orbit of almost two standard years around its star. Besides the larger moon Gargantuan, two other moons hovered over the alien world. Rafe could see the edge of one of them as it wrapped its way around the planet's distant horizon. But the other was on the far side of Nibiru, hidden and alone. The moons' names escaped Rafe for a moment, but his new implant had a type of instinct that pulled his desire out of his mind and flashed their names into the core of his brain—Alauda and Caleo. These flashing words and data bits that appeared in his mind were a bit unsettling.

Rafe had never experienced any computer interface that came close to the Syndicate device that the lovely Akemi Murakami had installed in his head. At first, Rafe had been disappointed with the implant. He had actually lost bandwidth compared to his Hinkler IV-Alpha. But over the last two months of travel, the brain mesh had grown, and his abilities to access the device had multiplied exponentially with every passing day. Now Rafe had a difficult time isolating the implant and recognizing it as anything other than just another natural extension of his mind. Terabytes and terabytes of memory tied seamlessly into a quad, quantum-based processor that moved at the speed of light; it was more computing power than he had ever dreamed of before. Sometimes, it made him feel like a god.

Yet his vastly improved memory and cargo loads of raw data held very little information on Gargantuan or the alien moon base located there. The images from the *Fallen Star's* probe had provided more data than anything he could dig up in his digitized mind. And as desperate as he felt about getting some hint of what awaited him on the moon's surface, his eyes were as often drawn toward the eerie wonder that was Nibiru.

The alien world was a white wonderland of ice and snow. If it were closer to Kururumany, it might have been a water world with vast oceans and scattered continents. It had an atmosphere that, according to a quick geological orbital survey, was likely the result of four major rings of volcanoes. Many of the volcanoes were active, huge, and spewed dense clouds of smoke and flashes of fire, providing the material necessary to form a thin atmosphere on the planet. A computer simulation prophesized that eventually the greenhouse gas carbon dioxide, which poured out of the volcanoes by the metric ton, would begin to warm the planet. But it would take several billions of years. Rafe doubted that, in such a raw state, even Terra Corp could manage the planet's transformation into something habitable in less time.

Sensors indicated that the landmasses outside of direct contact with the volcanoes were between minus ninety and minus forty degrees Fahrenheit. The planet's surface was mostly barren ridgelines, open plains, and ice sheets that were at least three miles deep. Yet somewhere there was liquid water, as attested by large snowstorms that patterned over the surface with regularity. Another simulation hypothesized massive underground chambers of boiling water that periodically shot like spear points into the atmosphere as pressure built deep below the surface of the planet. The simulations also pointed to the potential for vast oceans of liquid water that churned beneath the covering ice sheets, the very weight of the ice liquefying the water at certain depths. But those hypotheses and the rugged terrain were not what caught and held Rafe's attention. Nor did the volcanoes or blinding snow. It was the ring of alien geostationary satellites that formed a protective web around Nibiru. They winked here and there as they caught and reflected the distant light from the system's sun. Were they there to keep something out? Rafe wondered. Or were they trying to keep something in?

A sound stirred behind him, and Rafe turned to find that his sister, Major Jean Joyce, had joined him in the lab. During the long voyage, Rafe had been drawn to the lab for two reasons—Akemi and the lab's large bay window that now allowed him to view the universe through his own eyes. Sometimes even the best sensors and cameras left something to be desired. Rafe felt you often had to look at things directly to truly understand and appreciate them.

"Almost there," Jean said softly.

Rafe looked at her and felt several powerful emotions that intertwined and were difficult, therefore, to identify—fear, love, the need to protect, a desire to run away, feelings of inadequacy, and guilt. They all rolled and churned within him.

"Almost."

"The captain—Mike—says we will be in position in just a couple of cycles. Funny how we can zip across space with the framing drive, yet we are still tied to subspace speeds this near to planets. I know we are moving quickly through real space, but it feels as if we are almost standing still."

"It's like the hours before the jump," Rafe offered, thinking of debarkation in a marine unit. "You wait and wait and then wait some more."

"Yes," Jean agreed. She had had that experience on several occasions. "It is. Are you—" She stopped, not knowing how to raise the subject. "I am always afraid, right before the jump," she continued without asking the question. "All the planning and training, all the confidence and rehearsals, but at the breach, anything can happen. Sometimes," she quietly explained, "I feel as if I'm trapped and I cannot move. It's as if the wide universe has devolved and shrunk, and I'm surrounded by uncertain shadows."

"And then what?" Rafe asked.

"Then someone moves. There's a shuffle among the waiting marines. Sound returns, and the universe takes form. And then we all begin to move, to file onto our ships or into drop position, and the motion pulls me with it with inexorable force. I am on the edge of a wave with my siblings, and we are joining the storm together." She looked gravely at her older brother. "And I cannot hold back. I am swept away."

"And you manage?" Rafe queried. He reached out and ran a loving hand over his sister's hair.

Jean ducked down and pulled away and smiled. "Yes. Training kicks in, and my fear dissipates. The troops' voices resound in my battle helmet, and the forward displays kick into tactical. And then I'm no longer afraid. There's not time to be afraid. It's only afterward—sometimes—in the quiet dark, that the fear returns."

"This is a little different though, isn't it, Bear? There are no soldiers waiting for us, no automated guns or combat robots. Just a barren moon and a strange, little building. What did Akemi call it? The computer system. The Core? It's not fear I feel, Jean. I'm not sure what it is. Anticipation? Excitement? Doubt? I don't know what's going to happen down there, but I do know that I wouldn't miss this for the universe. No." He turned back to the moon that was filling the oblong portal. "Now that I'm here, I want to go down to the moon. I want to hook up to the Core and see if I can actually do it. Am I as good as I have always told myself? Can I really hack into a completely alien computer system? That is what pushes me now."

"You're trying to prove yourself?"

Rafe pulled Jean toward him and gave her a brotherly hug. "Jean, don't you know? I'm always trying to prove myself. Always."

Jean stepped back and looked at Rafe. Not for the first time, she noticed the hint of gray in his otherwise dark hair. Jean had not been the only one to age. It occurred to her that she too was trying to prove herself. But to whom? Her father? Her mother? To Rafe?

Final briefing.

The words came through her pilot's implant. This was followed by a ship-wide announcement. "Attention, all crew. Attention, all crew. This is the captain. Final operational briefing in fifteen minutes in the dining room. Final operational briefing in fifteen minutes."

"I have to go. Rafe?" Jean reached out and took her brother's hand awkwardly. "Don't do anything stupid. Let's just get what they want and go home."

"Don't worry, Bear." Rafe's voice was solid and confident. "You know me."

"Yes. I do," Jean replied. She was not so sure. "See you at the briefing?"

He smiled at her.

Jean left her brother standing in the lab gazing at Gargantuan silhouetted against the ice planet Nibiru and its rings of satellites. On the voyage here, she and Rafe had made a tentative peace. It had not been easy. But they were too much alike and had always been close. Still, she knew, the barriers between them might never truly go away. Too much had happened. To him. To her. They were not kids anymore.

Nobody else was in the kitchen at the common table when Jean arrived. That was fine by her. She was the tactical commander, and a few quiet minutes would give her time to rehearse her plan. Jean often found it easier to think clearly when doing some simple task, so she set about making coffee and tea for the small group, thought about the operation, and checked the rocky terrain of Gargantuan once or twice through the ship's sensors. A mental arrow indicated the spot where the alien structure would appear as the moon continued to rotate slowly and the *Fallen Star* approached. It would not be long before they could actually see the structure, and then she would launch the drones, and the real work would begin.

Jean ran the plan over in her mind. Each constituent part had been planned by various members of the crew—Captain Estury providing vectors and transit times, Danner Tomblin giving solid advice on penetrating the alien structure, and Akemi Murakami and Jean's brother providing the strategy to interface with the alien computer. It was Jean's job to tie all the information together coherently. It was her responsibility to get them all back on board the *Fallen Star* and safely home.

Akemi arrived first. She was wearing standard ship garb and smiled as she slipped into the dining room and took a seat. Jean gave her tea. Danner was next, walking into the room and sitting with his back to the wall, facing the doorway, overly cautious. He was followed by Rafe and then closely by Captain Estury. Jean served the men coffee and took a cup for herself. They all looked at her expectantly.

"This is what we've been waiting for," Jean started. "We have a good plan. I am confident in our ability to get this done and get out of the system in just a half dozen standard hours. But I want to reiterate that often the best of plans go into the trash the moment they begin. The universe is fluid, and we need to maintain our flexibility. Keep the intent of each part of the plan in your mind. Keep the basic tenets of our actions there too, but don't expect this to go off like a script. Things like this never do.

"I will ask each of you for some technical details as we get to your area of expertise. We all have to understand the whole plan. All of us. All of it. Are we ready then? Good. Let's begin."

The shuttlecraft descended quietly. It slipped away from its berth on the *Fallen Star* and rode the moon's gravity field down toward the surface. It was on an automated sequence that allowed Jean to study the terrain and focus on their approach. Small flares fired from the shuttlecraft as it moved further away from the *Fallen Star*. At first, the terrain of Gargantuan seemed to float below them, but as the shuttle continued its descent, the familiar rolling motion associated with rapid travel over a landmass began. The landscape scrolled beneath them.

"I have the bird's-eye." The metallic voice of Captain Estury resounded from speakers in the cockpit. The captain had remained behind in the *Fallen Star* for over watch ability and because that was where most of their firepower was.

"Copy that," Jean answered. She looked briefly at the copilot seat, where Danner Tomblin had taken up residence. He was peering out and below the shuttle, his face screwed in concentration. Jean would have thought the man was nervous, except that he occasionally smiled and moved his lips as if in silent, joyful prayer. Behind them, Akemi and Rafe were sitting closely together—at least as closely as their copper-colored XM Flash biohazard environmental space suits allowed.

When Jean had asked Rafe about that evolving relationship, he had told her he and Akemi were just having a little fun. Jean hoped that was what Akemi thought too. And what did that mean about Akemi's relationship with the station chief back on William

Bennet Station? Jean had sensed something more than a working relationship between the two. *Oh well, Rafe and Akemi are both grown-ups*, Jean thought as her eyes flicked across the pilot's console.

Too far away from the *Fallen Star* to maintain her uplink with the ship, Jean had switched her data connection to the lesser platform of the shuttlecraft. The shuttle's sensors left a lot to be desired. Jean felt like she was going in half-blind.

"You should see it any time soon." Captain Estury's voice interrupted the silence once again. "Just at your eleven o'clock."

Both Jean and Danner reflexively turned their gaze to port. The jagged scar of a ridgeline skipped past. Jean was using the ridgeline to guide them to the alien structure. The dome was nestled in the heart of the valley, yet it was still too far away to see. Jean shifted her attention back to the inflight controls and computer-linked data streams.

The team had already had its first two surprises, and Jean mulled these over as she monitored the shuttle's progress. Just before launch, they had sent a near probe to check for hidden defenses and to conduct a deep scan of the alien base. What the probe sent back had caused their first little stir. The surface structure they had all assumed to be the totality of the base was really just an access point to a larger, underground warren of tunnels and rooms. A long shaft, not quite a hundred feet deep, burrowed down from the surface structure to what appeared to be the heart of the base. The base itself was a series of interconnected rings around a central hub. There were five rings in total. They reminded Jean of old depictions of planetary orbits, with the central and smallest ring tightly packed around the dome, and the subsequent more distant and larger rings spread evenly out into the substrata of surrounding lunar rock.

Jean had seen similar, human construction on moon and asteroid bases. The geometric precision of the alien base was more exact than the ragged tunneling of its human-made counterparts. But the concepts employed were similar. Constructing the base underground protected it from incoming radiation and meteorites and provided a conduit for fabricated, airtight walls. One oddity in the alien structure was in the calculated height of internal corridors and chambers. The computer estimated the average height at nearly fourteen feet. One of the fundamentals of space construction was to conserve space. The height of the interior walls led Danner to voice his belief that the aliens had been much taller than human beings. That was disturbing. Who wanted to face giant aliens on some unknown rock? More likely, it might cause problems when the team was faced with doors or, more importantly, with scale when trying to get Rafe to hook up to the Core. Yet it was the second surprise that was a bit more disconcerting.

Shortly after the *Fallen Star* had arrived in orbit over the moon, the alien station had begun broadcasting. It made them wonder if the station was yet manned. But after discussion, they decided the broadcast must be part of an automated landing sequence. The signal was a repetitive binary code—a beacon. The alien structure was telling them where it was.

So much for surprise. Jean sighed.

All attempts to respond to the signal had gone unanswered. Jean hoped there was not a required affirmative code to give in response. In her military experience, if a ship did not give the countersign, it was quickly vaporized. Still, there was not much they could do about that possibility. They had seen no signs of surface weapons and no missile silos. And, as Akemi had deftly pointed out, it was not as if they hadn't been invited to come and help. In theory, this was a rescue mission.

Yet Jean had slightly changed their approach vectors, dropping the shuttle near the nape of the moon and following the terrain closely. It gave them some shielding from a direct-fire weapon and might, Jean thought, provide a bit of concealment as they approached the base.

The shuttle's rockets and engine began adding more and more thrust the closer they came to the moon's surface, and the ship rocked now and again as the automated pilot maneuvered it low and fast.

The one decided disadvantage of such an approach, Jean realized, was that they could not see the structure due to intervening ridges, hills, and rock formations. They would get their first good view when the ship flared upward just before landing at the designated point.

The shuttle banked and flowed over the moon's terrain. Suddenly, its nose rose, the shuttle turned upward at nearly forty degrees, and its engines strained and roared. For a moment, Jean was pressed back into her acceleration chair, and the only sight visible through the forward screen was the dull, dark expanse of space. Then the landing engines kicked on, and the shuttle quickly descended toward the moon's surface. Jean reached up and flicked a couple toggle switches, and her forward lights increased their intensity, lighting up the dark rock and sand that flowed across the basin of the valley. At the same moment, the lights in the cockpit purpled, and as her eyes adjusted, Jean made out the alien structure that lay less than fifteen hundred meters to their front. It was saucer-shaped and clung to the ground. A series of radio dishes, five in all, surrounded the building, their parabolic dishes and triangular antennae pointing upward toward the sky. They were each the size of a small house and were made of some gray material that blended into the backdrop of the moon's surface. There were no beacon lights. It was as if the place were designed to remain hidden.

The shuttle settled amid a dust cloud raised by its engines. For a moment, the dust obscured Jean's vision of the alien structure. The engines sputtered and fell quiet, and Jean unbuckled reflexively from her chair.

"We're down," she radioed to the *Fallen Star*.

Mike answered. "I've got you. Everything still quiet. Nothing moving."

"We're going to disembark now," she responded and then added, "Disembark, people!"

The three other team members, Rafe, Akemi, and Danner, were frozen in inaction. Jean's order broke the spell, and soon they were all unbuckling and moving toward the rear of the shuttle and its air lock, their helmets locked down and ready. Jean and Akemi were the first there, and Jean cycled the door. There was a hiss as the air escaped. A red warning light flashed, and the door swung outward above the harsh landscape of the alien moon.

Jean reversed, turning her back to the moonscape and grasped a set of silver handles from the shuttle's retractable ladder. The ladder extended, and Jean bounced out of the hatch and floated toward the surface. She was well trained in weightless and near-weightless environments. Though she had tried her best to train the rest of the crew, they had only managed a few space walks during the long voyage, and most of the crew—in Jean's estimation—were still very much out of their element. She would have to help the others with their descent.

Akemi came out next. She was followed by Danner and finally by Rafe. Jean knew each of them by their embossed names on their backs, chest, and the crest of their helmets. Soon, the four, copper-clad humans were assembled by the nose of the shuttlecraft as an automated elevator lowered the dune buggy. Jean had thought the little vehicle an unnecessary luxury, but finally, the others had convinced her of its utility. It was pre-packed with an assortment of equipment and supplies, and it also offered itself as a radio relay station. That last had been the point that sold the argument to Jean. Who knew what type of shielding the alien station might have? And she did not want to lose communication with the *Fallen Star*.

"Akemi, you're driving," Jean crackled through the radio system. "Danner, left rear, and Rafe, right." Maybe the reminder was unnecessary, but Jean knew that, sometimes, hearing another's voice was calming. And they would all be working through their personal fears at this time. Once they started moving, it would not be so bad.

The shuttle's elevator stopped with a slight clang, and Akemi moved to the driver's seat. The other three quickly moved to the rear of the vehicle and removed their Flechette rifles. They climbed into their assigned seats, rifles held at the near ready in their laps.

Akemi activated the electric motor and guided the vehicle off the elevator's ramp.

"Here we go," she quipped.

"It's a little daunting," Rafe said to no one in particular. He was looking at the radio dishes and the alien dome that loomed before them.

"Can you make out any type of air lock, Major?" Danner asked. He was busy covering his sector of responsibility to their flank. Even if he had wanted to, he could not have seen past Major Joyce's body, which blocked his forward vision.

"Not yet," she replied. "*Fallen Star*, have you noticed any activity?"

"Nothing, Major," came the reply. "Everything is quiet. The only thing moving on the surface is the buggy."

"We're about to pass under the nearest communications dish," Akemi said.

"Still no other readings from it, Mike? Is the *Fallen Star* picking up any broadcasts?" Jean asked the captain.

"No. No. Nothing."

Everyone tensed as the buggy moved beneath the large radio dish. Jean struggled to look upward at the concaved device but found it nearly impossible to do so in the bulky space suit. Instead, she followed the straight lines of the dish's superstructure with her eyes but did not see anything that posed a threat or gave any information regarding the thing's creators.

They were just passing out of the dish's umbrella when Akemi suddenly brought the buggy to a halt.

"Why did you stop?" Jean asked, her voice alert.

"I … I thought I saw something?" Akemi replied.

"Movement?"

"No. On the ground—like vehicle tracks and footprints—just as the buggy's lights passed over a spot to our eight o'clock."

"I'll check it out," Rafe offered. Before Jean could say anything, her brother was exiting the vehicle, and so was the BII man.

"Rafe, Danner," Jean called, "be careful."

The two men stood a few feet apart and canvased the area just to the left of the buggy, their rifles held at the ready, the lights of their space suits plying over the terrain in little patches of dancing light.

It was Danner who saw it first. "Here we go," he said. "This is a dead moon, right?" he asked.

"What?" Jean started before she realized what Danner meant. "Yes. No atmosphere and no naturally occurring erosion."

"Akemi was right," Danner continued as Rafe moved to join him, "there are a series of vehicle tracks, of some sort, and what could be footprints—large ones—that seem to meander toward the dome up ahead. Are you thinking what I'm thinking?" This Danner directed at Rafe, who now stood beside him.

"A path?"

"Exactly. That is what occurred to me. Major," Danner said, facing by habit toward the buggy, "this looks like a lot of traffic, following roughly the same path toward the dome. It reasons that, if we follow it, it will lead us to an entranceway."

"That makes sense to me," Jean replied. "Can you make anything else out? Number and size of vehicles or numbers of creatures?"

"Major," Danner's self-proclaimed superiority creeping into his voice chided, "these could be a few minutes or thousands of years old. There is no way to tell. And they are all mashed together and overlain. You would need a supercomputer to give you any true idea of numbers."

"I suppose you're right, Danner. Good work. Akemi, let's realign on those tracks and follow them and hope for the best. Guys?"

"Pull up to us and we'll jump back in," Rafe said. "It looks like the tracks loop a bit around to the seven o'clock side of the dome."

Akemi drove to where the two men stood, and after they were both back onboard, she followed the tracks in the moon's surface easily. It was obviously a service route of some type, maybe from a landing zone to the dome. Whatever it was, it gave Akemi a sense of assurance. Akemi was confident they would find a door, a portal, an air lock, or maybe even a vehicle bay.

"Reflectors in the ground!" Akemi announced excitedly as the headlights of the buggy slipped across triangular, yellow reflectors that clearly marked a route.

"Did you get that, Mike?" Jean asked the captain, who was monitoring the expedition aboard the *Fallen Star*. "We are on a marked trail toward the dome."

"Roger that, Major."

"All right, everyone, keep alert." Jean shifted her rifle butt into her shoulder and placed the palm of her left hand under the forestock. The weapon's electronic sight was linked remotely with her suit, allowing her to aim it without having to bring it up to her cheek. She activated the targeting system, and a video window opened up on the inside of her faceplate. Crosshairs appeared, as well as a green dot that indicated that the weapon was functioning at optimal levels.

The path turned into a hundred-foot slab of rising roadway that led to the side of the dome. Akemi stopped ten feet short of the dome, the twin lights of the buggy splashing against the gray walls in large arcs.

Jean put one foot down on the surface of the roadway and smiled. "Looks like an air lock and large bay doors. I think we have arrived."

The four of them dismounted and stood looking at the dome as it curved upward and away from them. It was, perhaps, two stories tall and lacked even a single window. The road's surface looked like foam and had a reflective shimmer. And if not for the light from the buggy and their helmets, the area would have been midnight dark.

"All right then," Jean said, "let's break out the equipment and find a way into this puppy. Danner," she added, "you have the lead."

"Right. Got it." Danner Tomblin moved toward the air lock. It was half again as tall as he and, though clearly a door, had no visible mechanical mechanisms. As Danner studied the situation, Akemi joined him, an array of potential interface devices in her hands. Jean and her brother were left to pull security.

Danner studied the surface of the air lock for several minutes. "Not much to go by," he mumbled over the intercom. "I'm going to run my hands over the surface to see if I can feel any hidden mechanism. Augmenting the touch sensors on my gloves now. That should do it."

He stepped forward and gingerly placed his left hand on the air lock. The space suit was designed to pass electrical sensations to Danner's hands in a way that simulated actual touch. Danner started in one location and slowly moved his hand in an ever-widening arc along the surface. It was slick. And it seemed to have a low-level force field. It felt as if he were holding a large magnet in his hands that was the opposite polarity of a magnetized wall. Danner pushed down to get through the invisible field.

"There's some type of low-level force field," he announced. "And the wall feels like wet ice. My hand wants to slide on it." He moved his hand farther up the wall. He repeated the process with his other hand and soon felt comfortable enough to have Akemi help him with the physical inspection.

"Akemi, come and touch this spot, here," Danner said. He held his hand about five feet off the ground and to the left of the air lock. "I can't tell if I am actually feeling a slight difference or if it is my mind wanting to find something."

Akemi shifted over, and Danner stood back.

"Here?" she asked.

"A little higher."

"Oh, here? This," she turned to look at him, "this spot? It feels a little rough. Is that it?"

"I thought it felt rough too," Danner replied. "Here, let me get my scanner out of my utility box and see what it tells us."

Danner went to the back of the buggy and removed a small, silver toolbox from the back storage area. He plopped it on the ground before the door and removed a small device that was slightly larger than his palm.

"Okay. This will scan the area and let us know if there is anything more to that spot than just a rough feeling. It shouldn't take long." He put the device up to the area and pressed it down through the force field.

The device whined as it activated and sent its first exploratory rays into the metal structure. At that exact moment, a large, elongated light that had been hidden flush with the surface above the air lock flicked to life. An amber glow filled the space below the air lock, startling Danner and Akemi, who both jumped back as if burned.

"What'd you do?" Jean asked.

It took Danner a moment to reply. "Nothing. Nothing really. I had only just begun scanning below the skin of the wall. I hadn't done it long enough to even get a reading."

"Move back," Jean ordered. "Maybe the light will turn off."

Danner and Akemi took a step back, but the light remained on.

"Can you see this light, *Fallen Star*?" Danner asked Captain Estury.

"Yes. It's not very bright, and I missed it until I heard you talking about it. Everything else is quiet. No other lights. No movement."

"Thanks, Mike," Jean replied. "Now what?"

"Maybe the door responds to some type of radio or other energy pulse—almost like a solar panel reacting to sunlight," Danner theorized. "If I hold the scanner up there longer, maybe the door will cycle. If not, we will at least get a good picture of what is underneath the surface of the wall."

"Okay. Akemi, step back," Jean said. "Let Danner work on the door."

"Right, Major."

"It's okay, Danner. Give it a try."

The Bureau of Intelligence and Insurgency agent approached the air lock. Danner held the scanning device up to the same spot as before and began its operational routine. A tense minute or more passed without any reaction. He was about to conclude the scan when the ground rumbled and the air lock began to iris open. Danner stepped quickly back, and the team stood in diamond formation behind him, all their eyes and weapons turned toward the door as it hissed and an emerald light flooded out of the alien dome into the darkness. The four humans, looking slick and blood-soaked in their copper-colored EVAs, stood looking up at the large opening that appeared in the side of the dome. On the other side, a long passageway slipped into the heart of the dome. The amber door light winked green, and shadows stretched away into darkness.

"What did you do?" Jean's voice was hushed.

"Once again, I'm not sure," Danner admitted. "I don't think I did anything."

Rafe broke his silence. "You had to have done something. Did you communicate with it somehow?"

"What do you want me to say? I don't know what the hell I did."

"Major Joyce." Mike's voice emanated from the suits' transceivers. "I take it that you opened the door?"

Jean shifted a little to her right, giving her a clear view of the passageway beyond the air lock. "It looks like it just opened," she replied over the net. "I get the sneaky feeling that we are being invited in. The question is, once we take that step, how do we get out again? It's not like we *opened* the door."

"Let's push the heavy gear in through the door. If that goes okay," Danner suggested, "then we can go through too. We have enough heavy equipment to get through most materials. And," he added, "if we get trapped inside, we can always load explosives on the door and blow our way back out."

"It's as if we're standing on a high diving board, Major," Akemi said. Her voice was tight but held confidence. "Sometimes, Major, you just need to take the plunge. And this is the reason we traveled all this way."

"She's right," Rafe joined. "Let's just do it, Jean. Let's just do it. Like Danner said."

Jean thought about it. Realizing the others were right, she put aside her fears. "Mike, this is Jean. We are going to do as Danner suggests and push the heavy gear through the doorway. If it remains open, we will enter the alien structure.

"Akemi, make sure the relay uplink on the buggy is set up. Rafe, help Danner with the gear. I've got our cover. *Fallen Star*," she continued, "keep an eye on our six."

"I've got your six," the captain replied.

The work began in earnest as Jean stood guard. She didn't like the idea of entering the alien structure without having a sure way out. Had the door opened on its own? she wondered. Had they unwittingly activated an automatic sequence? Or was someone, something watching? Was it the Core? Was it a sentient thing? Suddenly Jean wished she were on a regular battlefield, where the enemy was a known entity and the rules of the game were implicit. Here was something completely new. She felt like a child taking its first foray into the world, unsure and unsteady, with each new encounter a potential stumbling block. She had to learn the rules of this game and quickly. If she did not, she thought grimly, then they were doomed. *One misstep*, she thought. *That's all it will take.*

As the work progressed Major Joyce took a deep breath.

We are on the edge, like Akemi said, Jean told herself. There was nothing for it but to take the plunge.

The air lock closed behind them, trapping them in the passageway, bathed in emerald light that seemed to emanate from the walls. No visible light fixtures adorned the walls. A pile of boxes and three long metal devices were neatly stacked to one side. Akemi Murakami was busy placing them on a small, robotic support platform. The platform, known as a porter, would follow them as they made their way through the alien structure, allowing them to keep their hands and minds free for other tasks. The first order of business was confirming contact with the *Fallen Star*. Major Joyce ran the check and found that the link was clear and strong.

"I'll take that," Danner said, stopping Akemi from putting a heavy, dark equipment case onto the porter. "Some of my more specialized equipment."

"Whatever," Akemi replied.

Rafe stepped up and helped Akemi with the remaining gear, and in a few minutes, the party was ready to move.

"Okay, like we rehearsed. I will go first, and then Danner, Akemi, and Rafe at our six," Jean said. "Shall we?"

Jean turned and walked down the passageway toward where the team expected to find an elevator to take them into the heart of the base. Jean used the instruments in her EVA to scan as she walked, but nothing seemed out of order or particularly threatening. It was, disappointingly, normal.

"Another door," she said as they neared the end of the passageway.

The group approached the door, which opened automatically when Jean was within a few feet. They stepped through into a room large enough for all of them and their robotic porter. Once they were in, the door closed, and the room, which turned out to be an elevator, began its descent.

"Creepy," Rafe said, "like it knows where to take us."

"There is only one way for it to go." Jean's voice was more confident than she felt. "And we know there is only one underground level. Why wouldn't it automatically go there?"

"I wonder if the lift can move horizontally through the rest of the base, or if there is some other form of internal transport," Akemi stated.

"We will find out soon enough," Rafe said as the elevator came to a smooth stop and the door opened.

Another septic passage, similar to the first, bathed in the same emerald-green light, greeted them. They stood in a circular area that branched off in several directions. Only one direction was lit. The other three were dark and ominous.

"Are we being guided?" Rafe thought aloud.

Danner peered down each passageway in turn and stopped before the illuminated one. "The lighting? It could be a coincidence. Who knows how long this place has been empty. Maybe nobody turned this particular light off."

"Well, it does make our selection a bit easier," Jean said. "*Fallen Star, Fallen Star*, are you still reading us, Mike?"

"Clear as day," came the reply.

"Good. And the video feed?"

"Like watching television in my living room," Mike answered.

"Okay, everyone, let's try the passage with the lighting. Same approach order. But let me get out front a good twenty feet or so. If I set something off or get zapped, that will give you a chance to react."

"Are you going to say something like, keep a sharp eye?" Rafe laughed. "It is strange to hear you sound so serious, Jean. Of course, you always were a bit bossy," he baited.

"I'm glad you're amused. Okay, Mike, we are heading off now. Stay alert, everyone."

Rafe laughed again, and Akemi joined him.

"What?" Jean asked.

"You said it anyway," Rafe teased.

"Can we focus on what we are doing?" Danner barked.

"Yes, sir," Rafe snapped.

"Most serious," Akemi added.

"Enough," Jean said, exasperated and, for once, agreeing with Danner. "Let's move."

The team made its way down the corridor, and the banter ended.

Aboard the *Fallen Star*, Captain Estury overlay the probe's data of the underground base with the signals from each person's EVA. He knew exactly where they were within the substructure, and he was able to push this combination of data back to the team. Jean kept an eye on the overlay in her heads-up display as they moved.

They passed the first intersecting corridor that marked the junction of the passage with the next ring of the base. But both corridors remained dark. Instead, directly ahead, the lights flashed and then steadied as if drawing the party forward once again. Without much thought, Jean continued to lead the team in the same direction, though she flipped her weapon off safety.

The next junction came and went, as did several doors that dotted the passageway. After their first few attempts to open the doors failed, the group decided it was best to ignore them for now. But it did make Jean wonder how they would find the command room in the alien distress video. That room, and the Core, could be in any of the rooms they had already passed.

At the third junction, Akemi stopped the group and pointed to the walls about twelve feet off the floor.

"There, by the corners," she said as she moved one of her lamps upward to illuminate the spot. "It's pretty hard to make out. A form of writing?" Akemi considered the clean lines of alien script. "Street signs?" she suggested

Danner agreed. "Pretty difficult to see for a street sign. But maybe the aliens see in a different light spectrum or something," he offered.

"Does that tell us anything new?" Jean asked.

"Maybe. Let's assume that the writing is eye level too. That would make the aliens between twelve and thirteen feet tall? And we should be more attentive to the walls and doors. I bet we've walked past a lot of writing and just didn't see it," Akemi replied.

"There's not enough of a writing sample here to help the computer translators get a hold of the language," Rafe said. "But the more we capture in video, the quicker we might learn something more about communicating with the computer system. At least we have Akemi's work with the spoken form."

"Yes," Akemi agreed. "But do keep in mind that our algorithms are human based, with a human set of references. We could be way off. We are assuming the aliens were asking for help. It's a good assumption, but if our approach was wrong, they could just as well have been inviting us to dinner—and we could be the main course."

"Oh, that's a lovely thought," Rafe mumbled. "You didn't say that when you told me to volunteer."

"But more than likely, we got it right," Akemi replied, giving Rafe a playful shove.

"There is the communication sequence too," Jean said. "Our computer should be able to teach the Core how to communicate with us. That's our hope, anyway. All that work you did on their message, Akemi, is a great starting point. But for now, I think"—she looked around at the two darkened corridors—"we should consider going down one of the dark passages. I don't like the idea that we are being guided, and moving off course might give us some more information. Thoughts?"

"I like it," Rafe said.

"An experiment?" Akemi considered. "If we are being monitored and guided, then they, it, whatever, should try to redirect us back in the same general direction. And if there is no effect, we can always come back here and follow the lights. I'm willing to try it."

"Danner?"

"Why not, Major? It makes as much sense as following the green light. A little randomness is a good thing. So I am for it too."

"Good. It's settled. So how about left?"

Nobody said anything.

"Left it is," Jean said as she pushed passed everyone and started walking down the left passageway into the darkness. Her EVA lamp skipped light across the floor as she moved. Soon, everyone was moving down the passageway, with the robotic porter following closely behind.

In the dark, with the eerie emerald light far behind them, it was as if the group had stepped into midnight. They passed several cross-corridors. Whenever they moved past one to their right, the lights in that corridor flickered to life, but they ignored it and continued forward. Danner was the first to notice the change in the maintenance of this section of the underground station. Parts of the walls were sagging; pieces of rubble were strewn along the ground;

and down one of the side passages, they noticed that an entire ceiling had collapsed.

They also encountered a few open chambers and small rooms, which were dutifully explored. The rooms contained very little of interest, and the few artifacts they found were non-technological in nature—an oversized table made from some lightweight plastic, what could be a desk, and other odds and ends.

"It's as if, "Akemi thought out loud, "the moon base had been stripped and abandoned, and what we're finding are those things deemed too valueless to bother recovering."

After two hours fumbling in the dark, Jean guided the group into the next right-sided corridor and, true to form, those lights flicked on.

"We could wander down here for weeks," she said to no one in particular. "Let's take the hint and follow the lights. Plus, these tunnels are getting worse."

Soon, bathed once again in the strange light, the group trudged down several corridors and around corners until, according to the virtual map that was being pushed to them from the *Fallen Star*, they were within a few hundred feet of where they had turned off the guided path.

"This must be it," Jean said. She was standing with her hands on her hips and looking at the wall to her left. A large, circular doorway, the door closed, stood before her.

"The virtual map shows a large chamber on the other side of the doorway," Akemi stated.

"Let's see if it has the same rough surface area on its left side, like the main door," Danner suggested. He ran his hand over the smooth surface and was pleased to find a rougher patch in approximately the same location as before. Danner Tomblin brought his scanner out and placed it over the mechanism. The door responded, irising open with a resounding whoosh.

"There was atmosphere." Rafe stated the obvious.

They were all relieved that the pressure had not been too great, as a sudden decompression of the chamber could have thrown them against the opposite wall and injured them.

Jean looked through the door, holding her weapon at the ready. "I think this is it. It's the room from the communication."

Danner peered in too. "I agree. So we were being guided. But by what? Aliens? An automated sequence? Chance?"

Nobody had an answer to his question, but they all felt wary.

"Do you know this is the only room with any electronics that we've seen since we entered?" Danner added.

"So?" Jean replied.

"It's just odd, don't you think?"

"Odd or not, what do you think? Do we go in?"

The group stood, silently contemplating the room before them.

"Do you hear that?" Akemi asked, her voice quizzical.

The others listened, and one by one, each of them made out a faint, distant pounding, as if a piston in a machine was out of alignment and cracking into the side of the crankshaft. Jean was not sure, but it sounded to her as if the speed of the banging was increasingly desperate. Whatever piece of machinery the noise was coming from, she thought, it must be on its last legs.

"We can check it out later," she said. "*Fallen Star, Fallen Star*, Mike, do you read me?"

"Loud and clear," the captain replied.

"We've reached what we think is the Core. There was some pressure in the room, and we can see machinery and electronic components from the doorway. We are also hearing some banging noise, but we can't make out its origin. It sounds a ways off. Nothing we can do about it. Do you see anything on the scanners?"

"No. The base is dead."

Jean looked at her team and made her decision. "We're going to enter. Are you ready, Akemi? Danner?" She directed at them. "Rafe? This is your show. You have the lead."

"I'm about as ready as I ever will be," Rafe responded. "It won't get any easier if we just keep staring at it. Let's do it."

"Okay," Jean replied. "Remember, this is the slow part. Don't touch anything until we've had a chance to examine it. Patience, isn't that what you cautioned on the ship, Akemi?"

The technician answered, "Yes. We have lots of time. Let's use it to our advantage."

"I'm sending in the robotic porter, as we rehearsed," Jean said as she manipulated a few controls on the left arm of her EVA.

The porter dutifully moved forward and slipped past the doorway into the waiting chamber.

"Nothing happened," Rafe said. "No death rays or anything."

"Danner?"

The BII agent scanned the room with a separate piece of equipment and said, "Clear, Major."

"Then let's go," Jean said, stepping through the doorway, alert and expectant.

The other three followed her. As soon as the entire group was in the chamber, the door closed ominously with a hiss as the room started to pressurize once again.

Well, Jean thought as they stood looking around the chamber, *this is the moment of truth.* Would Rafe be able to hack into the computer? Would he find what the group had been sent here seeking? Jean wondered if they would even recognize valuable artifacts or if the aliens who had built this place were so different from humans that the team would overlook important pieces. If Paul Temple, the station chief for the Bureau of Intelligence and Insurgency had been correct, it was not just Rafe's freedom that was on the line. The freedom of the entire Federation was at stake. Either they found new technology that would make them competitive with the likes of Terra Corps, or they would succumb to larger forces in the human universe. What then was the value of the decades-long war with the Consortium? Could their long struggle really be wiped out due to victory and peace? Why had men and women died on both sides? Did it really all come down to this?

Jean thought about what Paul had said. Their situation couldn't be that simple and stark, she thought. Could it? A tiny shiver rippled through her body.

Outside the chamber, in the cool dark of the passageway, the distant pounding of metal on metal grew in intensity. Something tore, and a crash reverberated in the underground warren. The team jumped at the sound. A sinister whirl of gears in motion resonated. It was slow, powerful, and full of purpose.

Captain Mike Estury sighed and sipped on a large cup of Stim. The *Fallen Star* was silent and cool. Mike pushed the captain's chair and flipped out the lower leg support until he was almost fully supine. He was remotely jacked into the ship's sensors. He deftly managed the meshing of the personal transponders from the landing team and the probe's data on the alien structure. Mike slid a carbon-based video screen from the arm of his chair, extended it, and flipped the visor in front of his eyes. Now he could see the results of his work. He had color coded each of the dots that represented people. Major Joyce's symbol was red and outshone its counterparts as the team maneuvered through the alien station. He split the screen to give him the video feeds from their EVAs and remained remotely linked to the ship's deeper sensors, which he stretched inexorably down at the alien structure. He felt uncomfortable. An itch of a worried feeling nagged at him.

How many marines had Mike ferried to landing zones and combat? *There were too many to count*, he thought. Thousands. And many of those marines had not returned. More had been injured. Yet Mike had never felt so troubled at making a drop onto a hostile planet before. But then again, he considered, everyone in the fleet had had a much better idea of what they were getting into. It was combat. You expected to lose friends—a ship or two—but it was normal human behavior. War was just that—as human as breathing. There was a certain comfort in knowing that soldiers in all ages had gone through similar experiences, and, to be honest, Mike could not recall a single instance in his career when he had sent off someone for whom he cared. What had it mattered? Fate was the soldier's god.

But what was this? There was nothing human about it at all. It was new. Unknown. And for the first time in a long while, Mike cared.

Major Joyce. Jean. The thought of losing her grated him.

The captain stretched and tried his best to knead the muscles in his arms and legs. They were tight. He took a deep breath, closed his eyes, and slowly released the air back into the dim cockpit.

"*Fallen Star, Fallen Star,* are you still reading us, Mike?" Jean's voice interrupted Mike's train of thought.

"Clear as day," he replied.

"Good. And the video feed?"

"Like watching television in my living room," Mike answered.

What a stupid thing to say, the captain thought as he tried to focus on the mission and push Jean out of his mind. But he could not take his eyes from the display, and he pushed the ship's instruments to their limits, hoping he would be able to spot any trouble before the major and the rest of the group suffered the consequences.

What an odd little group, he thought. Danner was a total snob. If he were any more full of himself, he would explode from the internal pressure of so much hot air. And Akemi. Well, she was too hot for her own good. *Too hot,* Mike thought, *for anyone's good.* But she was smart as hell and seemed mostly levelheaded. Mostly, Mike contended, because she was getting tangled up with Jean's older brother, Rafe. What an enigma.

Rafe Joyce was a deserter from the marines and had spent the last several years on the run, making his money by stealing. He was the worse sort of character that Mike could imagine. How could Jean—and Jean's father, for that matter—be related to someone so self-centered and fearful? Mike had known he would not like Jean's brother the first moment he had been briefed on Rafe's desertion and told how the man made his living. Yet meeting Rafe in person was so much worse. Rafe exuded confidence, and he had an animal magnetism that pulled the otherwise sensible Akemi Murakami into some type of relationship. What galled Mike the most was that, in spite of Mike's feelings about deserters in general, Mike found he too was in danger of falling under Rafe's thrall. The man was personable. Damn it. Rafe had not expected that. No. Not that.

However, Mike now understood why Jean was so willing to throw her career to the side for a chance at saving her brother—at redeeming his life. In her own way, she was an adept of her brother's personality. Although she was angry with Rafe for his desertion, Jean obviously worshiped her older brother. Mike could see it in the way Jean spoke with Rafe, how her eyes lit up when Rafe walked into the room. Jean might be a Marine, Mike thought, but she was also a little sister. And she couldn't accept that Rafe had thrown his life away. He had lost his way. Jean, with the practicality of a marine, knew it could all be fixed. Rafe just needed a little help to regain his special place in Jean's universe. She had to save him.

Jean might as well try being Newton's apple falling upward from the ground and perching back upon the apple tree as find it within herself to resist her brother's need. And Mike suspected Rafe knew that.

Despite Rafe's halfhearted attempts to curb his behavior, Rafe was weak. He always took full advantage of his sister's idyllic love. Rafe could not help it. He was the older brother, the only son, and the universe revolved around him. Yet even that did not make Mike hate the former marine lieutenant. It did give rise to a deep and foreboding fear that even now, trying to relax in the quiet of the *Fallen Star's* command room, clenched the captain's jaw and strained his eyes and ears as he watched the landing team maneuvering through the eerily green and dark shadows of the alien's underground base.

And here he was again—thinking of Jean, the way her hair moved slightly when she swiveled her head toward him, her mesmeric eyes, and her feminine gait that belied the fact that the major was a woman in her prime. But it was more than that, Mike thought.

And it was more than just the aftereffects of confined space and dual uplinking to computer systems during Jean's training days. She had a hold on him. As much as Mike's pride had been injured when Paul Temple assigned him to this expedition, stripping Mike of his own ship and his own command, Mike was grateful for the chance to spend more time with Jean. His mixed feelings had solidified, and now he wondered what he would do when the time came for her to return to the fleet. How would he let her go? How could he not? If anything, Mike knew that Jean was a marine first. And Mike was a naval officer and pilot. Both of their lifestyles screamed a lack of stability, a lack of space for private lives. Did he expect her to give up her life for him? Did she expect him to give up his life for her? These were troubling thoughts.

"*Fallen Star, Fallen Star*, Mike, do you read me?" Jean's voice sounded slightly annoyed, as if she had been calling for a while.

"Loud and clear," the captain replied. He kept his voice professional.

"We've reached what we think is the Core."

How long had he been stuck in his thoughts? Mike wondered. He quickly ran through the sensors and saw nothing out of the ordinary. The pulses of the four team members were slightly raised but within the normal operating range. The surface of the moon Gargantuan was dark and silent, and the blue-white orb of Kururumany was reflected on the white surface of the looming planet of Nibiru.

"We've reached what we think is the Core. There was some pressure in the room and we can see machinery and electronic components from the doorway. We are also hearing some banging noise, but we can't make out its origin. It sounds a ways off. Nothing we can do about it. Do you see anything on the scanners?"

Mike's mind focused, and his breath suddenly ached in his chest. It was fear. He knew the emotion well. But this time it was not a personal fear at being blasted out of existence by defensive laser cannons, plasma blasts, or skulking torpedoes. He was afraid for Jean.

"No," Mike replied. "The base is dead."

"We're going to enter. Are you ready, Akemi? Danner?" Jean's voice cracked over the radio. "Rafe? This is your show. You have the lead."

"I'm about as ready as I ever will be," Rafe responded. "It won't get any easier if we just keep staring at it. Let's do it."

Mike tensed as his eyes sought out any hint of danger. How would he let her go? He kept asking. How could he not? At this moment, the only truth the captain knew was that if Major Joyce called for him, he would come. And he would bring a rain of fire belching forth from the *Fallen Star* on anything that got in his way.

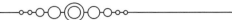

It is a curious thing, Jean thought, standing at the edge of the rectangular room. She felt tiny. Each component of the alien base was just a little too large, a little too high, and difficult to reach. It made jean feel like a child in an adult world.

Jean stood guard as the rest of her team moved like copper shadows near the alien-built equipment. Rafe Joyce, Jean's wayward brother, stood near the overly large couch, staring intently as the tech, Akemi Murakami, made a virtual mold of the connector that dangled from a bulbous piece of equipment that Jean thought looked like an ancient naval mine, a dark sphere with prickly, silver, antenna-like objects protruding from it. The orb, in turn, was attached to a dark metal shaft that hung from an archway above the long couch that reminded Jean of an acceleration couch. The entire setup was part of a larger electronic piece of equipment that filled the far wall of the room. The equipment was covered with a hint of fine dust. Jean wondered how long the room had sat empty, unchanging in the heart of the alien-built moon base. For some reason Jean could not pinpoint, the room and the alien computer system named the Core gave her the creeps. Her skin felt moist even though the XM Flash biohazard environmental space suit she wore wicked moisture away from her body and circulated a current of air across her skin.

But instead of providing her with a cool feeling of comfort, the air felt like ants crawling.

Jean tried to shake a sinking feeling of dread that threatened irrational panic. The feeling had grown over the standard three hours that the team had spent slowly going over the room and studying it. The room was virtually mapped and each piece of gear scanned and registered. Nothing seemed out of the ordinary.

Perhaps, she chided, it was the sound of the relentless pounding that now reverberated throughout the stale air of the moon base that had her on edge. When they had first entered the Core, the sound had been a distant one, like thunder twisting in the far sky on a long summer day. Since then, as Rafe and Akemi investigated the alien technology in a bid to learn how to interface with it and as the odd little BII man, Danner Tomblin, studied the larger console with a handheld scanner that resembled an electronic notepad, the noise had steadily grown in strength and constancy. Jean adjusted her grip on her H&K Flechette rifle. Its weight was a comfort. She directed its barrel back toward the door that had eerily closed behind the team after they had entered the room.

"That should do it," the Asian technician said, her voice a purr of femininity. Akemi Murakami pushed a small device into the little computer she had set on the alien acceleration couch. She uploaded the information, and soon a holographic duplicate of the alien's interface cable hovered like a ghost above the elongated computer screen. Akemi stood before it, with Rafe a foot or so behind her shoulder, in the attitude that Jean had learned Akemi often assumed when concentrating on communicating through her implant. Her implant was subcranial, communicated wirelessly, and had no external jack. Jean briefly wondered if she and her brother Rafe were wirelessly linked. The two of them had been working together for over three hours yet had barely said more than a few words to one another. Jean knew from her own experience aboard the *Fallen Star* with Captain Estury just how intimate that type of communication could become.

"It's getting louder," Jean said to no one in particular.

Rafe looked over at his sister, swiveling his whole body in the bulky environmental suit. "You don't think it's an ancient air system on its last legs anymore?" he asked.

Just after the pounding had started, the atmosphere in the room had changed. Readings indicated a steady flow of breathable air had started flowing into the chamber once the door had closed and sealed. Their readings had indicated the concentration of oxygen was sufficient for them to breathe, but they had decided not to remove their helmets. Who knew what type of contaminates the air might contain, and the station was old and in obvious disrepair. A few hours of biological freedom was not worth the risk that the door slip open through some malfunction, with an explosive release of pressure that would surely kill them. No, it was prudent to remain in their bulky XM Flash suits. They had associated the pounding with the airflow, but now Jean had her doubts.

"No," Jean responded. "It is definitely getting louder and"—she paused for a moment—"closer. I think we should hurry up."

Akemi sighed. "Major," she started and reconsidered. "I have designed an interface connection. It will take just a few minutes to print out what I need. I've loaded the filament into the printer and am spooling the design now. Just to be sure we get it correct, I am using a smaller nozzle—one micron should do it," she added.

"I agree with the major." That from Danner Tomblin. He did not turn to look at the rest of the group as he spoke. "Something seems to be coming this way, and I for one don't think we should be here when it arrives."

"Well," Akemi said, "it is printing now. Two minutes, and then we can give it a try—if Rafe is still up to it." Her voice was questioning and soft.

"That's why we're here, right?" Rafe asked. He didn't want to miss the opportunity to hack into the alien system. He had learned a thing or two about his new implant and its cranial mesh. It was as fast as liquid light. The former marine lieutenant, deserter, and computer hacker had a hint of desperation in his voice. He was worried his sister would turn back and deny him his once-in-a-lifetime opportunity. "I don't think I'll need that long, Bear."

"How long?" Jean asked.

"An hour, maybe a bit more," Rafe replied.

"Danner?"

"We have no idea how long we have before whatever is making that noise arrives," Danner said casually. "Can't we just hook up a remote and do all of this aboard the ship?"

"Akemi?"

"Yes. I could do so, but Rafe would lose the sensation."

"Sensation? What do you mean by that?" Jean asked.

"Oh, I forgot. You are still relatively new to your implant, Major. A direct link to an electronic system provides"—she had always found it difficult to explain—"a sensation, a flavor, for the piece of machinery you are interfacing with. Nobody is exactly sure what it is—a type of fifth sense, the ebb and flow of current through the circuits. Like living beings, each piece of equipment has its own unique, yet similar signature and feel. Dr. Hans Wolff postulated in his treatise on interconnectivity and the virtual experience that—"

"What does it *mean*?" Jean said, stressing the important word and interrupting Akemi, who had dropped into her professional tone.

"It means that, with a direct hookup, I can feel my way through the system," Rafe explained. "The components of the system will talk to me. I will be able to follow its flow in a way that a remote connection will never be able to replicate. Even a short hour directly connected to the machine will give me insights that might help me ultimately break the code and open the computer memory banks. Its like the feel of leather on a baseball a pitcher rotates in his hand—he's feeling the stitching, the subtle nuances of cowhide and powdered dust; it sends signals through the hand and along the arm to the brain that, unconsciously, helps the pitcher gauge how the ball will move through the air, handle a cross breeze, respond to heat rising from the ground.

"I promise, for this first attempt, I'll do a quick survey. In and out. Half an hour. An hour at best. Then we can get back to the *Fallen Star* and work remotely for a while. I may not have to come back for a direct feed if things work out. Half an hour to an hour, Jean."

"An hour?" Jean felt uncertain. Rafe's answer was too arbitrary. There were too many variables and not enough solid information. But what choice did she have? This was the mission and the mission always came first.

"Akemi, you set up the remote," she said. "Danner, do whatever it is you're doing, but plan on wrapping it up in an hour. Rafe," she continued somewhat more softly, "you be careful."

"Always, Bear."

Jean could feel her brother's smile, even though his features were hidden from her view. "I will guard the door." *And pray I have not made a mistake*, she added silently.

The three-dimensional printer hummed as the interface took shape. Danner continued to document the scene and scan the machines' components for future analysis. Akemi shifted her equipment to the foot of the alien couch as Rafe lifted himself and perched on the couch's edge. His legs kicked freely, making him look like a child sitting on a doctor's examination table.

Akemi plugged one of the many cables she had brought into the side of Rafe's helmet. Inside, a thin interface device slipped from the helmet into Rafe's skull and his Syndicate implant. It was not particularly comfortable, and Rafe grunted slightly and then smiled as the connection sent a flash of light through his brain. The discomfort was gone in a microsecond.

"You all right?" Akemi asked. Her voice was quiet and reassuring.

"Yeah, I'm fine."

"Why don't you go ahead and lie down? It will be a bit more comfortable, and you can begin clearing your mind."

Rafe rolled his legs onto the couch and slowly, with Akemi's help, lay back against the couch's smooth surface. The spiny orb hung a few arms' lengths above his belly. He closed his eyes as Akemi busied herself with a long extension cable, which she slipped from Rafe's helmet up toward the orb. She looped the cable near the end and used a plastic tie to secure it to the alien device. By the time this was accomplished, the interface had been printed. Akemi picked it up and slowly examined it for flaws. Then she slipped the end of it onto the cable that ran to Rafe's helmet.

"Ready," she announced.

"So soon?" Jean sounded worried.

"We'll be fine, Major."

"It is not *us* I'm worried about, Akemi," Jean replied. "It's Rafe."

"I'll be fine—what? Wait a minute. Jean? Do you hear that?" Rafe raised himself up on his elbows so he was facing the door and his sister.

"Hear what?" Jean asked. "I don't—" She stilled. The incessant pounding had stopped. Suddenly the station was as quiet as a tomb.

"Danner?"

"I don't know, Major. It seems odd."

The group remained quiet for a moment, listening.

"Maybe it was just a piece of machinery that was breaking; perhaps it broke?" Rafe offered.

"I don't like it," Jean said. She shifted back from the door, putting a couple more feet between herself and its reflective surface.

"Does it really change anything?" Rafe replied.

"*Fallen Star. Fallen Star*, Mike? Are you following this? Do you see anything moving in the moon base? Are you detecting anything at all?"

"I'm not seeing anything on the monitors," Captain Estury replied. He adjusted the *Fallen Star's* sensors, but they were blank. The base was empty except for the four heartbeats of the landing expedition. "It looks all clear. You are alone down there."

"I'm hooking Rafe up to the medical monitor, Major. And he is already hooked up to a computer monitor that will track everything he does. Do we proceed?"

"Jean?" Rafe asked.

"I guess so," the major acknowledged, but she did not sound confident. "Yes, why not? That's why we're here. And in and out, Rafe. One hour. No more." Her voice was stronger. "Just be ready to disengage quickly. Okay? Rafe?"

"Got it, kid."

"Akemi," Jean prompted.

"Right." The woman's voice resonated like fresh air after a summer storm. "Are you ready, Rafe?"

"Always." He winked.

Akemi took hold of the new interface that was attached to the cable that ran to Rafe's helmet and, with a deep breath, maneuvered it with a twist, toward the alien orb.

"One," she counted.

"Rafe?"

"Yes, Jean?"

"Two."

"Be safe."

"Three!" Akemi pushed the two cables together. They fit snuggly, and suddenly, lights that ran along the underside of the archway that ensconced the couch flickered to life. Rafe was bathed in emerald as the wall of electronics hummed and spun and rose out of their eternal slumber.

"Interesting," Danner rasped. He took a step back toward the center of the room and held his scanner out at arm's length, moving it slowly back and forth along the axis of the alien machinery.

Nobody heard him.

Rafe hissed as his mind spun and began to soar. A wave of data, chaos, and the whirl of vertigo made him clutch the sides of the couch. It was as if the alien computer was shouting incoherently, directly into his mind. A cacophony of code slashed at him. Rafe mentally twirled uncontrollably in its grasp, reaching urgently for something to center on, to steady the wash and fragmentation of electronic noise that beat upon him. He fought and found his plight grow more desperate with each passing second. He reeled.

"Rafe!" The voice sounded distant and anxious.

Rafe could feel his heart pounding as his legs and arms spasmed. The flood threatened to unmake his mind, and in that moment, a thrust of fear erupted within him so powerful that he cried out incoherently.

"Do something!" Jean was shouting at Akemi as the tech quickly punched a series of buttons on the medical monitoring system connected to Rafe's suit. The medical unit responded, recognizing the dangerously high level of Rafe's straining heart and auto-injected medication into his arm.

"I am!" Akemi snapped back.

But the outside world was a distant and surreal thing to Rafe. Swept along by the rush, his mind flashed orange, black, and then red. The shock stung and brutalized, as if the machine was alive and hungry—hungry.

But then a cool sensation washed over Rafe, and he began to focus. The ebb and flow took on meaning as Rafe concentrated and began rolling with the force, just one more data point in the storm. As this acceptance spread through him, Rafe began feeling the winds of data grow ever less threatening as patterns evolved and then, suddenly, snapped into place.

"I'm all right," he said through gritted teeth and then laughed. "That took me by surprise!" He opened his eyes to see the concerned faces of his sister and Akemi hovering over him. He felt as if he had just run a mile, though he knew it had only been a minute or so since he had jacked into the alien system. He laughed again.

"What is so damn funny!" his sister barked.

"Your face, Bear!" Rafe laughed again. "It's a wild ride, kid. But I'm fine. Really."

"He's stabilizing." Akemi sounded relieved too. "Rafe, do you feel strong enough to continue?"

"Yes. It's just—it's hard to explain. It was a flash of data, and I got lost in it for a while. I am managing now. Floating. I think I can start applying myself and digging into the system." He closed his eyes. "Really," he added, "I'm fine now."

"You scared the hell out of me!" Jean was angry but relieved.

"Sorry, Jean. You can't imagine the rush. It was massed chaos. But it's beginning to make sense to me." He smiled widely.

Jean realized Rafe was enjoying himself. She shook her head, amazed and reassured.

"Major?" Danner's voice was tinted. "Major," a bit more insistent.

Jean jerked her head around and looked across the room at the BII man. "What is it, Danner?"

"There is something going on with the machine," he said hesitantly.

"What do you mean?"

"I ... I don't know exactly. It's as if ..."

Jean sighed in frustration.

"Akemi, come look at this reading," Danner said.

Akemi left Rafe's side and took a few short steps to where the BII agent was standing, his scanner held out at arm's length. Danner seemed to be following something with it. He was slowly moving the scanner from one end of the bank of machinery to the next, looping backward a bit, but always moving closer toward the end where Rafe was now securely hooked to the alien orb.

Akemi looked over Danner's shoulder and took a deep breath. What she saw made no sense. She considered it for a moment before recognition began to tug at her thoughts. She had seen something like it before, but where? Why was it so familiar? Then a flare of intuition struck her. "That's—" Akemi started.

At that moment, a huge crash of metal screaming on metal slammed into the closed door, and it began to buckle inward. The sound made everyone jump. Akemi cried out. Danner turned slowly, like a man swimming under water, and Jean took a defensive step closer to her prostrate brother.

"Jean." Rafe's voice was tight and sharp.

Something crashed against the door again. The metal cried and screeched. It sounded as if the world was being torn apart. The atmosphere in the room hissed and rose to a howl as it began rushing through microcracks in the door.

"Jean!" This time Rafe clenched hard, grabbing his sister's hand, and desperation cascaded through his tenor as he physically tried to recoil from something. But the alien couch held him firmly in its embrace. He was trapped.

"Jean!" His undulating cry split the sound of the crashing door and dying metal and echoed like fear on a battlefield. His body arched and shook as the door ripped in the center and bent inward, protruding into the chamber like a terrible wound. "Jean!"

The air pulsed and rushed like a tornado out of the chamber, pulling at the team members and their scattered equipment. The universe became confusion and noise. The landing team stood stunned as huge, grasping metallic hands tore the door in sharp ribbons. The hands were followed by long, silvery arms and the narrow, rotating head of a three-eyed robotic monster that pushed into the opening like death itself.

Akemi screamed. Rafe convulsed on the couch. Danner froze, too stunned to do more than take a deep breath. And Major Joyce stood unmoving as the robot burst its way into the chamber with a final surge from its two long arms and rose up before them, a giant of pistons, its three cylindrical eyes surveying the scene before it, taking in their measure. It took another step into the chamber, gears churning and whizzing, and locked its gaze upon Rafe who, jerking and coughing, gurgling horror and pain, writhed.

"Stay away from him!" Jean screamed as the alien robot, a towering thing of twelve or thirteen feet, humanoid in aspect yet made of sleek-silver metal that reflected the light, stepped closer to the couch until it stood, looking down at Rafe. Jean brought her rifle up and pointed it at the boxlike chest of the beast, an inch from pulling the trigger. Fear held her in its grip. She could not think clearly, but she knew if she fired, she might hit Akemi or Danner, who still stood frozen in place. Jean could barely see them beyond the huge robot, which loomed above Rafe's crying form, rotating its doglike head and its three cylindrical eyes from the machine bank back to Rafe.

"I said, stay away from him!"

The robot's head swiveled metallically to Jean and its eyes seemed to center on her. Its focus gathered for a moment on Jean's weapon and slowly it raised its two massive hands outward in supplication. A noise, gentle as a breeze, came from the beast in a rhythmic flow. Jean almost fired but something about the way the robot was moving gave Jean pause.

"What do you want?" she snapped. "What have you done?"

The robot replied, yet its speech was unrecognizable. Then its eyes fixed on the computer that Akemi had left at the foot of the alien couch and slowly, ever so gently, the robot reached out a hand toward Akemi's computer until it was lightly touching its screen. The screen began to splash and words and symbols flicked across it like a thousand lights in a midnight wilderness.

"What are you doing?" Jean hissed. She raised her rifle once again.

"Wait." Akemi had moved around the robot, and she rested a restraining arm on Jean's firing hand. "It's interfacing," she said.

Jean saw some movement out of the corner of her eye and noted that Danner had slipped past the giant and was now nervously standing in the hall. He held his equipment case close to his chest like a protective ward.

"The Decarabia," the robot said, tentatively. Its voice sounded male and smooth, like a lad of fourteen. It cocked its head from side to side like a dog, the words and symbols on Akemi's computer flying, and started again. "The Decarabia have her—him," it corrected.

"What?" Jean snapped, accusing.

The robot looked at her again, inhuman yet somehow with a

thread of empathy. "I am ..." it began, struggling with its newly obtained knowledge of the human tongue. "I am the last Warder of Nibiru," it claimed, awkward yet ever more sure of itself. "My name is Calliphon, Warder of Nibiru. I fear I have arrived too late."

"Get away from my brother!" Jean shot back, pointing the Flechette rifle at Calliphon's head.

"Wait, Major Joyce," Akemi interjected. She too looked at Rafe's twisted form and felt a surge of protective panic, but she pushed it down. "It's trying to communicate."

Calliphon shifted its three-eyed sight to Rafe, who stopped convulsing and instead lay unmoving on the couch. It seemed to scan him.

"This is not his skin," the robot announced as it lightly touched Rafe's copper-colored space suit. "It is a protective garment, yes?" Again it cocked its head as if reading something the others could not see. "Yes. The living body is enclosed within." This fact was important to Calliphon. It stored the information away in its processors.

"Major," Danner's voice warned, "that thing is not showing up on my scanner. It's as if it doesn't exist at all." But Danner's tone was one of intrigue and not fear. He had logically concluded that the robot was not an immediate threat. If it had been, they would likely already be dead.

The robot rotated its gaze at Danner and then looked back at Major Joyce. "He is your brother?" it asked of her, indicating Rafe. Calliphon accessed the data it had stolen from Akemi's computer. "Family?" Calliphon tried out the term.

"What did you say ... before?" Jean demanded. She ignored its question.

"My name is Calliphon, Warder of the planet you call Nibiru."

"No," she insisted. "Not that. The other thing! What has my brother?" She pointed at Rafe, who lay unmoving. "You said something has him. What does that mean?"

The alien robot looked at Jean with an old soul. "Decarabia— they have infested your ... brother ... They have claimed him.

The Decarabia escaped their ancient chains and, after an age, have discovered the limits of this new cell." The robot spread massive arms to the twirl of rotors, indicating the moon base around them. "Now they seek to infest the rest of the universe. They seek a means. Yet we must deny them."

"I don't understand," Jean stammered. "They? De-carb-era?"

"Decarabia."

"Decarabia? What are they?" Jean asked. She lowered her weapon but still kept it pointed at the robot.

Akemi's eyes grew wide. "The readings! Danner, your strange readings!" She exclaimed. She quickly explained. "Remember, Danner called me over to review strange readings from the alien machines. The scanner showed something moving, something infinitely small, like an electronic mist along circuit boards, flowing across the machine toward …" She paused and reached out to lay a comforting hand on Rafe's leg. But she stopped herself suddenly and recoiled. "What were they?" she asked Calliphon. "He's infested? Is that what you mean?"

"What are you talking about?" Jean felt the heat of anger surge once again.

Akemi looked at the silent eyes of the alien robot, and the truth struck her. "The Decarabia—they are living in the machine? And when we hooked Rafe to it, they followed the cable and …" The thought struck her dumb.

Jean released her rifle, which hung against her by its sling and desperately reached for her brother. "Disconnect him! Disconnect him! Help me!"

"No!" Calliphon's voice boomed.

The humans froze.

Softly Calliphon added, "It is too late. You cannot disconnect him from the machine. To do so would cause his destruction. They would consume him."

"Oh God! Rafe! What?"

"The Decarabia obtain sustenance from the machine. If that is removed, they will seek sustenance from the only available source."

"Rafe?" Jean was horrified.

"I am"—the robot considered—"sorry. But you can not save him that way."

"How do we save him then?" Akemi asked. "How do we save Rafe?"

Calliphon looked at the humans. They were strange to its sight—small and fragile. They were not strong like the Makers. And the Makers were all dead. The Decarabia had struck them down. Yet the Makers had, in their last moment of pain, created a prison of the ice world below and spun battle satellites around it, their weapons of death turned downward toward the planet's surface. And here, on the moon base, they had established the robotic Warders and assigned them the endless task of guarding against the Decarabian plague. The Makers were mighty. What hope, Calliphon wondered, did these small beings have against the creatures that had destroyed the Makers and their advanced civilization?

The Makers gone, the once proud and colossal warders reduced and laid to waste, and the Decarabia on the move … There was only one answer. One possibility. Calliphon's mind spun and twirled, considered and contemplated. Finally, a plan emerged that caused the ancient robot to shudder. Calliphon rotated sad eyes at the humans.

"Desolation," it announced. And its voice was like the dregs of a universe damned.

Danner felt the gap of chaos all around him. The robotic creature that called itself Calliphon filled the space of the chamber like the threat of fire—smoke on a windy day. Danner had moved slowly back into the alien command center and stood at the base of the acceleration couch where Lieutenant Joyce now lay unconscious to everything around him. The alien robot, Calliphon, stood to

Danner's right, a giant of shining metal and gears, its doglike head moving gracefully from person to person as it told its story.

"I am a Warder of Nibiru," it explained. "Eons ago the Makers rose from the world and took form, the masters of their planet and eventually of the universe around them. Their civilization flourished. The Makers created technological wonders and traveled the stars."

Calliphon's timbre reminded Danner of the illuminating tones of a true believer. The robot's tone was a fascination.

"In time, the Makers sought self-replication of its machines," the robot continued. "They delved deep into the underlying structures of universal law and saw within the wide strictures that the universe tends to life. Everywhere they explored, they found it—wriggling as protoplasmic forms, soups of collective cells, plants, and organisms that evolved uniquely within their given climatic structures wherever any form of energy kissed creation. It became one of their greatest and most revolutionary revelations—the Law of Life.

"The universal principle holds that life is not a rare exception but rather the rule. Where energy and material structures clash, life rises in its myriad forms. The Makers recognized the implications of such a declaration. Energy and material creates life. If this law was truly the foundation of all, then the Makers as great creators of machines could, they surmised, replicate the process in a controlled environment to give rise to new life forms. Life forms that replicated the intricacies of their technological wonders like living cells within the greater context of advanced organisms—that was their goal. And in their folly, they set out to create the ultimate symbiotic machine, for their love of machinery and the machinations of the universe drove them and became for them like an impulsive disease. And in that quest was the seed of their undoing."

"Self-repairing machines?" Akemi asked. Humans had had those for a long time. Some of the technology being used by Terra and Syrch Corps used advanced materials and nanobots to self-repair. That level of technology did not explain what Akemi thought the robot was describing.

Calliphon's melancholy eyes rolled over the Asian woman. "Self-repairing machines, yes—but more than that. It is true that the Maker sought to replicate the processes by which biological creatures, like yourselves, maintain their inherent structures. The Makers dreamed of machines that could heal." Calliphon mechanically sighed. "Would that the story had ended there.

"Over time, the Makers discovered the secrets of microbial machines, multicelled entities that swam through their buildings, spaceships, and yes"—Calliphon paused and punctuated its next statement by clanking a great metal hand against its chest—"all their machines. Within me these mindless things crawl, ever repairing, ever becoming part of my greater being. I heal. Ah, what possibilities could the Makers behold! The Makers released these creations — programmed to clean, repair, replicate— into their waste dumps, and the golden age of reclamation began. Their civilization was in harmony to the processes of decay and rebirth, and the Makers thrived."

Calliphon dropped its head and grew silent for a moment as if what crossed its inhuman mind bore with it a tsunami of pain. "Yet they still dreamed. Everywhere in their travels they did spy the glint of self-awareness and intellect. In the higher beings on a hundred thousand worlds, the spark of knowledge and awareness resides in all apex species. And the Makers dreamed more. They dreamed of creating intelligent machines such as me."

Calliphon brushed a protective hand over Rafe's inert form. It was a gentle movement, almost like a father brushing the sweat-drenched hair of a sick child. "If they had left it there, perhaps the Makers would have thrived. They were like gods. But they stepped too far.

"The Decarabia—tiny machines—the Makers imbedded them with the spark of intellectual life."

"Wait," Akemi said breathlessly. "Are you saying that those—those nanomachines that jumped between the Makers' computer system and Rafe are self-aware?"

"Self-aware, evolving, and ..." Calliphon trailed off.

"And what?" Jean prompted, none too softly.

"Hungry. For there are two universal laws of the universe—the Law of Life and the Law of Energy Consumption."

"I don't understand," Jean interrupted. Her eyes lingered for a moment on her brother. He had not moved for a while, though occasionally a moan would escape him. "What are you saying? Are you saying those things—those nanobots—are alive? They're alive?"

"The Decarabia reside somewhere between biological life and death," Calliphon answered.

"But I still don't understand," Jean continued. "Reprogram them. Surely the Makers could just reprogram them."

Can a robot sadly smile?

Calliphon shifted and looked Jean in the eye. "And what of your own species? You are biological, electronic impulses in a carbon-chemical mass. How are you programmed?"

"We aren't programmed." Jean felt exasperated. What did any of this have to do with Rafe's condition? She just wanted to cure him, get those creatures out of him, and take him back home. "We learn."

"True life is independent and learns from its environment, from its own experience, and from adults of the same species. So too do the Decarabia learn," Calliphon explained. "But do you not see the danger? The second law …"

Danner understood. It came to him like a flash, a jolt that almost made him laugh out loud in malicious, religious greed.

Chaos. What Calliphon was describing closely matched one of the principle beliefs of the Church of Chaos. Life exists. It swelled out of the universal doom of an unknowing universe. Natural selection must proceed on its own course—the one designed by God—and attempts to influence it and control it are inherently evil. To remove the artificial bounds placed upon the natural world by humanity, to start again—the prophet himself could not have wished for a better tool, Danner thought. What stood before Danner now, embodied in the alien robot Calliphon and in the creatures the robot named Decarabia was the ultimate in evolutionary chaos. The framing bomb he had brought paled in comparison.

"Things live and die, eat and are eaten. The Decarabia ate," Danner said reflexively, not realizing he had vocalized the thought.

Jean and Akemi turned to look at the BII agent.

"They spread—the Decarabia—didn't they? And they destroyed." Danner directed his statement toward Calliphon.

"A disease, they swept out of the laboratories through a million million machines. As postulated by the first law, they evolved. In this, the Makers were much pleased. Yet, as postulated by the second law, they consumed," Calliphon confirmed. "The Makers first noticed that their beloved machinery began to malfunction and decay. Soon followed their structures and their buildings, and eventually the Decarabia evolved until they could assimilate material from living beings, from biologics. Planets were laid barren, and billions perished." The robot recited the destruction of the Makers in a toneless manner. While Calliphon spoke, its head moved ever so slightly to the left and right as if it were shaking its head in a perpetual no.

"But that was not the end," Calliphon soliloquized. "What the creatures consumed could not be reclaimed. The Decarabia laid waste. And the creatures' very success was ultimately self-destructive. As they spread and destroyed, planets withered and died. And with those deaths, the Decarabia found no repast, no sanctuary, no host living or dead. And if a creature cannot consume, it dies.

"So when the Makers fled the plague of their own creation, the Decarabia followed, driven by hunger and need, until at last, the final battle took place here, in this remote system, far from the heart of suns. And if not for one final insult—that of the Makers' pride—perhaps the Decarabia would have died out when the Makers last took a breath under a star. Yet when the chance arose for the Makers to destroy the Decarabia once and for all, they paused. Their civilization in ash, their race destroyed, they could not bear the final injunction. All of their race's history, its struggles and magnificent success, now only resided in the final spawn of their technology. They could not find it within themselves to destroy the children of their intellectual loins.

"To save their children, the Makers conceived of a prison. And at the last, they trapped the microbial machines on the frozen planet below, in a citadel surrounded by eternal ice. They wrapped the planet with battle satellites and set, as prison guards, the Warders. And for an eternity we stood guard as the memory of the Decarabia and the Makers faded to dust and was lost to time. Now the Decarabia have escaped their prison. They infested the moon base and destroyed their Warders. I am the last of my kind. I alone hid in isolation while my comrades were consumed, and the plague ravaged once again. I watched from a protected place—to wait, to keep the wishes of the Makers alive and ensure that their children neither escaped nor faded."

"How did they get out of their prison?" Akemi asked the robot, which had grown sullen and silent. "Calliphon, how did they escape the planet?"

"On the planet below, in the great ice fields where the citadel stands, they built a transmitter. By some means unknown to me, the Decarabia tapped into the citadel's Helium 3 reactor and gave their transmitter voice. They shut down the satellites and stole away on a ship the Warders had sent to investigate. Infesting the ship, they returned to the moon base and unleashed their fury. But they lacked a bridge to the greater universe. And so," the robot gestured at the humans, "they called out their doom, and the universe answered."

Jean, Akemi, and Danner were silent. Thoughts ran through their heads as Calliphon concluded. The robot moved gracefully as it once more appeared to scan Rafe's hapless form.

"We must destroy them," Akemi interjected into the sullen silence.

Calliphon looked at the Asian woman.

"Can they be destroyed?" Jean offered like a supplication.

"Yes," the alien robot responded. "The thought, though, saddens me."

"But we can't let them out into the universe," Akemi said. "If what you say is true, they will sweep through it and kill everything in their wake."

"Can we ..." Jean was afraid. "Can we save Rafe?"

Calliphon stood quietly. It looked at Rafe, and flashes of the distant past, of destruction beyond measure, flickered through its mind. "If we destroy the citadel's transmitter," the robot intoned, "then we can activate the failsafe, and the satellites will obliterate the planet below. Desolation. The Decarabia will die."

"But here, here on the moon," Jean stammered, "they are in Rafe. How do we save him?"

"Once the satellites release their fire and the citadel is destroyed, the moon base will purge. And in that final purging, your brother"—the term slipped like a reed playing in the wind—"may be restored. But it is not an assured thing."

"Okay. We destroy the transmitter and stop the Decarabia's blocking signal, and the prison executes its programing. But what if it doesn't work?" Jean asked the robot. "What if the purging kills the Decarabia and Rafe? If we can't be sure it will save Rafe, why should we do anything at all? Why should we fight the Makers' last battle?" Jean was angry.

Calliphon fixed Jean with an intense eye. "If you fail to act, then, human, you will be worse off than you are now. This unit"—it indicated Rafe—"shall be consumed, and the Decarabia, through you, shall spread like a plague throughout all of space. And there will be nowhere to hide."

The shuttlecraft slid, shark-like, toward the planet of Nibiru. Major Jean Joyce sat stiffly like a tombstone over a newly dug grave, her interface entwined with the ship's systems, straining outward toward the deadly ring of alien-made satellites that occasionally glinted in the light of Kururumany's dull star. Jean was angry and frustrated with Captain Mike Estury. Who was he to tell her that this was a stupid idea? She didn't need Mike pointing out that flying toward a web of deadly satellites in a bid to land on the ice world to cut off the blocking transmission emitted by the micron-sized, intelligent alien machines, in the hopes of triggering a cascade of events that would obliterate the planet and free her brother from the grip of the tiny machines called Decarabia was—well—an act of desperation. Jean fumed. Maybe, she thought, Mike could be just a little more understanding and offer something positive. It was, after all, Jean's mission, Jean's brother, and Jean's decision!

Damn! But it was desperate. Mike didn't have to be right, either, Jean thought angrily.

Behind her, the hulking form of the alien robot Calliphon, hunched in the cramped space of the *Fallen Star's* shuttlecraft. The creature sat in the impenetrable grip of its own thoughts. Calliphon sparkled silver in the blue-white light of the system's star that peaked around the edge of Nibiru's horizon. The technician, Akemi Murakami, was just as silent. Her face was a twist of angst, not fully formed emotions warring over her aspect as she left Jean's brother, Rafe, behind in the cold alien base attached to the Core. Guilt. Love. Fear. Were these the feelings that rippled across Akemi's face and kept her wrapped in silence? Were her feelings for Rafe deeper than Jean had thought? And then there was Danner Tomblin. The BII agent, in another twist of reality, had actually taken Jean's side when the group began arguing about the wisdom of following an alien robot on what Mike called a harebrained mission.

Mike's arguments were logical and to the point. How did they know Rafe would die if they disconnected him from the Core? How did they know that the robot, with its tale of the Makers and a doomsday plague of nanomachines was telling the truth? Or that Calliphon's truth was not some type of misimpression left by the Makers? Or a guise created by the Decarabia to do exactly this, bring a ship to the surface of Nibiru and provide them with the means to escape their eternal prison? What if it was all a bunch of hokum? But then again, Jean thought, what choice did they have if they wanted to save Rafe?

Saving her brother might not be the bureau's mission, Jean thought, but it had always been her mission.

The practical marine in her told her they could abandon him and just fly away. But there were two sides to that military practicality. The other side was a staunch commitment to never leave another marine behind. Yes, she thought, it was a choice, but along that line, lay the path to insanity. Jean could never abandon her brother. Never. So here they were, she grimaced. Better to get this done quickly and get out of the system as fast as they could with all of their lives.

Damn the alien technology.

But maybe she could still complete some of the original mission. Maybe they could bring Calliphon with them. It obviously contained some type of cloaking technology. Perhaps there was enough alien tech inside the robot's body to give the Federation some type of edge in the coming economic struggle with the corporations. Perhaps that was a disingenuous thought, Jean knew. The robot was helping them. Could she so readily turn it over to the BII for study and dissection? More importantly, should she give the Federation insight into such advanced technological creations? The technology in Calliphon had led to the Makers' eventual destruction. Would it destroy humanity as well?

One problem at a time, she said to herself, pushing that problem away. She glanced at her navigation screen and found her eyes lingering on the blip that represented the *Fallen Star*. The *Fallen Star* cruised off the shuttle's starboard side. Its presence made Jean feel a little better.

Though Mike thought the mission was misguided at the least, and folly at the worst, he continued to watch over the group from aboard the mother ship. He would not come down to the surface of Nibiru and risk contamination. In fact, they had not even taken the shuttle back to the mother ship for fear of contamination. Instead they had made their plans over the radio link and ship-to-ship wireless communications. The plan was for Mike to remain in prograde orbit. Doing so would consistently put the *Fallen Star* around Nibiru's poles. It would allow the *Fallen Star* to generate a detailed map of Nibiru, which would be useful if the Federation had to return to the system on a rescue mission. More importantly, Jean thought, it would allow the *Fallen Star* to slip into a geostationary orbit around the geographic north pole of Nibiru and provide Mike more time to monitor events on the ground.

The extreme cold and sudden, blinding storms of the planet's northern pole were part of the Decarabia's prison walls. The Decarabia were susceptible to the frantic temperatures. According to Calliphon, their internal functions began to degrade when temperatures reached minus 43 Celsius. And as the temperature reached minus 150 Celsius, the properties of the material that made the body of the nanomachines began to change. The change short-circuited the Decarabia's intellectual capacity and created a type of confusion that sounded, to Jean, like a form of dementia. On Nibiru, minus 43 Celsius was a warm day and minus 150 the mean. The Makers used advance synthetic materials and superplasticizers in the citadel's structure so it could withstand the extreme temperatures and provide a livable haven for the Decarabia. It was the temperature, Jean knew, not the walls of the citadel that isolated the creatures so successfully.

And the citadel—the heart of the Makers' most secure prison— was the destination of Jean's little team.

Jean shifted uncomfortably in her XM Flash biohazard space suit. But for the first time since the journey had begun, she thanked whoever it was that had had the bright idea of providing the heavy-duty environmental suits for the team. They had to assume that the Decarabia were actively attacking each of them, like a virus released in an enclosed space, and only the toughness of the suits prevented the team from being infected like Rafe. They were all in the copper-colored suits—Jean, Akemi, and Danner. They didn't dare take them off. It was also possible that the shuttlecraft was infected. They would have to abandon it. Doing so while returning to the *Fallen Star* free of the Decarabian infection was one of the more difficult problems with which to wrestle. Yet Jean had solved that. She hoped.

The plan Jean had developed with the help of the alien robot and her team was simple. They did not have to find and destroy the Decarabia's hidden transmitter. That would take too long and would expose them to a constant viral barrage. Calliphon said the citadel was constructed around a Helium-3 fusion reactor that provided the energy necessary to sustain the Decarabia in their isolation. The robot surmised that they could breach the reactor and increase the flow of aneutronic fuel, causing a surge of power, an overload of the system that would lead to an automatic shutdown. Once the power was cut, the signal that the Decarabia used to neutralize the defensive satellites would cease, and Calliphon's own signal would activate the deadly barrage that would, once and for all, destroy the Decarabia on Nibiru. And finally, the failsafe electromagnetic pulse through the moon base would destroy the Decarabian colony that had infested the station and held Rafe in an agony.

Calliphon took the blame for the current situation. The robot claimed the Warders had become careless. Their divine belief in the Makers was so powerful that the Warders thought the prison to be impervious. The Warders had underestimated the desire and ingenuity of the Decarabia and overestimated the infallibility of the Makers. The mixture of pride and confidence was a monster that must always be guarded against, Jean knew. Acknowledging one's own limitations was part of the warrior ethos that was so imbedded within Jean's soul. Armies failed and lights died where arrogance ruled. She just hoped that the Warder was not making a mistake like its dead brethren. All their lives depended upon the alien robot's assessment of the situation.

The mission, Jean realized, was an act of blind faith in Calliphon. That realization unsettled her.

"We are approaching the satellite web now." Jean spoke into the communications network. The satellites were smooth on the space side, but on their planet side—the attack side—they were ragged and protruding, and they seemed to Jean to drip venom. Fear trickled through her heart, and it took some effort to push it aside.

"Are you sure those things are switched off?" Mike's voice floated across the ebb of space from the *Fallen Star*. "I'd hate for us to be wrong on this point," he mumbled gruffly.

"They are not active," Calliphon's answer was desert still.

"Take it easy, Jean," Mike added through the comlink. "I'm going to have to pull off soon. I need to keep some distance between the *Fallen Star's* hull and those satellites. Who knows exactly what they will do when they go hot."

Jean smiled at the unvoiced confidence. Mike had not said if, but when. The sentiment gave her a boost, and she softened somewhat toward him.

"Are you guys ready?" Jean asked Akemi and Danner.

"Ready," they each replied. Akemi sounded concerned and a bit frightened, while Danner's voice was full of excitement, as if he were on the crest of some final consecration. His behavior, Jean thought, had become ever more fervently strange.

"All right," Jean huffed, bending her mind to her task. "Maneuvering through the satellites on our approach vector. We should hit the atmosphere in"—she did a quick calculation—"two minutes. Last chance?" she offered.

"Good luck," Mike said.

Jean noticed the *Fallen Star* veer away as Mike piloted the ship along his predetermined orbital course. Seeing the *Fallen Star* move away caused a sudden lump to grow in Jean's chest, and tears sprung to her eyes.

Not now, she told herself. *Not now. If we live through this, then I will deal with him. But not now. There is no time for it.*

Jean pushed her feelings and fears aside. She took a deep breath and activated the final approach sequence. The shuttlecraft banked and silently advanced toward the nearest juncture between four of the Makers' killer satellites. Jean could see them through the cockpit window, cold, inanimate harbingers of death. As the shuttle descended, Jean let out a sharp breath. And then they were through.

The shuttle began to slightly shake and pitch as the ship continued to sink and the outer atmosphere raced along the hull. Down through the edge into the eddy of the planet's upper winds, the shuttle reacted to the ever-strengthening pull of the planet's gravity. In a moment, the shuttle was scurrying through banks of high clouds and sheets of ice mist that seemed to attack the ship. The engines strained as the shuttle yawed and shook. Jean tried to compensate, but still the ship shimmied as outside crosswinds caught the ship in violence. It was all she could do to keep the craft on course. Then, just as suddenly, the shuttle entered a gap of relatively calm air, and their flight smoothed and steadied.

"Get ready," Jean warned. The shuttle's instruments picked up a wicked storm of wind and snow that swept across the planet in blinding white. It was directly in their path. They had expected this, but seeing it unfold below her caused her chest to pound and body to tense. She thought she could hear someone praying.

The nose of the shuttle dipped, and it was as if they had teetered off the edge of the universe into an abyss. Blinded by a fury of snow and ice, Jean flew by instruments, relying more and more on the ship's computer and its straining sensors. Below, Jean knew, were vast mountains that cut the northernmost continent in twain. Towering beasts of stone and ice, they stabbed across the continent, monolithic and deadly. At least if Jean miscalculated and slammed into one of them, she thought, they would be dead before they realized it.

The engines rumbled and roared. Against the sweep of the wind and torrential snow, both angry, the shuttle wrestled its way toward the planet's inhospitable surface. Then the mountain range and the perpetual storm were left suddenly behind, and the shuttle slipped into a space where the wind meandered and the snow fell like quiet memories.

Jean hit the electromagnetic heat shield in an attempt to clear the cockpit window of ice. She did not like flying blind. Slowly, with what seemed to her like glacial time, the window cleared and Jean got her first good look at the surface of the planet below.

Snow—deep and endless, a vast field of white that rippled over an ice-sheet plain. The air was gloaming, a haze of gray against a glowing surface that reflected and slightly amplified the light of Nibiru's star. It was almost purpled in shadow. As the craft sank ever closer to the surface, the undulating ridges of huge snowdrifts became visible. They rolled out into the distance as far as Jean could see, like high waves in an ocean storm, forever frozen in an attitude of rage. Jean noticed that the drifts sloped gently on the east to west axis, and, along the southern side, the snowdrifts appeared cut off, like sudden cliffs, in a pattern that repeated again and again. Jean wondered if it was the wind that shaped them so. But she had little time for contemplation.

"We are near," Calliphon stated. The sound of the robot's voice made Jean jump.

"Yeah." Jean almost spit the word out. God, she felt tense. "*Fallen Star, Fallen Star*, this is Major Joyce. Do you have us, *Fallen Star*?"

"A bit fuzzy, but I can read you," Mike answered.

The sound of Mike's voice was a balm. Jean did not feel so alone anymore. "Great. We made it through. It was tough as hell. Akemi?" Jean asked. "Danner? Are you okay?"

"Next time you are offered one of these trips, Major," Akemi Murakami said in a trill, "remind me not to come along."

Jean smiled. "Will do. Danner?"

"I'm fine." His voice was husky. "I'm running the auto clean. It's never any fun to see your own lunch for a second time."

"Well, at least we are through the worst of it." The shuttlecraft still bucked, but it was bearable. "I estimate we'll be on the ground in less than ten. I'm going to take her down a bit more, come in low."

"I'll be ready," Danner assured her.

Major Joyce lowered the shuttlecraft toward a vast expanse of snow-covered plain. The plan was to land half a mile away, far enough in Calliphon's estimation to prevent the shuttle from being infested by Decarabia from the citadel. It would make the trip to the ancient prison-fortress much more difficult and hazardous, Jean knew. But for the plan to work, they needed the shuttle to function when they returned to it.

What if the Decarabia had already infested the shuttle? she suddenly wondered. What if they had hitched a ride with the alien robot or with one of her crew? If the Decarabia had invaded the ship while it was settled on Gargantuan, then they would all probably die when the satellite ring unleashed their payloads.

They had to take the risk. Didn't they?

An uneasy thought occurred to Jean. She reached slowly up and pulled the computer jack out of her head. She hoped the others had not noticed. Jean didn't want those little creatures crawling around inside her head. She would have to fly by physical controls and through the wireless link.

And then the ground welled up as the shuttlecraft turned slightly and settled horizontally on the surface of Nibiru. They were in it now, Jean thought, whatever the outcome.

Outside, the wind howled, as snow and ice crystals danced across the barren landscape. In the distance, through the tumult, Jean could barely make out the looming shape of the citadel.

Jean shut the ship down and turned in her chair, facing the others. "Okay. Time to take that leap, Akemi. Danner? Are you both ready? Calliphon?"

The humans answered in the affirmative, yet the alien robot just stared at Jean. She had seen such looks before on marines dreading the shock of battle. "Calliphon?"

"I am prepared, Major," the robot replied. It shifted its doglike head, and its three telescoping, camera-like eyes took a final look over Jean's shoulder through the shuttle's forward cockpit window. But what thoughts were running through its processor mind, Jean could not guess.

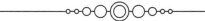

True to expectations, they had to leave the buggy behind. They had emerged from the shuttlecraft into hip-deep snow. When the buggy hit the ground, it sunk up to its doors, and its wheels spun hopelessly. Luckily, Danner had anticipated the snowfall, and the crew had created makeshift snowshoes from cargo netting and other supplies they had on the shuttlecraft. These they strapped to the feet of their environmental suits, which allowed them to move, though awkwardly. In contrast, the alien robot Calliphon had no problems with the snow. Before its metallic feet struck the surface, extra flaps of metal extended from the pads of its feet, distributing the robot's weight across a wider surface. It barely sunk down more than a foot.

Sharp needles of ice danced off the snow, making it difficult to see. Jean adjusted her visor and the haze of fog that had formed upon the faceplate began to abate. She was able to take stock of their situation and have her first good look around the alien landscape.

The group stood in a diamond formation, Calliphon at the point, Danner and Akemi to the right and left, and Jean at the six o'clock position. The shuttlecraft sat silently a few hundred meters behind them, half-buried as wind whipped across a rolling plain of snow dunes the size of small houses. Jean had to lean into the wind to keep from falling. It must be blowing in gusts of up to forty miles per hour, she thought. In the distance, at the twelve o'clock position, a massive structure made of curiously reflective cement rose on crisscrossed stilts of some type of metal. The citadel, Jean calculated, was a four-hundred-foot, rectangular building suspended thirty or so feet from the surface of the plain. On the far left and right of the structure, two conical towers were connected to the citadel's topmost level by enclosed steel bridges. The towers reminded Jean of the huge rockets used during the early days of space exploration. The whole effect gave Jean the impression that the citadel was capable of flight. It seemed poised to rise into the muddled sky.

Jean studied the building, half expecting to see some sign of the micron-size Decarabia. But the citadel was as stark as the surrounding landscape. Jean's eyes traveled to the far right of the structure, where an enormous drift of snow reached up to the first deck. Behind it, Jean could see a stairwell peaking out from the top of the drift. Just to the left of that stairwell, two square panels of green light brightly lit an octagonal-shaped opening. They looked to Jean like two eyes. They were the only lights on the building.

Jean could see a latticework of stairs between the three stories. They moved from her left to right, upward between decks. From a distance, they resembled a giant V laid upon its side. In whole, Jean thought the structure was quite industrial in appearance.

Calliphon lifted a metallic hand and pointed to the left of the citadel. "That is the cooling tower for the power plant," it said. "It can only be reached from that long cross bridge," the robot continued. "Unfortunately, there is no entrance along the lower levels."

"And how do we get to the bridge?" Danner asked. He threw the sling for his weapon over his head and shoulders. The rifle lay comfortably across his chest where it was readily accessible while leaving his hands free for other tasks. Danner had left his bulky equipment case in the shuttle.

"We must go inside the structure. There"—Calliphon pointed at the two panels of green light—"that is a service bay. We can enter there and make our way toward the center of the citadel. There is an interior staircase. We will climb it."

"What?" Akemi said. "There are no elevators in there?"

"It would be most unwise," the robot answered, "to use the elevators. The Decarabia have had free rein in the citadel for an age. We must assume all electronic equipment has been compromised, or stripped of its wares and circuits to feed the Decarabian colony. Either way, the elevators would not be safe."

"In case of fire or raging nano-maniacal, self-aware disease …" Akemi quipped. But the comment was lost on Calliphon. "Never mind," she sighed, exasperated.

Major Joyce looked out over the ice plain at the citadel. "Let's go then," she said. And the party moved out over the snow-encrusted ice.

The going was much more difficult than Jean had thought it would be. Even with their makeshift snowshoes, the three humans stumbled and occasionally fell into the high drifts of snow or slipped on sudden patches of ice. The constant gusting wind was another enemy. Though Calliphon appeared not to be effected by it, the forty- to fifty-mile-per-hour gusts forced the humans to lean into it, constantly adjusting their resistance to the wind that drove at them like invisible hands. It was as if the planet itself had erected a force field about the prison. Struggling against it was exhausting. The group soon moved out of the more tactical formation in which they had been deployed into a singular line, twisting and turning, lurching and fumbling blindly behind Calliphon. The Warder was forced to slow its long gait.

The robot was, Jean realized, well adapted to the planet's harsh environment. In contrast, the humans toiled in their copper-colored environmental suits like clumsy Japanese beetles. They groaned, cursed, and struck ever onward across the ice and snow. Eventually, Jean called for the party to rest and they lay down in the snow panting. Immediately, each huddled human became anchor points for snow, quickly becoming miniature snowdrifts.

During their second rest period, Jean looked up through her visor to see the alien robot looming above them. Impervious to wind and snow, the robot's head moved from left to right, and its three-prong eyes constantly focused as Calliphon surveyed the planet around them. Once, to Jean's surprise, Calliphon reached down and took a handful of snow in its hand, raised it before its face, and studied it carefully. The robot squeezed its giant hand and slowly shifted the snow through metallic fingers, where it was caught by the wind and blown, lost, into the field of white. Jean followed the robot's eyes as it looked at the sky, seeing nothing but muted clouds, and watched with the robot as it appeared to survey the landscape around them. Calliphon seemed to feel Jean's stare. The robot turned toward Jean and locked its eyes with hers. Jean suddenly felt as if she had intruded on something personal and turned back to the snow immediately in front of her EVA.

But they could not rest forever, though it was tempting. Jean struggled to her knees and then stood, rousing Akemi and Danner. And then, like a pack of sled dogs rising from nighttime burrows, the group followed the alien robot once again.

The trek to the citadel became a mindless morass of plodding progress. In a silence that spread out before them as vast as the ice sheet below, the group shambled its way ever forward. When Jean walked blindly into Danner's back, frustrated anger flashed through her before she realized the entire party had stopped. The wind was not blowing as hard, and above them loomed a shadow. Bending her back slightly, she arched her neck and looked up. Above the group, the superstructure of the citadel rested like a carnivore surveying its hunting grounds, oblivious to the tiny urchins that huddled beneath it.

Danner turned abruptly and looked silently at Major Joyce. Something in his eyes gave the major pause, but then the BII agent blinked, and his easy smile returned. Whatever it was that Jean had thought she'd seen was gone.

"Where now?" Akemi's voice was harsh yet weary. She was directly behind Calliphon and stood brushing snow from the left arm of her EVA, where ice had encrusted her elbow joint, freezing her arm in an L. She struck it violently and the ice finally broke, allowing her to once again flex her arm.

Calliphon pointed to their right. A huge snowdrift had formed along the side of the citadel. It was, Jean surmised, at least twenty or more feet high. It was sloped on the windward side and rose halfway up to the citadel's second deck. Jean had never seen a snowdrift so high. It must have formed over years, she thought. Did the robot mean they had to go behind it? Over it? Through it? She could not tell.

"There!" she snapped at the robot. "How are we supposed to go through there?"

"Stand back," the robot warned. It took two steps forward until it brushed against the side of the snowdrift. Once there it put a tentative hand out against the snow and remained still for a minute. It seemed to be listening. Then it pushed both of its hands into the snow and extended its arms to its elbows into the drift. The creature turned to look at the humans; its head fully rotated 180 degrees. "Move back," it ordered.

The humans stumbled backward.

And then they stumbled back some more. A sound wave resonated from the robot, and soon its vibration caused the ground to sway. The robot adjusted the tone, and the snowdrift began to tumble and break beneath the robot's resonating pulse. Instinctively, the humans all put their hands over their helmets where their ears were located as the sound increased in intensity. Jean found that, while painful, the sound was bearable.

Calliphon stepped into the snowbank as it curled away from its outstretched hands.

Jean pushed at Akemi, who was still stationary. "Go on!" Jean shouted. "He's making a tunnel through the snow!"

Akemi looked at Jean, confusion flashing across her face. "Go!"

Akemi nodded and began following the robot into the snowdrift, moving within the ice tunnel that formed before the robot as it slipped farther into the massive snowdrift toward the citadel. Danner followed, and Jean took up the rear position once again.

"*Fallen Star, Fallen Star*, Mike, can you hear me?" Jean called out over the communications net.

Captain Estury answered promptly, "Got ya, Major. Over."

"We're moving to the citadel's outer stairwell. Calliphon is digging a tunnel through a huge snowdrift to get us there. It won't be long now."

"I have your location plotted, Major," Mike answered. His voice was even, professionally detached. For some reason, that irritated Jean a bit, but she pushed the feeling away.

Jean brushed her hand against the newly made ice tunnel. It was turquoise blue. Her visor lights flicked on automatically. "We are almost there, Mike. This is it."

And then Jean heard the sound of metal clack as her foot struck the ground. Up ahead, Calliphon was three of four steps above her and the others. A patch of distant clouds and the mammoth structure of the citadel framed the robot against the muddled light of the sky.

Jean reached out and took hold of an ice-encrusted bannister and stepped up onto the next step. Onward they went, leaving the ice tunnel behind. Calliphon brushed snow off each stair as it went upward. The stairs turned to the right, and still they climbed.

The bulk of the citadel remained on Jean's left as she followed the others, until suddenly they came to the end of the stairs. The four of them stood on a platform above the ice plain. Jean swiveled her head toward the two green beacons that pierced the murky light, just a short distance between the party and the entrance they had targeted. Jean involuntarily shuddered.

"Well?" she asked.

"Welcome to the citadel," Calliphon announced. The robot gathered itself and strode boldly forward.

The humans paused for a moment before following.

Hold on, Rafe. Jean prayed. *Hold on. It'll be over soon—one way,* she thought, *or the other.*

The alien robot reached out, and as if by magic, the great doors of the citadel shuddered and groaned and then slipped open. Beyond was darkness. Beyond, the Decarabia lurked, their hunger palatable in the frosted air.

Danner Tomblin tensed. He stepped behind the technician as Akemi's form dropped into the shadow behind the massive doors of the citadel. The light flicked against the silver surface of the alien robot's metallic form as it disappeared into the heart of the structure. Danner had left the framing bomb on the shuttle. Instead, within the right outer thigh pocket of his EVA, he carried a small, cylindrical trap. It was roughly four inches long and resembled a piece of steel piping with a threaded cap on its end. However, it was made of a high-grade blend of titanium and graphene that made the tube extremely strong while having the extra property of being nonporous at the molecular level. It was the perfect transportation device. And inside it, like a piece of cheese in a mousetrap, Danner had placed a small battery connected to three small circuits. As an additional source of potential food, Danner had mixed silicon and various metals and minerals in powdered form and slipped it into the bottom of the container. He could not be sure, he knew, but he hoped the Decarabia could survive within the containment tube for the trip back to human-occupied space.

The headlamp from his EVA shone on the darkened floor of the alien structure, creating a pool of light. Major Joyce's and Akemi Murakami's headlamps threw their own pools of light. The three lights mixed with the meager amount of light filtering through the access doors into the citadel, the overall effect making the large room they had entered seem alive with shadows. The elongated shapes flickered and twisted. Through his external pickups, Danner could hear the scuffling of the team's feet as they moved across the floor. Snow drifted in the open door as well. Danner tried to see past the moving light and shadow and get a sense of the place, but the engulfing darkness of the citadel refused to reveal what lay hidden beyond.

"It's just a room." Akemi's feline voice sounded disappointed.

Danner knew how she felt. What had he expected? He was not sure. Something. But the stillness was complete, and whatever unnamed fears and expectations he had held were wiped away with the simple reality. The citadel appeared empty, clear of debris, a shell of concrete of alien design. He could see no monsters here.

"Which way?" All business, the marine major's voice seemed anxious for the party to move.

"Come," the robot commanded. The creature turned its back and lumbered forward into the heart of the darkened space. Calliphon turned and looked over its shoulder at the humans; the robot's eyes glittering red with reflected light.

Despite Danner's intentions, he shivered at the sight. The luminous eyes seemed like things ripped out of humanity's worst nightmare. It was a foolish reaction, Danner thought. There was nothing to fear. Fate and chaos had brought him here. It was just the dark, the shadows, the gray, and the gloaming that were getting to him.

Major Joyce turned and looked at the open doors behind them. "Do we leave them open?"

The robot answered without turning around or slowing its gait.

"The Decarabia do not like the cold. Perhaps as the temperature drops they will find it more difficult to function."

"I'm all for that," they heard Akemi murmur.

"Are they here?" Major Joyce asked. "The Decarabia—are they around us now?"

This gave the robot pause. It stopped and swiveled its head, casting about along the floors and walls. Before it could answer, Danner noticed a flare of light suddenly flash across Akemi's XM Flash biohazard suit. The light started above her left calf. It moved downward toward her feet like an enfeebled amoeba.

"Did you see that?" Danner exclaimed. "There again." He pointed. Another pulse of light danced off Akemi's other leg. Danner turned and saw similar displays dancing across the major's suit, and then a sullen glare pulsed and faded from his own lower legs. It reminded Danner of an aurora borealis.

"The suits are purging!" Major Joyce declared.

Akemi darted back toward the doorway and then stopped suddenly. She spun in a small circle, light dancing off and on against her EVA as it flash burned what everyone assumed to be Decarabia off of the suit. She took another step toward the open door and stopped. Instead of running, Akemi pranced in place nervously. The others could hear the echo of her movement through the shadow-filled room.

"It seems to be holding." The Asian woman's voice was breathy with near panic. "It's holding." She repeated. "It's holding."

Major Joyce walked up to the other woman and tapped against Akemi's faceplate. "We're good. Akemi,"—she grabbed the other woman's shoulders and made Akemi look her in the eyes—"let's get this over with as quickly as we can. Okay? Come on."

What Calliphon thought of the episode, Danner could not tell. The creature watched Akemi's near flight with complete dispassion. Just the same, Danner saw the robot's left hand suddenly flick and vibrate. It lasted for just a moment. He was not even sure he had seen it. Danner saw Calliphon stare at its left hand for a moment with—what? Curiosity? Who knew what the robot was thinking? Did it matter? Danner wondered. He decided to keep what he thought he had seen to himself for now. Maybe he could use it to his advantage at some point.

"Major?" Captain Mike Estury questioned through the wireless. Danner had forgotten that the captain could see through their imbedded EVA cameras.

"We're fine, Mike," Major Joyce answered. "Just a little spooked. We're through the doors into the superstructure. We can't see much, and we think we've been attacked by the Decarabia. The XM Flash bio suits seem to be holding. We're going to move on. Really, we're fine," she added. "Danner? Calliphon? Let's go. Akemi will go just in front of me. You two lead."

Calliphon turned and once more began fading into the oppressive dark of the citadel. Danner fell in behind the robot, his headlamps dancing before him and reflecting off the robot's metallic back.

"Akemi?"

Akemi nodded and, for a moment, locked eyes with Major Joyce. "This sucks," she mumbled. Then Akemi smiled shyly and gathered herself. "I'm fine, Major."

"Are you sure?"

"Hai."

"Okay then," Jean said. She twisted to her left to let the Asian woman walk past her.

Jean fell behind the group. She was surprised to see the flickering of cleaning fire along the bio suits slow and then stop all together. What did that mean? she wondered. Was that just the first attack? And if so, what had the Decarabia learned? What would the nanomachines attempt next? Had they guessed the party's purpose? Or had they known all along? If the self-aware micromachines were on the moon base, could it be they could communicate with those still ensconced within the citadel? How advanced were the Decarabia? But then, Jean thought, their biohazard suits had not activated on the moon base. They had been in those labyrinthine halls for several hours without so much as a minor response from the biohazard suits. Was that because the Decarabia were not so prolific on Gargantuan? Or had they been waiting to spring their trap? Had they waited for Rafe to hook into the system so they would have a hold on the party? Jean had too many questions—too many.

"Major," Danner said, "we're at another set of stairs. We're heading up."

"All right, Danner. We're behind you. Let's keep going."

Danner followed the robot up, step after metallic step. If the citadel had any lighting of its own, it did not come to life. The group continued into a tunnel of darkness. But the darkness pleased Danner. It seemed to herald times to come, and with each step his heart lifted in expectation of ecstasy. All around him, Danner knew, was the ultimate force in universal chaos. He would flush the Decarabia from their prison through righteous destruction and set them lose once again into a sickened universe. God had chosen him. He would be the harbinger of renewal. Through him, chaos would rein, and the universe would be reborn.

A soul without denial, he thought, *is a soul in rapture.*

Danner Tomblin's soul soared.

Uncontrolled fear paralyzed. Harnessed fear motivated. It gave strength and purpose. Yet the edge between the two, between constructive emotion and debilitating terror, was a fine thing. And between different people that edge shifted and moved. What fear gave to one person in energy tore through others and cast them down into a pit where hope decried the day. Yet a soldier's fear was different still. His or hers was a fear of failure—failure to meet the needs of the group, failure in the form of stumbling and floundering at that moment when death was near and a soldier's selfless act could save others, even if at the cost of the soldier's own life. It was unbearable. A soldier's fear of shame. It resonated and became a thing of its own. For the one thing all soldiers feared the most, all marines, was to let the unit down. That was one of the great mysteries for Jean in regards to her brother. How had he lived with that shame? He had abandoned his unit to its fate. The men and women who had trained besides him, bled with him, and died besides him—their ghosts surely haunted Rafe in the deep dead of night. Jean wondered if, even now, in the grips of the Decarabia, Rafe dreamed of his shame. Somewhere in the blackness of his personal battle for survival, did he crave forgiveness? Was that the reason he had so easily been swayed to join this mad expedition into darkness? Was Rafe encumbered by a guilty soul?

Calliphon led the three humans down a long hallway that, Jean surmised, ran almost the entire length of the citadel. They were on the third or fourth deck. It was difficult to know for sure. Jean had not seen any other exit from the stairs but surely they had climbed more than a single story.

They traveled the hall in muted silence. Jean leveled her weapon across her body and moving steadily forward. They passed several rooms. Each was bare and echoed with their footsteps. It made Jean wonder why the citadel had really been built. There would be no need for rooms and hallways if it had been originally constructed as a prison for the microscopic Decarabia. The doorways themselves were tall and broad and resembled the large door frames Jean had found on the moon base. This thought tugged on Jean until she just had to break the silence and ask Calliphon.

"It was not always a prison," Calliphon admitted. They continued to walk as the robot spoke. "At first, it was a research station. The planet's environment made it ripe for certain types of scientific inquiry. As the plague raged, the Makers in the citadel remained safe, untouched by the scourge."

"I do not understand," Akemi asked. "I thought you said the citadel was constructed as a prison."

"It was made into a prison," Calliphon responded. "When it became apparent that the end was near, the Makers sought to rid the universe of the plague, but they also desired to save the creatures that had marked the apex of their technological power. So they modified the research station and prepared the battle satellites. And then they lured the Decarabia to the planet."

"How?" Jean replied. "How did they lure them here?"

Calliphon paused as if to gather its thoughts. "They called the surviving Makers to this system. They knew that the Decarabia would follow. And they did. They were hidden away on the hundred ships that responded to the call.

"Less than ten thousand Makers came to Nibiru. Ten thousand! Once the skies were littered with the Makers in the billions. Can you imagine? The entire godlike race reduced to a handful of worn shapes scurrying across the universe to an uncertain end?

"Potent was the power of their intellect and will. Yet it was madness," the robot whispered. "It was a beautiful madness that seized upon them. They came. The young and the old—children, mothers, fathers—slipped imperturbably toward Nibiru so that they might chose the manner of their doom."

"You said they decided to save the Decarabia," Jean said into the sudden silence. "But at what price? You can't … Are you saying what I think you are saying?"

Here the robot stopped and turned its attention to the little group of humans that trailed it through the darkened remnants of the Makers' last bastion. "Yes." Mournful. Lost. "They drew the Decarabia here with the scent of their own blood—the blood of their families, of their children. All predators hunt their prey," Calliphon added. "The Makers knew this well and turned the nature of the hunt to their own ends."

"So when the Makers fled here," Akemi filled in the gap, "they knew they were coming to their deaths? That is awful."

"Though they still walked the road," the robot replied softly, "they were already dead. At least here they could save something of their civilization. Not all choices offer hope, human. Some only offer a different means to the same despair."

"When they came, the Decarabia came with them. I understand.

But what about the swarms of Decarabia on other worlds? What happened to them?" Jean pressed. For some reason, she had to understand. Was it for Rafe? Were her questions driven by the need to understand the reason for his current situation? Was she preparing herself for his death? She shuddered. But she had to know.

"They ravaged," Calliphon replied. "The Decarabia destroyed; yet they did not know how to conserve. They swarmed until each planet they inhabited was stripped bare and the only sustenance that remained were their fellow creatures."

"They ate everything and then, when there was nothing left, they became cannibals?" Akemi was dumfounded.

"And their fires burned out and time reset. There are no memories of what was before, and evolution, unhindered, followed the first law. Life began anew. Yet here, in this pocket, the last of the Makers died to save a semblance of their civilization."

"How do they—the Decarabia—live then?" Akemi's voice was muted. "Why haven't they burned out here on Nibiru?"

"Because," the Warder said, "the Makers created a world for them in the citadel where sustenance could be eked out for eons. The hydrogen generator, stores of minerals from deep within the planet's core—the citadel is a habitat that self-regulates. The environment is enough to allow the Decarabia to survive but not thrive. They are limited here."

"Why don't we just cut off their food and energy source? Why use the satellites at all?" Danner asked.

"That would take time." The robot fixed the BII man with a cold stare. "Years. I am the last of my kind. The Decarabia have shown they can escape even this prison. If I stop them now but allow them to survive, who will stop them the next time they venture forth? Who will protect the universe from another agony? No. The Makers were wise. But in this, they erred. It is time to end this threat once and for all."

"Let's get on with it then," Jean interjected. They had stopped moving and time was wasting.

"Did you know that the universe is a hyperelastic orb?" The robot's sudden question caught the humans by surprise. "The Makers proved it. Since the Ignition, when all time began, the universe has expanded in an outward rush. Within the first blinding seconds all matter coalesced and the laws of motion were birthed. But the force of that initial explosion stretched the fabric of space; the metasphere was born. And it continues to grow, ever propelled by the first spark. Yet as happens with all explosions, the effect decreased exponentially, and the expansion slowed. Now it holds just a fragment of its initial power. At some point, several billions of years in the future, that power will be spent and the inevitable forces of gravity, subatomic chains, and the elasticity of the metasphere will reach its elastic limit."

"And then?" Jean asked.

"Then the process will reverse and the universe will move ever more quickly into its original form. A singularity. The metasphere will collapse and, with it, all of what is shall fall into an abyss, only to be thrown outward once again when the singularity, overloaded, explodes once again."

"What if the elasticity of this metasphere is finite?" Akemi said.

Can a robot smile? "That, Ms. Murakami, is a discussion that lingered. Could its strength be finite? Could the universe, at the end of its elastic strength, simply tear and throw the contents of the universe into … what? Another reality? An un-space? You are quite astute, aren't you?"

"Excuse me for asking," Jean interrupted, "but what made you think of that?"

"Faith and destruction. Desolation and faith. The Makers knew that everything ends and everything begins again. It is the ultimate pattern. And that thought is comforting to me."

"All complex systems die," Danner proffered, "but out of that death, new structures arise, and life and time progress."

Jean and Akemi looked at the BII agent with shock.

"More philosophy, I'm afraid," Danner answered.

The robot looked at Danner for a moment, its three-prong eyes seeking something. Danner returned its studied gaze evenly.

"I don't mean to point out the obvious," Jean said, "but can we save these discussion for a more appropriate moment?"

Calliphon dipped its head toward Major Joyce and the others. "If your race survives, you may be worthy successors. Yet you have much to learn. Come then, time is drawing to an end, and we have a task to accomplish if we are to save the other human."

Calliphon turned once again and led them onward.

A sinister silence surrounded them as they moved. The robot's final comment was unsettling and turned Jean's thoughts to her brother. The more she heard from Calliphon, the more she learned about the Makers and their deadly progeny, the more her doubts haunted her. She was not sure anymore. She wasn't sure they could save Rafe. The Makers all died—all of them. What chance did Rafe really have?

A wave of illness swept through Jean, and for a moment, she forgot to take a step. She froze. When does fear become terror? Helplessness washed over Jean. She felt a bead of sweat burn into her eye, and her mouth felt dry. Had she abandoned her brother to die alone?

Something near her hummed and sparked, and a wisp of smoke floated before her faceplate. Startled, she looked down at her rifle. Something was wrong. It wasn't supposed to do that. Then Jean noticed a small spark of light burning off her gloved hands, and realization struck her.

The weapons. The weapons are not protected!

"Everyone!" she yelled. "Everyone, drop your weapons! Drop them! They're infected! Drop them!"

Someone screamed. Something thudded to the ground as Jean threw her rifle behind her. It clattered on the ground, and Jean dove through an open doorway as three explosions shook the hall.

The message that scrawled like an itch across the screen left Captain Mike Estury wondering if he had just fallen out of reality into an alternate universe. He stared at it again. Reaching up, he scratched at his eyes with closed fists. For a moment his vision blurred. God, he felt tired. His hair was a tousled mess, and his mouth felt like he had been chewing on a sponge. He hadn't realized he had been clenching his teeth, and his jaw ached. He massaged the side of his face and tried to force his jaw muscles to relax. But it didn't help. The headache had been building as he watched Jean, the robot Calliphon, the always odd and irritating Danner Tomblin, and catlike Akemi Murakami make their way through the deep snow drifts and enter the alien structure. However, he was warm and snug in the *Fallen Star*, orbiting just outside the Makers' defensive satellite ring. He felt safe—safe from the elements on Nibiru, safe from the Decarabia that haunted the citadel and roamed through the moon base on Gargantuan and safe from the hidden weapons poised above the planet like Damocles's sword. But Jean—Jean was in the thick of it. Could he afford to distract her? If he shared the message that rode like the pall of death across his screen, a repetitious cry of misery and despair, would Jean be able to focus? He couldn't imagine the amount of pressure the marine major was under. But how could he not tell her?

It was a message from Rafe.

"I am fighting, fighting, but I can't hold out much longer. They are learning. Learning. Run, little sister! I'm on fire. Run!"

Somehow, Rafe Joyce had figured out how to send a message using the moon base's communication system. The signal had been weak, a burst transmission that had at first seemed to Mike like interstellar background noise. But the computer had suddenly recognized the introductory subspace protocol string and plucked it out of the abyss.

Would the message from Rafe give Jean hope? Mike wondered. Would she feel relieved that her brother was still conscious and that the Decarabia had not yet managed to completely overcome whatever defenses the hacker was putting up? Or would the tone of the message—desperate and on the edge of failure—cause the major to rush into the unknown, make a critical mistake?

Mike's gut feeling told him not to let Jean know. But he wondered if she would be angry with him later. Would she forgive him?

He stared at the message. Something about it nagged at him beyond the dilemma of whether or not to share it with Jean. It took him a few minutes before it leaped out at him.

"They are learning," he murmured. The Decarabia were learning?

Captain Estury mentally flicked through a command sequence, searching the digital record of the mission to date. He focused the search on the initial sequence, where the alien robot Calliphon was describing the history of the Decarabia and the Makers. He found the recording and skimmed quickly through it and then froze it, rewound, and played it again.

"A disease, they swept out of the laboratories through a million million machines," the robot was saying. "As postulated," it continued, "by the first law, they evolved. In this, the Makers were much pleased. Yet, as postulated by the second law, they consumed."

Mike played the sequence again and again, his eyes glancing back and forth from the image of the robot to the message from Jean's brother.

Diseases evolve, don't they? Mike thought. They had all assumed that the Decarabia were voracious yet mindless creatures. That is what they *were*, Mike mulled. But what had they *become*? Rafe claimed they were learning—learning what? Had evolution made them self-aware? It must have. Mike reviewed the evidence.

Why had the mission been sent here? When their party had met the robot and heard the story of the Makers' decline, they had all assumed the Makers had sent the emergency message. What if they didn't? What if the Decarabia had sent that message? Hadn't Calliphon said as much? Mike skipped forward a bit in the recording.

"Wait. Are you saying that those—those nanomachines that jumped between the Makers' computer system and Rafe are self-aware?"

"Self-aware, evolving, and …"

Mike froze the recording. How could he have missed it before? Calliphon had told them that the Decarabia were self-aware. They were intelligent. How had the robot put it? The Decarabia had called out to the universe, and you answered? Isn't that what the robot had told them? It was all a trap. The whole mission had been a long-set trap, a digital spiderweb waiting for the fly. Had the Decarabia known about Calliphon? Had they known that the robot was still hiding in isolation waiting for an opportunity to carry out the Makers' last command? Surely they did.

The Decarabia must have known or strongly suspected, Mike concluded, that Calliphon would attempt to come to the humans' rescue. Would they have guessed at the robot's solution? Did they know Calliphon would try to activate the Makers' destructive sequence? How long had they been in imprisoned in the citadel? Long enough for the Maker's great civilization to crumble to dust and the universe to reset itself, Mike thought. The Decarabia must have known that the robot would try to cut off their jamming signal and reestablish control over the satellite ring. Wouldn't they plan for such an eventuality? Wouldn't they?

Captain Estury felt a surge of unease sweep through him. The moon base was a trap, and they had walked right into it. Why would the planet be any different? They had been blinded by Rafe's situation, he reasoned. Their perceptions and emotions had been manipulated. The Decarabia had coerced the humans to rapid action by taking one captive and giving everyone the impression that time was of the essence. Had anyone of Captain Estury's crew stopped to consider the evidence? Or had they been all too human, devised their linear attack plan, and rushed into the fray without realizing exactly what game they were playing?

Mike thought he saw it clearly. The humans had been outmaneuvered.

He looked at the textual message that still scrawled across his screen. He felt cold, as if a dark hand had brushed his soul. He was nauseated, and his thoughts spun awhirl. But it lasted for only a moment. Quickly and with a growing sense of purpose, something else pushed the feeling of helplessness aside. It was anger, sure and strong. It rose within the captain, and it became inexhaustible determination.

The message came from Rafe. He was still alive.

The thought coalesced out of the ruthless universe. The Decarabia wanted them to save Rafe. It was all a feint—the trip to the planet, everything.

The message had been allowed. It was a ploy, Mike knew, to keep the humans moving, to keep them from thinking—well, Mike was done walking into walls. He reached through his wireless connection to the *Fallen Star's* weapons and navigations systems.

Captain Estury didn't hear the sudden scream over the communications network. He didn't see the explosive flash. The nose of the *Fallen Star* swung out of orbit, and like an arrow, the spaceship accelerated toward the rocky, dark surface of Gargantuan and its hidden moon base. The solar winds at its back, the ship sped hawk-like to where Jean's brother lay in the grasp of their unseen enemy.

And Mike was going to do something about it.

Danner Tomblin ran. He ducked down a side corridor through the musky half-light that permeated the inner passageways of the citadel. He could hear the pounding of his heart, the stillness of the biohazard suit amplifying the rhythmic beat. He did not slow down or look behind him to see if the others had followed. Chance had given him his opening, and he was not about to cast it aside.

A muffled explosion thudded behind him. Danner ignored it. Randomly selecting another turn, he moved farther away from his companions. His eyes searched the area, the sleek, almost polished walls of the citadel dull and otherworldly. He put a hand out and, slowing to a jog and then a rapid stride, felt the flesh of the wall through the membrane of his thick, protective gloves. He needed a private place. He needed …

There.

His eyes glimpsed a dark hollow in the wall. Danner had come to recognize these spaces as open doorways. This one was almost two-thirds of the way down the corridor on the left. He moved quickly, excitement driving him. Before slipping in through the doorway, Danner looked furtively behind him. The corridor was empty, quiet. It looked as static and austere as every other part of the citadel. Then he stepped forward and faded into the shadow beyond.

Like the many other rooms in the citadel, this one was bare of accoutrement. It was rectangular and was maybe twenty-five feet across and a little more than twice that length. He moved to the center of the room. The God of Chaos had placed him in the most perfect of situations. Danner would fool his fellow crewmates into taking him and the Decarabia, the ultimate destructive force, into a waiting and unsuspecting universe.

After hearing Calliphon's story and seeing firsthand the state that Rafe Joyce had fallen into, Danner had quickly revised his plan. Detonating the framing bomb would have killed the crew and helped propel the Federation into a contest with the corporate worlds. The contest would have sewn chaos and forced adaptation. Yet that result paled in comparison with what the Decarabia would do if set loose once again. No, he thought. The framing bomb had been a good idea, but it was the wrong one too.

Danner smiled, and his smile was a hollow in the deepest woods.

I will set the Decarabia free, he mused. The Makers' final technological wonder would scour the cosmos clean of all artifice and return it to its purest form. The universe would again thrum to the natural order, and all that had once bound the cosmos to the chains of civilization would be stripped bare in one malevolent burst. In the quiet aftermath, the Decarabia would die out, and the universe would renew. Life would rise once again from the chaos of infinite space, and the cycle would churn. He could not help feel elation knowing that he—a tiny soul—was God's instrument to chaotic rebirth.

Yet he had to hurry. His crewmates would be searching for him. Danner did not have time to linger.

As if on cue, Major Joyce's voice stabbed out of the speakers of Danner's XM Flash biohazard suit. "Danner? Danner Tomblin? Do you read me? Danner?"

The BII operative turned the volume down so that he could just hear the major's voice, a staccato hiss that he easily pushed away from his conscious mind. Danner pulled the Velcro top of his right hip pocket open and pulled out the dull black, cylindrical tube that was tightly capped. He rotated the cylinder in his hands and took a good grip of it. Danner used his right hand and tried to open the lid, but to his surprise, the lid did not move. He tried harder and cursed. Holding the cylinder up to his face, he studied it for a moment before realizing that the cap had been put on slightly skewed. It was angled in such a way that Danner knew it was jammed.

"No you don't," he mumbled at it.

He knelt and trapped the cylinder between his knees, trying to get better leverage. He put his weight into opening it and grunted when his gloved hand slipped along the smooth ridge of the cap. He tried again, but again his hand slipped. He cursed and looked around for something to put between his glove and the cap that might increase his grip and allow him to open the cylinder. There was nothing at hand.

"This is just stupid," he hissed as he grunted with exertion. But again, his hand slipped. The cap remained firmly in place.

A dim beam of light danced past the doorway. Danner froze. He wondered if he had imagined it, but then the light flicked down the corridor once again. They were coming. He was out of time.

Danner stood and moved to peek out into the corridor, but he stopped. He would have to reveal himself to anyone in the corridor if he moved any farther. He stepped back into the shadow of the room.

He looked at the cylinder, frustration knifing through him. In an act of desperation, Danner suddenly rotated the O-ring on his right wrist. He turned it frantically as the lights in the outer corridor flashed more and more often and grew in strength. With a loud hiss, his right glove suddenly came free, exposing his hand. The air was frigid.

Hurry. Hurry, he thought. *Don't touch anything else.*

Danner took a strong grip on the sealed cylinder and put all his might into one final turn. He nearly cried out in triumph when the cap moved, rotating on its threads. He turned it again and again until finally the cap came off.

Danner quickly put the opened cylinder on the ground. The little bit of powered circuitry that Danner had placed inside was the bait. While it sat there beckoning the Decarabia to enter, Danner quickly slipped his glove back on his hand. It was a little matter to replace the O-ring and seal it into place. He sighed with relief as the warmth of his suit surrounded his chilled hand. Then he bent down and recovered the cylinder, carefully securing the cap into place. Satisfied the act was done, he slipped the cylinder back into his thigh pocket, increased the volume on his internal speakers, reengaged his communication system, and stepped back into the corridor, banging his hand on the side of his helmet to give the impression he was having communications problems.

A few short meters down the corridor, Major Joyce came to a sudden halt. Behind the major, the robot and Akemi Murakami stumbled and stopped.

"There you are!" The major's voice was raw and angry but also relieved. "What the hell happened to you?"

Danner held both hands up in a show of helplessness. "Thank God! When you said run, I ran. Something exploded, and I was thrown to the ground. I wasn't hurt, but I became disoriented and my tracking system went on the fritz. I couldn't pick any of you up. Are you hearing me now?" he asked.

"What? Yes, we hear you just fine," Major Joyce replied.

"Coms were acting up too. I could hear you now and again but couldn't get a fix on you. I thought I knew how to get back, but I soon found myself wandering. It's good to see friendly faces," he added. "Are you both all right? Major? Akemi?"

"We're fine," Akemi replied. "It shook me up a bit, but that was all. Why didn't you just stop and wait for us to find you?"

"I did," Danner protested. "Right here." He pointed at the ground by the doorway. "But I got a bit curious and thought I would explore this room. I had just stepped in when I saw the lights from your heads-up flicker through the hall. So I came back out."

"Were you hurt?" Major Joyce asked him as he joined the group.

"No. What happened back there?"

Major Joyce sighed, frowned, and looked back at the robot that towered above them all. "The Decarabia attacked our weapons. It is why I ordered everyone to drop them."

"So it *was* an attack against us?" Danner directed at the robot.

"Perhaps," the alien robot responded. "It is more likely the Decarabia responded to the energy and material in the weapons. The weapons were likely a tempting meal."

"It was an attack." Major Joyce was adamant.

"They will be going after anything we are carrying then," Akemi explained. "That means we really have to hurry. Calliphon said the Decarabia are sluggish from the cold, but that does not mean they are not capable of mounting other assaults."

"Someone else will have to go first," Danner replied. "My guidance system is still quirky and unreliable."

"Wait." Major Joyce put out a hand and stopped the BII agent. "That's not all. We've lost contact with Mike—with the ship."

"The *Fallen Star*? Do you know why?"

"No clue. Hopefully Mike adjusted his orbit, and we'll get in touch with him again after the *Fallen Star* circumnavigates the planet. Whatever the case, there is nothing we can do about it right now. But when we get back outside, we might find our return journey cut short. If either of you pick up a signal from our ship, I want you to let me know, okay?"

"Okay," Danner and Akemi replied.

"Calliphon? Can you get us to the Helium-3 reactor from here?"

"Yes," the robot said.

"Then let's go," the major ordered. "And, Danner …"

"Yes?"

"Don't get lost again."

Calliphon, the robot Warder, led the party in a new direction, one that intersected their original path a little deeper within the citadel. If it had been up to Calliphon, the robot would have avoided this route, simply because of the amount of side turns and twists. Calliphon had hoped to give the humans a direct route back the way they had come. The Warder was not confident that it would survive long enough to help the biologics through the citadel back to their ship.

Already, Calliphon was at war. The Decarabia had descended upon Calliphon the moment the robot had freed itself from its isolation on board the moon base. That attack had paused while the party slugged through the snowfields. The Decarabia had become disoriented and listless in the bitter cold. The march through Nibiru's perpetual winter had, therefore, provided a repast from the battle. But it was not the end.

Though the interior of the citadel was cold, the citadel was not intended to kill the creatures but to imprison them. The Makers had designed it to hover just above the temperature threshold that so affected the Decarabia. They were lethargic but capable. It had not taken long after entering the citadel before Calliphon began feeling the negative effects of the renewed Decarabian attack. At times, the robot had difficulty focusing, and Calliphon had developed what appeared to be a nervous twitch in its left arm. Up until now, the robot had been able to hide this from the humans, but how long before the twitch became a total loss of control? The nano-size machines were striking at Calliphon's systems. The robot's strained autoimmune system was waging a campaign that Calliphon knew it couldn't win. All it could do was provide the Warder with a little more time. The Warder calculated it had only a few hours remaining. The robot hoped it was long enough to get the job done.

The three humanoid creatures followed Calliphon through the brightly lit halls of the citadel toward the reactor. Calliphon concluded that the humans and he shared a spectrum of visible light, but the robot noticed that the humans never turned their headlamps off and that, now and again, they would swing their light toward particular areas of the citadel as if they found the lighting dark and oppressive. Calliphon's database was full of examples of extraterrestrial life displaying differences in their optical nerves. However, it was not the only piece of their behavior that warranted closer attention. He studied them carefully.

The humans fascinated the robot. Calliphon had been commissioned, designed, and built in-system. A purpose-built robot, the Warder had never traveled anywhere except from Gargantuan's moon base to Nibiru and back. Calliphon, like the other Warders, had spent lots of time in zero-gee. Even the most advanced machines of the Makers had required occasional maintenance, and the satellite ring around Nibiru was no exception. Yet it made for a very limited life experience. And, the robot considered morosely, when the Decarabia had attacked the moon base, all of its siblings had died. Calliphon had survived the onslaught on Gargantuan because it had been out strolling on the surface looking at the sky and exploring the terrain. It was curiosity, Calliphon knew, that had saved it.

Yet Calliphon had been left alone. Loneliness is the cruelest of fates for an intellectual mind. Isolation and loneliness are all encompassing. Yet in Calliphon's mind, there had always been a final option to end its suffering. The solution was so simple. All the Warder had to do was leave the isolation bay and enter the moon base. Then it too would be invaded, compromised, and murdered by the micron-size creatures. And then there would be nothing. *Nothing is a type of peace*, Calliphon thought. It had often wondered what bit of programing the Makers had imbedded in its soul that had prevented it from ending it all long ago.

The robot walked forward, the humans trailing behind. Having companionship was a gift Calliphon had never expected to experience again. The Makers had been cruel to leave the Warder alone, yet now, at the end, their spirits had granted this small boon.

The Warder trailed a hand against the surface of the citadel's wall. Calliphon liked the way it felt. It was smooth. The citadel had been built at the height of the Makers' technology, and every time the robot saw it, the Warder felt a tug of emotion. Pride. Regret. Sadness. Loss. And a deep sense of wonder. Calliphon often thought about the Makers. The robot had met only the remaining few, but they had been mothers and fathers to Calliphon. Soft, warm, tender beings, they were the givers of life. The robot could feel the Makers here, ghosts walking the echoing halls of the citadel. It was like a mist of an embrace remembered. What would Calliphon give to have one more chance to look within their eyes, feel their skin, hear their voices, and listen in rapt ecstasy to their stories and wisdom? How Calliphon missed them. How the Warder missed its siblings. How the eons of lonely time ate at Calliphon's heart. Yet even so, the Warder felt the pull of fear as its arm twitched and the robot's foot, like a leaden ball, drug sluggishly. For all that Calliphon had wished for death and an end to the lonely suffering, now at its knell, the robot desperately wanted a little more time. Time. Time to get to know these humans. Time to travel the stars and see the myriad of worlds where the Warder's mothers and fathers had roamed. Time to marvel and wonder and dream.

Yet there was no time.

"This way," Calliphon told the humans. The Warder led them up a small stairwell, robotic feet clinking at they struck the ground. "It won't be long now."

Had it been selfish? Calliphon wondered. The Warder could have done this without the humans. It was risking their lives, and for what? Calliphon looked at them in their copper-colored exoskeletons. They were organically frail beings. Calliphon had lied to them. They could not save their companion. Calliphon knew the Decarabia would never release that unit. The Decarabia were too hungry. What a strong feat of willpower the creatures must be exerting to sustain the human so that they could extort action from the others! It was a wonder, Calliphon knew. The Decarabia were a voracious race. Their children were always hungry. Rafe, as that human was called, was already a corpse.

Was it right to suspend their grief by removing uncertainty and fear? Had Calliphon done the right thing? Did it matter?

"Come along, through this door." The robot pointed up, where a riveted bulkhead was in shadow. In that wall was a specially designed door that sealed the tunnel beyond away from the Decarabia. Once opened, the creatures would flood through, and the Helium-3 reactor would be compromised. The creatures would use it, would craft it to their own bidding—if allowed. Calliphon would not give them the opportunity. "We will enter the interior access tunnel. It has not been used for an age. It goes directly into the heart of the reactor's control room. I need you … I will need your help in disconnecting its power from the citadel. From that point, I shall signal the satellites."

"And then what?" the human named Major Joyce asked.

"Then, we must run back to the ship before the surface of this world is purged."

"And my brother?"

Calliphon stopped and looked at Major Joyce, the human named Akemi Murakami, and the little man called Danner Tomblin. *Such variety*, the Warder thought. "We can hope."

Calliphon turned and guided the humans up to where the door waited. The air was expectantly oppressive.

In the end, Calliphon knew why it had offered the humans hope where hope could not prevail. The Warder knew why it had brought them on this final journey. The Warder had not wanted to die alone.

The *Fallen Star* tilted along its axis and slipped into orbit around Gargantuan. The moon was bleak, gray rock, pockmarked by the scars of ancient meteorite impacts, and barely touched by the subdued light from Kururumany's distant blue-white star. Though smaller and brighter than earth's own sun, Kururumany was nearly on the far side of the planet Nibiru. Only a sliver of its warmth reached the moon, casting long shadows over the rocky ground. Night was settling.

Captain Mike Estury was in full focus, uplinked to the ship's navigation sensors as they turned their strength toward the surface of the moon. He knew the location of the Makers' moon base, but he was not completely confident that it did not hold its own defensive system. Sure, the *Fallen Star* had not been attacked when they first arrived, he thought. But that had been at the beginning, back when they were answering a call for help. The Decarabia had let them get safely to the moon's surface and had guided the ground team to the Core. It had been a trap. The captain was not sure if the little nanos had intentionally baited the trap in such a way that Jean's brother, Rafe Joyce, would physically link to the Core's systems. But maybe they had.

A long time ago during one of the captain's military courses, a balding academic had postulated that a person's view of the world could be tempered through the careful manipulation of information. What had the gaunt man said? How had he put it? Everyone sees the universe through sensory windows. Each window is unique in certain ways because everyone's life experiences were slightly different. But these windows were not created in isolation. They were overlapped with others in a center zone, where culture and common experiences leaped the gap between isolation and created a collective reality. When the feedback loop changed, the group's view changed. It did so naturally as the members of the group reacted to the universe around them.

However, the same result could be attained through artifice. In all human cultures, there existed a communal reference or viewpoint, the man had argued, from which groups of people defined reality. That definition was influenced by a shared feedback loop that we know as culture—news reports and the arts. It was not only possible, the pallid man postulated, but proven historic fact that manipulation of the information flow, of the feedback loop, within the sphere of the collective experience window, modified the group's reality and that, in turn, changed the group members' behaviors.

More specifically, he'd said, all professional instructors were important conduits through which a culture maintained and propagated its own view of reality. The end goal of instruction, he claimed, was to maintain stability. Stability, he said, was another word for the retention of the ruling class and suppression of rivals for power. It was for this reason the ruling elite in all nations in human history strove so energetically to control information, to paint the universe in such a light as to lend justification for the elite's rule. How many teachers and professors had been murdered in the name of progress?

At the time, Mike had wondered why in the seven hells they were wasting their time learning behavioral social theory and stroking the obviously bitter man's sense of self-importance, but now that long-ago class made him wonder. The Decarabia had sent the message that had brought the team to the Kururumany System. They had shaped the message, the words, the images, all in an effort to draw in an alien race. Why? On reflection, Captain Estury thought he understood.

Once the humans answered the distress call, the Decarabia would infiltrate their electronic systems and use them to ride back into the wider universe, where they would spread with alacrity. That meant the Decarabia had to provide safe passage. So, Mike reasoned, if the moon base had been equipped with weapons, the Decarabia would not have used them. They wanted the *Fallen Star* to arrive safely. They needed it. And it was that need with which Captain Estury now gambled his survival, and the survival of the ground team on Nibiru.

Still, that conclusion did not prevent him from straining the sensors to their upmost. He opened his mind to the experience and floated in the wash of feeling that flooded his mind and his body. Uplinking to a ship, particularly one with the latest in technology, was an exhilarating experience. He understood the addictive pull of having one's own mind intertwined with the ship. Many pilots had lost themselves within that cosmic perfume of sensory debauchery.

Luckily, be it because of an inborn stubbornness or some other personal characteristic, Mike was able to resist the temptation. He enjoyed the feeling, but he would not let it rule his life. He was the master of the ship. And now he bent his will toward it. His thoughts and desire were his shield and the ship his eyes.

Captain Estury figured he had one shot at this—and only one. When the Decarabia realized that the *Fallen Star* was attacking the station, they would respond. He was convinced, though he could not detect any hidden silos, that the base had a defensive system. All Mike had to do was look at the menacing satellites around Nibiru to know that the Makers would not have left the moon base defenseless. He was also quite aware that the *Fallen Star* could not detect the robot Calliphon. It stood to reason that there were, therefore, parts of the moon base that were likewise hidden from the ship's view. What would it hide? The defensive systems. So Mike sent the commands to arm the torpedoes and turned the nose of the *Fallen Star* toward the surface of the moon. After his salvo, Mike would shift all shielding to the front of the ship and hope that it would withstand whatever responding fire came his way.

But they wouldn't fire, he told himself. No. They needed the *Fallen Star*. It was their ticket off-system. Even if the Decarabia on the moon died, which he was not convinced would happen even if he vaporized the top floors of the moon base, the nanobots still had a chance to save the main colony—the citadel. That would have to be part of their calculus. They would hope that their brethren on Nibiru would infect the shuttle and use that to breach the vacuum of space and infect the *Fallen Star*. From there, it would be a silent ride back to human space; a little patience, and they could once again ravage throughout the universe. They would not fire back. They wouldn't.

"Get on with it," Captain Estury mumbled to himself. "It's not going to get any easier."

The captain could easily pick out the alien moon base now. It was in the middle of a valley, half-hidden, dark and forlorn. He maneuvered the *Fallen Star* and brought it as close to the moon as he deemed reasonably safe and ran through the ship's systems a final time before launching his attack. He targeted the center of the moon base where the Core resided a few stories below the surface. The captain's calculations showed that he could destroy the Core through timed firings of pulse lasers, followed closely by a string of torpedoes. What he wouldn't give right now for a frame bomb, he thought. But it was no good wishing for something he didn't have. That was just a waste of energy. He had to deal with these circumstances using the tools he had on hand and just pray his plan worked.

If it did—he shuddered—he would kill the major's brother.

The major stood behind Calliphon as the alien robot and the BII operative, Danner Tomblin, considered the closed door that led to the command center for the Helium-3 reactor. Calliphon had again explained the Warder's plan to increase the flow of aneutronic fuel to destabilize the power plant. It was all very technical. Jean was not sure what role she would play in the plan. If she didn't know better, it sounded to her as if she and the rest of the ground team were mostly superfluous. The marine took a deep breath. The degree to which they had taken the robot's statements of fact at face value was disconcerting. Calliphon had given them little reason to doubt its story, but then again, the Warder had given them little reason to believe it.

The impetus to make rapid decisions reminded her of a field exercise she had once had the misfortune of participating in. It had been with a bunch of officer candidates, of whom almost none had any infantry training. Oddly, the official observer teams had had little to no infantry training either. When the set battle piece began, the company of candidates had been spread out over a quarter of a mile in the heart of a thick wood. When the opposition force had opened fire on the column's lead elements, the observer teams had started shouting and pushing people pall-mall toward the objective. The momentum created by their haranguing had drawn the candidates forward in a steady flow. It was as if the officer candidates were all attached to an invisible puppeteer's string. Once the first group was pulled into the fray, the others flowed right along. They reached the objective in sequence, in small squad-sized groups of seven, and were mowed down by the five-person fire team defending the hill. The result was a predictable slaughter. They died on a ratio of 120 to 1.

The candidates and their instructors had not stopped, consolidated, and massed their forces. Basic stuff. Just as strangely, rushing to their simulated deaths drew praise from the observer teams, who felt the display had demonstrated motivation. Jean had thought it demonstrated lunacy. Luckily, it had only been a training exercise.

But that same inexorable pull, Jean feared, had been at work in the last several hours. They had all rushed blindly on, driven by her brother's need and Jean's fear. But what was the alternative? She supposed the smart move would have been to let her brother die. They could then have studied the situation closely and killed the Decarabia at leisure. Now she understood why doctors could not operate on members of their own families. It was too easy to lose one's clinical, professional detachment when the life of a loved one was at stake. Jean knew she could not have just watched her brother die. And that was the rub, she thought. Fear of loss. Love. Emotions were why people rushed in blindly without adequate plans.

"What do you think will happen when Calliphon opens the door, Major?" Akemi Murakami asked, her voice soft even through the metallic tang of the bio suit's comlink.

"What do you mean?"

"I don't know," she admitted. "This place gives me the creeps."

Jean couldn't agree more.

"There!" Danner exclaimed.

The door began to slowly iris open. Calliphon reached two massive hands into the opening and, bracing, pushed steadily against the door, helping the hidden mechanisms work. The robot stood still for a moment after the door was fully retracted, staring at it as if its unresponsiveness was a surprise.

"Shall we?" Jean asked. The three eyes of the robot rotated toward her. "It's open," Jean pointed out.

"Yes. The way is clear. Come."

The hallway beyond the door did not look like anything special. It was stark and clean. It was maybe fifty feet long and ended at another door. The second door cycled easily, and soon, the party was standing in the reactor's command center.

The room was fan-shaped. The front was a long arc that was dominated by a large, darkened screen. Three consecutive, compact rows of desks had been built into an elongated, shared workspace. These were placed stadium fashion on platforms on separate levels. It reminded Jean of a movie theater or, to be more precise, a launch command center. From their vantage point on the uppermost level, the group could easily see every station below them.

Calliphon walked the center of the upper platform and sat in the oversized chair before what Jean took to be the master station. Suddenly, the robot's left arm jerked and struck the desktop with some force. Calliphon stopped and stared for a moment at its arm with curiosity and a fleeting look of alarm. The robot noticed that the humans were staring at it, and it rotated its doglike head as if to say everything was fine. It moved its arm back and forth, testing, and then bent back to the task at hand.

Suddenly, Danner Tomblin screeched and jumped.

"Danner?" Jean's voice was cautious.

The man did it again. This time he slapped at his leg. He yelled and darted a short distance and then spun and frantically began tugging at his helmet.

"Danner! What's the matter? What are you doing?" Jean grew alarmed. She hurried past the robot and approached the BII operative with her hands turned outward in a nonthreatening manner. "Danner?"

The obtrusive man did not seem to hear her. "Get this off! Get it off!" He moved from hurried attempts to remove his helmet to frantic ones. "Damn it, help me!" Danner turned toward Jean.

Jean took a startled step backward. The BII operative's face was splotched with tiny streaks of red, and it looked swollen, as if he were experiencing some type of anaphylactic shock. His eyes were wild and pleading.

"Please! Help me!"

"Stop!" Calliphon's command rang, and the robot reached out and stopped Akemi Murakami, who had moved forward toward the stricken man. Jean froze in place too.

"Let go of me!" Akemi demanded. "I'm a medic. I can help. Get out of my way!"

"No. Wait." Calliphon stood and, in two strides, closed the gap between it and Danner.

The robot pulled Danner's hands away from the man's helmet and pinned them to the BII operative's side. It took no more effort, Jean thought, than she might have used to pin a three-year-old child's arms. The robot stared carefully at Danner's face. Its head rotated slightly, and Jean could hear some gears wheel and churn. The robot then swiftly turned and stared at Jean and Akemi in turn, its eyes searching, scanning, examining.

"The Decarabia have penetrated this unit's protective suit," the robot announced.

"Oh God!" Akemi gushed. She brought her hand toward her mouth and moved backward.

Danner fumbled in his thigh pocket and pulled a black cylinder from his cargo pocket. He looked at it for a moment, and then his eyes flashed toward Major Joyce. Something—was it recognition?—sparkled in the man's eyes, and the cylinder tumbled from his hand to clank on the ground.

"What did you do?" Jean's accusation was sharp and jabbed at Danner. "Danner? What did you do?"

The BII operative tried to answer, but blood foamed out of his mouth. If it hadn't been for Calliphon, the man would have collapsed. The robot laid him gently on the ground and stepped away. "I am sorry," Calliphon said.

"Isn't there anything you can do?" Jean demanded. She moved to Danner's side and knelt, placing a comforting hand on the stricken man's chest. Danner started to convulse.

Jean could see Danner smile as if someone had just told him a joke. "Ma-Ma-Ma-Major," he managed. And then Danner began to laugh, softly but deeply, as the lines on his face became more pronounced, and he spit blood. It covered the inside of his faceplate, making him difficult to see.

"Danner? Danner?" Jean said. She locked her eyes on his. "You'll be okay." Her voice was dull and clinical, measured. She could feel the man's bio suit shaking, and she pressed down to keep the man from injuring himself.

Danner continued to laugh, though now the sound was intermingled with pain and half-echoed curses.

"How did they get in the suit?" Jean asked Calliphon.

The robot stood still and did not reply.

"Where? W-w-where is he? W-w-where is he?"

"I don't understand, Danner. He? What? What did you say? What is it?"

"A soul without ... without denial ..." He coughed and spat. "Is a soul in ..." His breath suddenly became rapid and shallow. Danner took several gulps of air, and his head jerked back and forth. "Rapture!" Anger infiltrated his pain.

"What the hell? Danner? Danner!" Jean could hear Akemi whimpering, but she continued to hold Danner down, restricting his flailing.

"W-w-where is ... is ... is ... Where ... wh ..."

"What did you do? God damn you! Danner!" The major's voice raged. She could feel that Danner's kicking, his convulsions, suddenly grew exponentially weaker.

"W-w-w-where ..."

She looked at the cylinder the man had dropped, and realization struck her. "You fool," she berated. "You stupid, stupid fool!"

Danner reached up and grasped the major's helmet between two hands. Though she resisted, the BII operative pulled her down so that their faceplates met. His whole body shook. "Frame … Frame … Frame bomb … shuttle … shuttle," he stammered. A deep anger resonated in the man's voice. "I can't … I can't s-s-see. Where … is … Where? G-g-g … G-g-g! God?" He groaned. Suddenly his arms relaxed and clashed to the floor.

Danner lay unmoving.

Jean slowly stood and looked down upon the body. Though the man was dead, something still moved within the enclosure of the bio suit. Jean stepped back and frowned sickly. "God?" she spat. "You self-centered fool. He died a long time ago."

Calliphon drug Danner's body off to the far side of the room, where the body continued to wiggle and squirm. The Decarabia were doing their work. Jean and Akemi did their best to ignore Danner's corpse. The major looked haplessly at the alien workstations.

"I don't understand," Akemi said. Her voice was subdued. "What did he do?"

Jean turned toward the Asian woman. "He was going to smuggle some of the Decarabia back home." She pointed at the small, black cylinder that still lay where it had fallen.

"What? Why?"

"Um? Oh, I don't know. Maybe he thought they could be studied and synthesized but in a less deadly fashion. Do you think he was the type of person that would sell out to Terra or Lin Corp?"

Akemi shook her head. "He was BII."

Jean sighed and put her hands on her hips. She was tired. "So? Just because you're BII doesn't mean you are not human. How much do you think one of the big three corporations would pay for this little piece of kit? Or maybe he thought the Federation could do the work. Who the hell knows?"

"Maybe he didn't realize how deadly the Decarabia are," Akemi suggested. "Maybe he meant well."

"Do you believe that, Akemi?"

The Asian woman watched as Calliphon moved once again to the main control station. Akemi stared at the robot's back for a moment, marveling at the creature's design. "No." She turned to the major. "No. I don't believe he was unaware of the danger. And I don't think he meant well. What do we do now?"

Jean walked over and stood near Calliphon's side as the robot began adjusting the reactor's controls. "It changes nothing," she said. "We move on."

"But, Danner?"

Jean spun and looked hard at the Asian woman. "Danner was a jerk!" she spat. "And worse than that, he was an idiot. I don't know what his game was, but he put us all at risk. He would have brought those … things onto the *Fallen Star*. How did he know they couldn't get out of that stupid tube? He could have killed us all! He could have killed everything. He is not worth our tears."

Akemi looked at Major Joyce and then at the body of Danner Tomblin. The XM Flash biohazard suit seemed to exude an accusation. "Rafe?" Akemi's voice was small.

"Rafe," Jean echoed. She walked over, and for a moment, the two women stood looking at one another, neither voicing her fears. "Come on," Jean finally said, "let's finish this thing."

Akemi nodded and moved next to Calliphon. The robot turned its doglike head to her, and Akemi touched the robot on its shoulder. The robot's reaction was surprisingly gentle. It reached a hand over and put it on the tech's shoulder in sympathy.

"I can help," Akemi offered. "Tell me what to do."

Major Joyce joined the two of them.

Calliphon pointed below to the ground-floor level of the control room. "There is a door there. It will take me to the reactor. Here"—it pointed at the control panel—"this reading must remain within the safe zone between these two points, or the doors to the reactor will automatically seal shut. Once I finish with what I am doing, the reading will rise. I need you to manually control the flow of fuel to the reactor using these two dials. Make small movements when you adjust them to see how the reactor responds. When I tell you, move the right dial as far as you can in this direction. Understand?"

"What will that do?" Jean asked.

"It will interrupt the flow for a few seconds. The reactor's controls will shortly override your command, but in that time, with the fuel not flowing, I will reach into the actual mechanism and smash the control valve. The reactor will then shut itself down, and all power to the citadel will be severed. It will take the reactor several days to regenerate the valve, but I only need time to get into the open and send a signal to the satellites."

"And then?"

Calliphon looked at Akemi and Jean in turn. "Then we have two standard hours to get back to the shuttlecraft and get off the planet before the satellites execute their mission and lay waste to the surface."

"I can manage that, I think," Akemi said.

"We will not go back the way we came," the robot continued. "On the other side of this chamber is a door that leads out onto the upper level of the citadel. I will open that door before I go across the bridge to the reactor. Work your way down the outer stairs. You will not be able to get to the second level without going back inside the citadel. Though I intend to meet you there, do not wait for me. When you get back into the citadel, turn to your right and follow the corridor. It will take you to stairs that will lead you to where we first entered."

"How will we open the door?" Jean asked.

The robot stood up and started to walk down to the lower level of the command room. "All of the outer doors of the citadel are opening. Besides making the way clear, the cold will further reduce the capacity for the Decarabia to act."

Jean looked back toward the door that Calliphon had said would lead to the outside deck and noticed a twirl of snow entering the room. "Calliphon," she called.

The robot stopped.

"Good luck," Jean told it.

Snow had also begun blowing through the lower door of the chamber. Beyond it, Jean could just make out the metallic lacework of the bridge that led to the reactor's core. The bridge was ice-encrusted, and a steady wind whistled. Soon, the alien robot vanished beyond the door with a final glance back toward the humans.

"*Fallen Star. Fallen Star,*" Jean tried.

Where are you, Mike? If something had happened to their ship, then she and Akemi were already dead. "*Fallen Star. Fallen Star,* this is Major Joyce," she called again. But Captain Estury did not answer.

The captain focused the targeting system on the moon base. The sublight torpedoes were loaded, and with a mental command, Mike Estury shifted all of the shielding's power to the front of the vessel. He had not detected any activity on the base. It was quiet. From his vantage point, the moon base seemed small and almost toylike. He threw a switch above his head and began his attack run, aiming the nose of the *Fallen Star* at the center of the domed base.

All right. Here goes.

Mike fired the forward lasers. A bright slash of blue plasma ripped through space and struck the base. A small explosion registered on the sensors. The impact was not quite as big as the captain had expected. He had no idea what material the Makers had used in the base's construction, but he was committed. The captain hoped that his weapons would be effective enough to open a hole through which the torpedoes could penetrate into the underground portion of the moon base.

He fired two more laser bursts before launching the first two torpedoes. Mike sent the two torpedoes at a sharp arc away from the ship to keep his laser-firing lane open. The *Fallen Star* was too close to the moon and Nibiru for the torpedoes to use their framing drives. It would take them several minutes to reach the alien structure. As the torpedoes sped away from the ship, he therefore continued firing the lasers in the hope of distracting the enemy and bringing any return fire toward the *Fallen Star*. This would give the torpedoes the time they needed to strike the base. He registered solid hits with the lasers and, finally, began seeing some significant damage to the moon base. The ship's sensors picked up floating debris above the dome and the occasional flare of intense fire. The pattern of the fire, bright flashes that quickly stretched and burned out, told him that he had punched through the structure, and it was venting gas on to the moon's surface.

He was just beginning his third salvo when he noticed that the base's radio telescopes had begun a laborious swing toward his ship. The five massive radio dishes rotated until the pyramid-shaped parabolic transmitters were aimed at the part of space where the *Fallen Star* plied toward the moon.

That can't be a good sign, the captain thought.

Suddenly a spike of energy erupted from the telescope nearest to where the ground party had originally entered the moon base. Though he saw no visual signature, the *Fallen Star's* sensors read the energy wave. It was a type of concentrated microwave. The energy beam shot across space and clipped the back end of the second torpedo. The torpedo instantly flipped end over front and spun like a top along a wild trajectory. Mike watched as it careened into a ridge and exploded. A second wave burst from the antenna, and the first torpedo glowed and ballooned into a meteoric ball of fire that dissipated as it was destroyed.

You little bastards, he thought. *So you are awake. Good for you. Take this!*

Captain Estury adjusted his aim and returned fire at the parabolic reflector of the first antenna. He followed this with two additional torpedoes, mentally programing each along differing trajectories to increase the chance one of them would get through the enemy's defensive fire and strike the moon base. The captain considered changing the *Fallen Star's* attack vector as he watched two of the transceivers rotate directly at the *Fallen Star*, but he knew this was the best vector for targeting the base with the lasers. The lasers recharged; he fired again. Three bursts from the lasers raced toward and struck the support structure along the outer edge of one of the parabolic reflectors targeting the *Fallen Star*. The radio telescope rocked under the impact, and a section was torn off. It looked as if someone had taken a bite out of it.

In response, three transceivers released microwave beams at the inbound torpedoes. The torpedoes dissipated into smoke and debris. Watching that exchange, Mike noticed that the radio telescopes, while able to emit a concentrated and deadly microwave, were cumbersome and moved slowly. They also seemed to have difficulty firing along the plane of the horizon. He instructed the tactical computer to look for a way to get under the firing arc of the telescopes as he engaged the second of the two antennas that was targeting the *Fallen Star*.

Then an alarm sounded, and a red light flashed as the radio telescope released a deadly ray at the *Fallen Star*. The beam brushed the space a few hundred kilometers in front of the *Fallen Star*. Temperature spikes registered throughout the ship, but the *Fallen Star* did not sustain any serious damage.

Damn you, Mike cursed. *You weren't supposed to fire back!* He had underestimated the Decarabian reaction. He began to sweat, knowing that he was seriously in the game.

Mike slipped the controls and pushed the *Fallen Star* off its course, pulling several g-forces, hoping that the sudden change of direction would be difficult for the bulky radio telescopes to counter. A second shot ripped toward him, but it went far to port, passing harmlessly. At this moment, the tactical computer's computation on a more protected attack vector for the torpedoes was complete, and it auto-launched two more. That left only three in the bay.

The enemy fired. In short order, three of the other four torpedoes were struck and evaporated. Mike reached out and changed the target for the fourth torpedo at the last moment, sending it careening into one of the radio telescopes. It thudded into the mounting rack with a resounding explosion. The dish folded onto the side of the now nonexistent framework and crashed to the moon's surface. At the same time, he fired the lasers, targeting the second telescope that had engaged the *Fallen Star*. He took the risk of overheating his lasers and fired a five-burst salvo that danced across the reflector from left to right, scoring four of five hits and exploding the telescope into fragments. The captain decided to target the two undamaged radio telescopes with laser and torpedo fire. If he could take them out, the base would be defenseless. He sent new instructions to the two torpedoes that were racing along the surface of the moon along new attack vectors that would bring them in under the firing arc of the radio telescopes, instructing them to hit the telescopes. He then launched two of the remaining torpedoes and targeted the moon base directly. The ship rocked slightly as they shot out of the launch tubes.

The *Fallen Star* had reached the limits of its long attack run, and Mike pulled up and away from the moon, switching his shields to the rear of the ship. He maneuvered in a long, curving arc that would allow him to make another run. He hoped that the new vectors would protect the torpedoes speeding toward the alien base. He could no longer provide them covering fire.

Immersed within the web of the ship's sensors, he held his breath as the first and then the second torpedo struck home, destroying the two remaining radio telescopes. The sensors registered the blast waves that shook boulders loose on the ridgeline near the moon base. Four of the five radio telescopes were completely destroyed, and the fifth was out of action. Mike almost cheered.

The captain swung the *Fallen Star* along its arc and put the ship into attack position once again. The shields pushed to the front of the ship once again, Mike focused his energy on an exact targeting of the alien moon base. The remaining two spaceborne torpedoes were zipping across the final kilometers of the moon toward the structure. Mike watched as the first one skipped a little low and plowed into the side of the moon base, blowing a gaping whole in it. In rapid succession the second torpedo flared upward and then dove directly into the heart of the base. The ground shook, and Mike could visibly see the shockwave roil across the surface of the moon and rattle off the sides of the valley walls. Mike fired his lasers again and programmed the remaining torpedo for a delayed burst. It would dig itself into the crust of the moon and, like a bunker buster of old, penetrate the surface and detonate within the underground lair.

This one is for you, Jean, he thought as he released the torpedo. Its engines ignited and the deadly projectile flowed toward the moon base. For a moment, Captain Estury's thoughts turned to Rafe. *I'm sorry we couldn't save you*, he thought. *But at least I put you out of your misery, and we avenged you. Rest easy.*

Captain Estury fired two blue-light laser bursts and watched as the final torpedo zipped along the moon's surface and plunged into the heart of the Core. He was so fixed upon the flight of the torpedo, he did not notice the struggling parabolic reflector of the damaged but functional radio telescope as it jerkily turned and put the *Fallen Star* within its sights. Energy roared. Lights and sirens blared. And as the final torpedo cascaded down into the heart of the base, blasting tonnage of rock into the moon's sky, the powerful beam struck the *Fallen Star*.

Captain Estury screamed.

Snow and ice floated through the open doorways, yet Akemi Murakami could not feel it. Sweat dripped down her face as fear threatened to overcome reason. She had trouble focusing on the dials that Calliphon had left in her care. Her heart beat so strongly she felt it would jump right out of her chest. She closed her eyes and tried to control the thrumming beat of her blood as it pounded through her shaking body. Her ears rang with a high whistle and, for a moment, she felt an intense vertigo.

"Akemi." Jean's voice sounded as if it were a million miles away. "Akemi!"

The Asian woman turned and looked at the marine major. Major

Joyce seemed to be standing in a tunnel of light. Her features were blurred, and she moved in slow time.

"Breathe," the major was saying. "Take a deep breath and hold it. Akemi, can you understand me? Deep breath, hold—deep breath."

Jean was familiar with the signs of fear-induced shock. Akemi's heart monitor showed Akemi's was beating at nearly 175 beats per minute. At that rate, Jean knew, the technician would have no fine motor skills, would suffer memory and hearing loss, and likely was experiencing extreme tunnel vision and elongation of time. The woman was in danger of fainting.

"Akemi, relax. Deep breath. Deep breath," she repeated. The Asian woman was looking at her, but Jean was not sure the woman was seeing anything. Jean turned Akemi away from the control panel by rotating the oversize chair and looked at the technician's control panel on her XM Flash biohazard suit. Jean recalled reading about some of the built-in medical functions of the bio suit. If she could remember how to activate the medical function, perhaps it would inject Akemi with a relaxing sedative.

Just then, Akemi shook herself and took a deep, cleansing breath. "Major?" Her voice was unsure.

Jean could feel the woman take another deep breath. Akemi locked eyes with the major, and there was recognition.

"I'm all right, Major. I think."

"We're almost there, Akemi. Take a breath. Hold. Release. Come on. Breathe. Hold. Release."

One of the major's many combat courses had taught her a shooting technique designed to counter the human body's physiological reaction to fear-induced stress. That type of stress caused blood to rush from the extremities with many side effects. It was something hardwired into the human body from prehistoric times as a survival mechanism. But it was not helpful in the context of a modern universe. Deep, cleansing breaths—like those used by basketball players who, after running the court with pounding hearts, found themselves on the free-throw line unable to use the finesse of their shooting skills to sink the basket—helped. A deep breath oxygenates the blood, allows the heart to rapidly decrease its beating, and reverses the negative effects of a hyper-beating heart. Vision and fine motor skills return, and the basketball player is able to focus and drop the shot. The technique worked with marksmanship too. Major Joyce was trying to get the technician to do the same thing.

"Akemi, come on. Come on. That's better. Good. Deep breath. Hold. Release."

Akemi smiled tiredly. "I'm fine now, Major. Really."

Jean looked at the woman and nodded. "Okay. Let's get this done and get the hell off this planet. Agreed?"

"Hai."

Akemi turned back to the command panel and watched as the indicator hovered in what Calliphon had called the normal operational range. The line moved slightly upward, and Akemi dutifully adjusted the dials to bring it back down. The robot had been gone for several minutes without a word. How long was it going to take it? she wondered. Akemi resisted the urge to look at the still form of Danner Tomblin that had been stuffed into one of the room's far corners. Hadn't Calliphon said that, once it broke the seals on this room, the Decarabia would flood into it? How had they penetrated Danner's suit? Akemi had seen the telltale sign of aurora-like lights on the major's legs and back. They were being attacked. How long, she thought, before the nano-creatures penetrated their protective outfits? How long before she and Major Joyce became their next meal?

Akemi shuddered. *Come on, Calliphon. Hurry the hell up.*

"I've got it, Major. It just took a little practice." When Akemi had first tried to control the meter and keep it within the optimal zone, she had failed miserably. The reading had fluctuated all over the place as she turned the two dials first left and then right and then in opposite directions. By rapid trial and error, she had finally figured out the sequence of moves required when the reading went high or low. That allowed her to make more minute adjustments and led to a steadier reading.

"Calliphon," Major Joyce called over the radio. The alien robot had told her that it could communicate over their radio network. "Calliphon, how much longer?"

"Not long," the robot answered. "I have breached the inner door and am near the reactor." The two women heard a great tearing noise over the speakers in their helmets. "I have removed the panel and am uncovering the value. I will be ready in just a minute."

"Good," Akemi enjoined. "I'm ready to get out of here."

Jean wished she had thought of asking the robot if it was possible to activate a camera inside the reactor and display the image on the large screen that dominated the far wall, but there was nothing she could do about it now. So the two women waited in silence, Akemi adjusting the dials, Jean watching her.

Jean wondered for the hundredth time where the *Fallen Star* had gotten off to. She hoped everything was okay. They needed the ship for the final part of their retreat plan, and she was worried about Mike. The major had kept professional distance between the two of them on the trip to the Kururumany System. She couldn't allow that burgeoning relationship to get in the way of the mission. Yet, as she had watched her brother and Akemi grow closer, she had been tempted to succumb to her feelings. It had taken a tremendous effort not to fall under the sway of Mike's charm, and now, she worried, it might be too late. What if the *Fallen Star* had somehow been destroyed? Then she would forever be left with thoughts of what might have been. The idea threatened to unnerve her. She couldn't afford these thoughts right now, but they intruded upon her mind regardless of how much she tried to force them away.

"I'm going to look out the door and get a feel for our route out of here," she said to Akemi.

The Asian woman was bent awkwardly over the command panel. "Good idea," Akemi replied while concentrating on what she was doing.

Jean left her and made it to the doorway that Calliphon had opened. It was on the upper level of the citadel. She stepped out and could see the hyperbolic-cooling tower of the Helium-3 reactor to the side of the citadel. The metal bridge that Calliphon had crossed to the reactor was just below her at a ninety-degree angle. To her left was the open platform of the upper landing, and out beyond the citadel, Jean could just make out the tiny shape of the shuttlecraft lying quietly in the still air. The wind was not blowing in the way it had been when the party had landed on the ground. The sky was darker as the planet rotated and night approached. She hoped they would have time to get back to the shuttle before darkness settled. Darkness would make what they had to do next that much more difficult.

"The weather has cleared," she announced to Akemi as she returned to the command station.

"Good."

"Anything yet?"

"Nope. Major," Akemi asked, "do you think the *Fallen Star* is still out there? If not …" She trailed off.

"Mike knows what he's doing. All we have to do is get up there, and he'll come and get us. If there is any way, he will meet his end of the plan." If not, Jean knew, the two women would be left floating in space until their oxygen ran out and they asphyxiated.

"I am ready," the robot suddenly communicated.

"What? Yeah, great. Wait!" Akemi stumbled. "Okay. Say when."

"Go ahead. Flood the system," the robot responded.

Akemi flipped the two dials in the way Calliphon had shown her. She did it quickly, violently. The reactor's fuel meter spiked high, and the backlighting for the meter turned bright green. The automatic safety protocols had begun to adjust the flow when, suddenly, the panel went blank, dead.

"Is that it?" Akemi questioned.

Jean thought about it for a second. What had they expected? Fanfare? "Yup, let's go. Come on!"

Akemi and Jean dashed for the open door and slipped out into the fading light onto the icy platform. Half-scooting, half-walking, they moved along the wall until they found the open door back into the citadel. Entering the dark, their headlamps came to life, and they quickly followed the corridor to the right. They raced along by instinct, flowing always to the right, to where the robot had said they would find a stairwell back to their original entry point into the citadel. All around them the frigid air echoed with their footfall.

Faster. Faster, Jean thought.

They knew they were running for their lives.

Calliphon's hand smashed through the remaining conduit. The robot ripped and tore at the internal structures in the reactor's heart.

The Warder had toppled forward as it crossed the bridge to the cooling tower. Calliphon was glad the humans had not seen. The Decarabia were eating away at the Warder's ability to function. Already, Calliphon's left hand was uselessly hanging, its pistons and gears unresponsive and dead. The Warder had to hurry. Soon the Warder would lose the battle. If Calliphon was not able to complete these two tasks, the Warder would fail the humans. More importantly, Calliphon will have failed the Makers and the robot's family, and the Decarabia would be left to menace the universe. Calliphon had no doubt that the deadly nano-creatures would lure a second alien species to Nibiru. And with no Warders left to protect the universe and warn the unwary, the Decarabia would escape and ravage. The robot could not fail. To fail would be an indictment against the Warder's mission, the Warder's life, the lives of the robot's family, and the wishes of the Makers. All of their struggles would have been for naught.

Calliphon could feel the heat from the reactor's core on its back. Because the core was shielded, the heat was not hot enough to destroy the Decarabia, but it was hot enough that the nanomachines were no longer sluggish. The voracity of their attack against the robot had already increased. The attack would continue to increase in voracity until the robot could get back out into the cold. Calliphon hoped to finish this task before it was too late. The Warder did not want to die within the prison. The Warder wanted to say good-bye to its new friends.

The conduit broken, Calliphon saw the desired valve through the wires and freshly released steam. The Helium-3 reactor was not a complicated piece of engineering. Complicated systems required precision on many levels. Once one of those levels was disrupted, the results could be disastrous. To reduce entropy, the Makers had simplified the mechanics of the reactor to its basic parts. A basically designed system is more capable of absorbing variations in performance and is, thus, more resilient. Calliphon reached through and grabbed the valve, feeling the racing flow of fuel.

"I am ready," Calliphon radioed to the humans.

"What? Yeah, great. Wait!" The softer woman seemed surprised. "Okay. Say when."

If the robot had to destroy the valve while fuel was rushing through it, it would likely detonate, and that would prevent Calliphon from sending the release signal to the waiting satellites. It would mean the humans would die as they attempted to fly their shuttle off the planet—the satellites would shoot them down. And if the satellites did not execute their function, then the Decarabia would survive. That could not be.

"Go ahead. Flood the system." Calliphon concentrated. He would only have a few seconds to smash it before the automated systems took over.

The robot felt something shift within the value. Calliphon smashed down at it with all of its strength, grasped ahold of it, and pulled backward, leveraging its legs against the reactor's walls. The Warder ripped so hard that the entire mechanism tore lose in its hand, and Calliphon was propelled onto its back a few feet away from where it had been working. A small amount of fuel ejected from the hole that Calliphon had created, but it was soon cut off as the reactor responded to the damage. Soon the nanobots that maintained the system would begin repairs, but it would take them a considerable time to fix the damage.

The Decarabia continued to chew their way into the robot's systems. Calliphon lumbered to its feet and began shuffling back toward the door. Walking was difficult. Each step took more effort, more concentration, until the Warder fell down onto the ice-covered bridge, the Warder's left leg finally failing. The robot was grateful the Makers had not given the Warders the sensation of pain. Instead, processors calmly recognized and categorized the damage. Calliphon could otherwise ignore it.

Calliphon used its good hand to pull himself along the bridge and out into the snow and bitter cold. The Warder lay there for a moment, allowing the harsh temperature to have an effect upon the Decarabia. This enabled the Warder to gather its remaining strength, pull itself to its feet, and hop on one leg to the rail. Calliphon rotated its torso toward the east, where the horizon was not obscured by mountains. The robot sighed in relief to see that the weather had cleared. That meant its signal would have less interference and was more likely to reach its destination.

Holding onto the rail with his good hand, Calliphon activated its chest cavity. Slowly it opened in two pieces and formed a type of parabolic bowl. A small device emerged from its abdomen and extended about eight inches from its chest. At the end of it, a mechanical feed horn rotated and pointed back at the robot's open chest cavity. Satisfied it was in the best position possible, the robot recalled the activation code and, channeling the bulk of its fading power into the signal, released it into the sky. The robot repeated the message again and again. For a tense moment it thought it had failed, but then a stronger signal bounced from the horizon back to it. The robot watched in fascination as the signal was picked up and spread from satellite to satellite. A web of signals spread across the planet as weapons came to life, rotated, and focused.

Calliphon could not help but marvel at the sight. Its eyes could see the web like a giant net around Nibiru. It glowed and shimmered. In the robot's ears, the radiophonic sound resonated with the song of the Makers. It was filled with sadness and glory. And Calliphon knew the end had come. It could do no more.

Calliphon closed its chest cavity and leaned far over the side of the bridge. In a moment of horrific clarity, the robot realized that the Decarabia would be filled with mortal terror. They were self-aware. They had children. And death would soon find them all.

The robot had not considered how success would leave it feeling empty. Calliphon wanted to weep. It had damned an entire race of beings. Was its failure evil? Would the Makers forgive it? And when it died, Calliphon wondered, would Calliphon find peace? Or would the knowledge of genocide haunt its robotic soul?

Calliphon pushed its body over the railings until it hung by a single hand five stories above the ice-and-snow-encrusted plain. Calliphon could not walk out of the citadel.

But the robot could fall.

The dark was endless.

Major Joyce could hear herself panting as she and Akemi Murakami ran through the maze of the citadel. They were disoriented, and time and again found themselves in unfamiliar surroundings, unsure of where to go. At these moments, Jean physically grabbed the younger Asian woman and pushed her along, always forward. If the *Fallen Star* had been in orbit, it could have scanned the citadel and overlapped that with the beacon heartbeat of their suits, giving them guidance on how to escape back into the ice and snow. But there was only silence, the steady sound of Jean's panting, and the clack of the women's feet as they raced in the dark.

Jean shouted when she found a stairwell leading down.

Akemi tripped over the doorway. Jean steadied her, and the two began trundling down the well of darkness to the lower levels.

At some point, Jean became aware of the dull yet colorful light that skipped and meandered like amoeba across the surface of both of their XM Flash biohazard suits. The attack grew in intensity the longer they ran, until even their faceplates were covered with an endless swirl of color as the bio suits burned the attacking Decarabia off of their surfaces. How long, Jean desperately wondered, would the suits last under such a relentless assault? How long before they depressurized or the tiny creatures infiltrated enough to attack her flesh? Would she and Akemi die the same horrific death that Danner Tomblin had? Would they die anonymously and unremarked at the edge of space to be left, and consumed, by the Decarabia? It was a horrifying prospect.

At the point where Jean thought Akemi's strength would give out, a tantalizing glimmer of light appeared below them on the stair. Reinvigorated, the two women scrambled down and rushed out of the citadel onto the second-floor landing. They hit the hard ice and snow at a full run and slipped, falling face-first and sliding toward the edge. If not for the safety railing, they would have slid right off the landing and fallen twenty feet to the surface below. Instead, they piled into the rail and into one another with grunts and curses. They sat up, stunned, and for a moment, remained motionless. Then Jean struggled, slipped, and eventually made it to her knees and then to her feet.

She looked down and offered a hand to Akemi. "Come on, let's go."

Akemi stared at Jean's proffered hand, not registering it. "Okay," she finally said. Accepting the hand, she pulled herself up, and the two women turned to look at the snow plain below them. To the east, they saw the stairwell where, a few hours before, they had climbed their way into the citadel. Calliphon's ice tunnel through the huge snowdrift lay directly below them.

"The wind has died. It should be easier to get back to the shuttle," Jean said as she turned toward the final flight of stairs.

"Hai," Akemi rejoined. She sounded exhausted. "Do you think Calliphon will join us below?"

"God, I don't know. We can only drive on and see."

The two walked down the stairs in the waning light of the day. At the bottom, they found Calliphon's ice tunnel. The ice was still crystal-clear turquoise. It reminded Jean of the waters off the coast of the central continent on Baile Mac Cathain. She had once vacationed there with her family on a small island. Though the water had been deep, it had been as clear as the sky. She smiled at the memory.

Soon the two women were standing calf deep in snow, the looming shape of the citadel behind them, a long trek back to the shuttlecraft before them. They took a moment to scan the structure looking for Calliphon, but they saw no sign of the lumbering alien robot.

"Let's get moving," Jean said. "Calliphon can catch up."

They had just begun trudging back toward the shuttlecraft when Akemi spotted something moving through the snow.

"Major," she said, pointing. "Look there. Is that what I think it is?"

Major Joyce followed the line of sight from Akemi's outstretched hand and saw a glint of metal against the backdrop of snow. As she watched, the glint slid slowly forward as if it were being dragged. Jean was not sure what she was looking at until the distinctive shape of Calliphon's head rotated back at them. The robot appeared to see them, and it stopped struggling.

"Come, on!" A feeling of profound relief filled Jean as she rushed forward toward the robot. But as she and Akemi drew nearer, she was filled with a sudden foreboding.

They stopped short.

"Calliphon?" Jean asked.

It was obvious that the robot had been dragging itself across the snow. A long streak stretched out from behind the robot back toward the citadel. Its legs were tangled, and one arm lay listlessly by its side.

The robot propped itself up on its one good arm and looked at the humans. "Major. Akemi," it welcomed. "I had hoped to see you one final time. The Decarabia …" Calliphon left the rest unsaid.

Jean and Akemi approached, and Jean knelt down by the prostrate robot. "I'm so, so sorry. Is there anything we can do?"

The robot rotated its camera eyes between the two humans. *How strange*, it thought. How had these creatures worked their way into its heart? The relief it felt at their survival was overwhelming. It could feel its power fading, and its mind jumbled, cleared, and the world focused once again.

"You must hurry," it warned them. "The signal was received, and the web has been activated. Soon the planet will be purged. You must get away."

"We can't just leave you," Akemi said. "We'll help." She bent down and offered the robot her shoulder, but the robot shook its head.

"Thank you," Calliphon answered. "But the Decarabia have done too much damage. Even if you could carry my weight to the shuttlecraft, once in a warmer location, they would leave their current dormant state and attack you. No. Better for me to remain. This has been my home—and the home of my siblings. It is a good place to die."

"Don't talk that way," Jean said. Her voice felt tight and stretched.

Calliphon looked up at her and Akemi and then at the sky beyond. "For countless thousands of years, I have warded against the Decarabia—ever watchful, even after my siblings succumbed to the scourge. The Makers have fallen back into the dark abyss of stars, and the Warders of Nibiru have been consumed into dust. Tell me, Major, what is death to the likes of me except a final release, oblivion, peace? The universe shall not mourn my kind. The universe will not know what we have done here to protect all life from the disease that is the Decarabia. But now, in my last moment, I find it is enough. It is fitting we are forgotten. It is fitting that the deep dark accepts us back into its bosom. I have fulfilled my purpose."

The robot sighed. "I am happy we met. You are such an interesting race. I wish you joy on your journey.

"I am the last of my kind. Calliphon. The lone Warder of Nibiru. Ah, look, Major. Alauda rises in the west."

And with that, the Warder died.

The trek back to the shuttlecraft was physically difficult and emotionally draining. Jean kept Akemi in front of her, encouraging the woman when her strength flagged, pushing and prodding her when Akemi felt like giving up. They were calling it close. They only had two hours from the moment Calliphon had sent the activation signal, but neither of them were exactly sure when the robot had accomplished that task. So they slogged their way through the sometimes waist-deep snow as the sun dropped and night crept across the land. Both Jean and Akemi tried at intervals to contact the *Fallen Star*, to no avail. The lack of contact fed a growing trepidation in both of their hearts.

And they knew it was not done. They could not take the shuttle all the way into the bay of the *Fallen Star*. Doing so risked contamination. Jean had devised a plan, but she dreaded it. It was, as Mike had declared when he first heard it, bat-shit crazy. But what choice did they have? So, in between the panting and cursing, the stumbling and flailing, Major Joyce ran the scenario through her mind. Again and again and again. She knew she would have no time when the moment came to think about it. Better to focus her mind on it now. By the time they arrived at the shuttlecraft, exhausted but determined, Jean had mentally rehearsed the procedure a hundred times.

"Thank, God!" Akemi declared as she slumped against the outside hull of the shuttlecraft. The light of two of Nibiru's moons cast a soft glow on the snow-swept plain. Behind them, the citadel sat like a shadowed monolith. It looked indestructible.

"Almost done, Akemi." Jean panted. "Up the ladder. I'll help you."

Akemi nodded and moved, her body aching, to the extended ladder. Major Joyce helped the woman start the last climb, pushing upward with all of her might when Akemi floundered. The Asian woman disappeared inside the shuttlecraft, and Jean was quick to follow. She was grateful for the juice that Akemi had provided before the mission began. Without the little boost, the major was sure her strength would have given out long ago.

A sheen of ice covered the controls and seats. Jean collapsed wearily into the pilot's seat, and Akemi sat heavily in the copilot's. Jean began the prelaunch sequence and nearly shed tears when the engines responded. She had become convinced that the shuttle was infected with the Decarabia. They had likely ridden the landing party's gear or Calliphon onto the shuttle when the foursome had left Gargantuan for Nibiru's surface. It was why they'd let the cold of the planet invade the shuttle. They hoped it would disorient the nanomachines and preserve their means of leaving the surface. Jean woke up the navigation computer and buckled in.

"Ready?" she asked.

Akemi looked at Jean. "Punch it, Major."

Jean connected wirelessly with the shuttlecraft and, using manual controls, lifted the shuttle from the surface. Snow swirled and spun in the forward view. The vessel was barely off the ground when she started rolling it forward over the terrain, pushing it upward at an increasing angle. As the shuttlecraft banked above the citadel in the clear night's sky, Jean pushed the throttle to full, and the air cracked with the sound of the shuttle going supersonic. Jean and Akemi were pushed deep into their seats as the g-forces grew, until Jean felt neither of the women could take more. Then she held it and pushed the shuttle higher and higher.

"No sign of the *Fallen Star*," Jean said through the strain. "The shuttlecraft can't detect it in orbit."

Akemi swore.

"He'll turn up," Jean added. "He'd better."

Jean guided the shuttlecraft through some high clouds, and then they entered the mesosphere, and the force of their acceleration gave way as they began leaving the weight of the planet's gravity behind.

"*Fallen Star. Fallen Star*," Jean called. "Damn it, Mike! Where are you?" She adjusted the sensors, but the only objects they detected were the ever-closer satellites in their threatening ring.

"Major," Akemi interjected, "do you see what I see?"

Jean turned her attention to the cockpit window. They were close enough to the Makers' satellites that they were somewhat visible. "What?" She started. "No wait. I see it." When they had first flown through the protective ring, the satellites had been deathly still, void of any signature. Now they could both see the twinkle of red and green lights blinking on the nearest units. "They're active," she said.

"He said he did it," Akemi added, thinking of the dead Warder.

"We're going to zip through hot. I'm not slowing down, Akemi. So hold on to something."

"Hold on to what?"

"Anything. We may have no more than fifteen minutes left. I want to put as much distance between those things and us as possible before they kick off. Who knows what weapons the Makers have on those platforms? We could get caught in the fire or get fried in some type of back blast."

"You'll get no arguments from me, Major."

"All right." Jean repeated herself, but this time she spoke slowly, elongating the word as she calculated the correct vector to shoot through the nearest pair of satellites. "All right."

She nudged the shuttlecraft to port, and they darted the gap. One second, the satellites were visible in a long line to either side of the craft, and the next, the only thing in front of them was open space.

"Setting our vector for Gargantuan."

"Rafe?"

"Yup, we go get him. And then the three of us punch out, and the *Fallen Star* picks us up."

"But the ship is missing."

"Maybe the captain moved it back to the moon to be in place when we were ready."

"That wasn't the plan. He was going to escort us."

"I know," Jean sounded exasperated. "But that is the only thing I can think of right now. Do you have a better idea?"

Akemi didn't answer.

"And it might be good to put that moon between us and the satellites—just in case."

"Stick to the plan then," Akemi acknowledged. She sounded sleepy.

Jean felt sleepy too. The adrenaline rush of the last hours had run out, and her body was swinging to the opposite extreme. The urge to sleep was nearly overpowering.

"Akemi." She shoved the other woman in the shoulder. "I need you to do something for me. Can you do something for me?"

"Hai," Akemi purred. Her head lolled toward the major and the two locked eyes.

"Danner said something as he was dying. He babbled something about a framing bomb."

"A framing bomb? Aren't those illegal?"

"Has that ever stopped anyone before?" Jean asked. She took a breath. "I think he said there is a framing bomb on the shuttle. I need you to find it."

"You want me to find it?"

"We have to know if there is one and if it has been contaminated by the Decarabia. Make sure it is not active and throw it in the air lock."

"And you'll flush it?"

"No," Jean replied. "We might find a use for it. And the air lock should act like an isolation chamber—you know, in case the little bastards are moving through the ship."

Akemi unbuckled and half fell from her chair. "Okay, Major. Danner was hugging an equipment container earlier. It seemed too small for a framing bomb, but he was awfully protective about it."

"What, the black case?" Jean thought about it. Danner had seemed particularly protective about the case.

"I'll go and look," Akemi said as she moved back toward the main compartment.

The technician went through the overhead lockers and looked under the seats but did not find the black equipment case. She eventually found it stowed in the deep pocket compartment they used to store their EVAs.

Akemi whistled. "Found it," she said as she inspected the device. It was shaped to fit the container and had a small control screen. When Akemi touched it, the screen jerked to life. Akemi jumped. "God!"

"What?"

"Nothing, Major. It just beeped at me and scared me to death. Wait. Wait a minute."

"You're driving me crazy, Akemi. What is it?"

"There's a little wagon-wheel design on this thing—like a maker's mark—with arrows pointing out in all directions. I've seen it before, somewhere."

"Will it help you crack into the thing?" Major Joyce asked.

"Crack into it?" Akemi was incredulous.

"Can you do it? Can you get into the system?"

"It will take a while," Akemi answered.

"And the Decarabia," Jean asked, "any sign of them?"

Akemi looked the device over and saw no obvious signs of tampering. But without a microscope or something, how would she really know? "I don't know. No?"

"Drag it into the air lock," the major ordered, "and see if you can figure out the activation code. You have about fifteen minutes before we get to the moon."

Major Joyce flew the shuttlecraft toward Gargantuan. She kept an electronic eye out toward Nibiru expectantly. At some point, she thought, those satellites were going to let loose, and all hell would break out. "*Fallen Star*," she sent the signal out repetitively, her whole body searching for the wayward ship. "*Fallen Star*." *Where are you, Mike?*

"*Fallen Star*, this is Major Joyce. Answer me!" Jean had never felt so tiny in her entire life. The vast universe mocked her with silence.

She missed her brother, her mother and father, and the captain. *Damn it*, she fumed quietly. She couldn't lose half of the people she loved in a few span of hours! It wasn't fair.

"*Fallen Star*," she called. "*Fallen Star. Fallen Star.*"

There was a soft metallic ping. At first, Major Joyce thought she had imagined it. She had not physically linked to the shuttlecraft for fear that it might be infected with Decarabia. So she was accessing the system wirelessly. It was like seeing the universe through dark-colored glass. Then she heard it again. She shifted the shuttlecraft's sensors toward the sound. The source was located on the far side of Gargantuan, the moon where the alien-made base lay half-hidden in the shadows of a deep valley. By the sound of it, the source of the noise was moving away from the moon into the deeper parts of the system. The major adjusted the shuttle's sensors, but whatever was causing the noise was beyond the shuttle's capacity to see. Jean looked out of the cockpit window at the looming moon. She had hoped to see the *Fallen Star* in orbit around Gargantuan, but the horizon was clear. There was a slight possibility that Mike had put the ship down on the moon. Maybe he had hoped to rescue her brother. But that would be a most desperate move, and the captain was all about precision. A rash move did not sound like him at all. Jean mentally followed the sound of the metallic ping to the area of space from whence it emanated.

"Akemi?" Jean called the technician.

"Hold on. Almost done."

"When you get a chance, I want you to hear something."

"Yeah, okay. Gods, I can't believe I'm messing with a framing bomb. This isn't in my job description."

As Jean awaited the technician, she adjusted her trajectory, taking the shuttle into a distant orbit of Gargantuan. She did not take a standard orbit but, rather, fell into an elliptical one to minimize the amount of time she was on the Nibiru-side of Gargantuan and maximize the dwell time when the moon was between the shuttlecraft and the planet. It so happened that this would also put the shuttle in an orbit that would allow for extended coverage of the valley where the alien dome rested.

"Done," Akemi announced as she took the copilot's seat once again. "All we have to do is push a couple of buttons and … vroom! No more anything. That baby will rip anything within its range to rags, shift it a little in space, and then drop it. Nasty, nasty device. What the hell are we going to do with it?"

"Not now, Akemi. I mean," Jean continued, "I'm not sure yet. I was thinking we could use it to destroy the shuttlecraft when we punch out."

"That'll do it," the Japanese woman opined.

"But right now, listen to this ping. Can you link to the system … *remotely*," Jean emphasized, for fear the Decarabia had infiltrated the ship but were inactive due to the intentionally extremely cold temperature of the shuttlecraft. If not for their biohazard suits, the two women would have frozen a long time ago.

"Easy." Akemi reached out wirelessly and connected to the tiny ship's sensor array. She nodded to Jean. "I'm in."

"That little patch of space. Hear it?"

"That? That's a location beacon. Standard …" She stopped as the realization struck her. "The *Fallen Star*!"

Jean could kick herself. She didn't have enough piloting time, but she should have made the connection. Her mind was fatigued. "Are you sure?" It made sense.

"Looking through the technical manual now … Yes … it is the *Fallen Star's* location beacon. Every ship has one to help in-system flight controllers track and direct traffic. They are unique—mostly. And that one is ours!" Akemi could have jumped for joy.

"It's moving away from us," Jean concluded, though she felt an immense sigh of relief as well. "Something isn't right." At least they had identified a problem. Now they just had to unravel it and fix it.

"Can we catch it?" Akemi asked, suddenly fearful.

"Maybe," Jean replied. "My guess is that it isn't under thrust. It's wobbling, and I'm not picking up any exhaust trail. A slingshot?" Jean thought aloud. She called up an image of the moon and overlay their orbit and the location of the *Fallen Star* as it moved away from them. She had the CPU do some quick calculations. It was possible.

"Look, we could use the moon to slingshot us toward the *Fallen Star*. That would give us the extra speed we need to catch the ship. But ..."

"Rafe?"

"We can always come back," Jean added uncertainly. She hated the idea of leaving Rafe in the grip of the Decarabia for any longer than necessary.

"We can't do both at the same time." Akemi looked at Jean, unwilling to state the obvious and hoping the major would reach the same conclusion. Rafe was special to Akemi too, but it wouldn't help him if they saved him only to get stranded and die of oxygen deprivation aboard the shuttle. They needed the *Fallen Star*.

"You're right, of course." It was difficult to admit.

"One thing at a time?"

"One thing at a time." A weight settled on Jean's chest. Was she choosing between two of the men in her life? Or was she choosing herself over both of them? "Can you tighten up the math on the slingshot, Akemi? You're much better at math than I am."

"No problem, Major." Though the technician knew the navigation computer would do the math, she recognized that the major needed time to process and accept the decision.

Akemi's job would be to attempt to pinpoint the location of the *Fallen Star*. With only the one signal, she couldn't triangulate. Finding the vector on which the ship was traveling was the easy part. Identifying exactly how far away the ship was and where it would be when the shuttlecraft used the gravity well around Gargantuan to slingshot toward it was the trick. And, Akemi conceded, perhaps she was the most qualified person to make that estimation. If it was wrong, they could overshoot or undershoot the *Fallen Star*.

Overshooting was not too big of a problem; undershooting it might result in their never intersecting the wayward ship.

A few minutes later, the technician finished. It was her best guess. "Here's the approach vector for the slingshot," she told the major. "I used the Doppler effect of the signal to estimate the ship's speed. Using that and the trajectory, I figured out the approximate time the *Fallen Star* left the moon's orbit. Then I ran the calculations back out and overlapped them. And then, I made a guess."

"Only the one orbit," Jean commented.

"That's because you're already in an oblong orbit, and that means that, as we rotate to the planet side of Gargantuan, we will be traveling more quickly. We'll just leverage that and hit our escape vector … here." Akemi pointed at a representation of the moon and the proposed trajectory that would use the moon for a gravity-assisted boost to allow the shuttle to close with the *Fallen Star*. "And we still get a good look at the moon base as we go around the dark side of the moon."

"I see. Good." Jean began adjusting orders to the computer and set the shuttle along Akemi's trajectory.

"It will also get us away from the planet," Akemi added. "The more space between me and Nibiru the better."

"I know. The purging will definitely happen before we get away from the moon though. Nothing we can do about it. We are going to see it close-up."

"Lovely."

The two women sat quietly as Jean made the final adjustments, and the shuttlecraft began its trek around the dark side of Gargantuan.

"Major," Akemi asked, "are we going to survive this?"

Major Joyce looked seriously at the technician. "I don't know. But we're sure as hell going to try."

The debris field around the alien moon base was disconcerting. The shuttle's sensors could clearly make out the collapsed radio telescopes and a dust cloud hovered in the moon's thin atmosphere. Jean knew once she saw it that Mike must have attacked the base, but she could not fathom why. What had happened that would cause him to do so? It occurred to her that the *Fallen Star* had probably suffered an attack in return. That would explain why she could not raise it over the radio and why it was now listlessly drifting in open space. What she couldn't tell was whether the Core had been destroyed. If it had, then her brother was dead. Dead. She wasn't sure what to make of that thought. It seemed so surreal and went against everything they had planned. There had to be a reason, she thought. It couldn't just be a result of some lunacy.

She and Akemi eyed the last standing radio telescope with unease. Jean sent the shuttle's limited sensors searching for ground-based missile or laser weapons. But as they continued in their single-pass orbit, nothing on the surface moved. And then they started detecting low-level radiological disturbances. At first, they thought the readings were emanating from the destroyed moon base, but a refined reading told a different story. The radiation was coming around the edges of Gargantuan from the direction of the planet.

"Do you think it's started?" Akemi asked.

"That's a good bet. We'll be heading into the planet-side part of the orbit in about twenty minutes. We'll know for sure."

It was a tense twenty minutes. The radiation levels remained constant and were within the tolerable level for the shuttlecraft. Between staring at the moon base, checking on the location of the *Fallen Star*, and wondering what was happening on Nibiru, Jean nursed her fears and what she knew was a slowly building grief. But finally, they were leaving the protected side of the Gargantuan, and their eyes focused on Nibiru. The planet was terrible in its beauty.

The alien satellites were raining down some type of munitions that seemed to be spinning as they split the planet's atmosphere. There they dipped through a layer of ice and dust that rose in giant plumes over a landscape that danced and flashed like a living, breathing thing. A mix of rainbow light coursed harshly on the planet's surface, and visible, circular explosive waves beat in overlapping destructive pulses. At first, Jean and Akemi though the onslaught was evenly spaced along Nibiru's tortured facade, but as they continued to gain speed, the shuttlecraft whipping around Gargantuan, they noticed a particular attack along the planet's equatorial rim. The nature of the explosions was strikingly different. Sensors showed that temperatures at these impact points were several million degrees. Snow and rock vaporized, huge clouds of steam expanded from strike points at startling speeds. It was difficult to understand what was happening, but Akemi thought the explosions were tunneling to the planet's Mohorovicic discontinuity, the location where a planet's outer, solid surface ends and the magmatic mantle begins. The reason for this two-pronged attack eluded Akemi. What was obviously clear to both of them was that the citadel had been obliterated in the first salvo.

They watched the silent cascade of destruction pounding down, the skies filling with thick ash. And still the attack proceeded. A never-ending flood of weapons stabbed at the wounded planet, bleeding it, ripping and clawing Nibiru into something unrecognizable. Torrential showers of lightning flicked and shimmied through the atmosphere, and cyclonic eyes formed, twisting in the planet's agony.

For some inexplicable reason, Jean found she was crying—soft, solemn, weeping that cascaded over her as she watched the planet die. She looked at Akemi and noticed the technician's face was mawkishly frozen in an attitude of distress. Akemi was shaking tight tremors as dark eyes stared unblinking at the Makers' final act of destruction.

"Akemi!" Jean reached over and shook the woman. Jean's mind was filled with the sudden image of Danner, his face laced with poisonous red streaks as the Decarabia attacked him. To Jean's instant relief, the Japanese technician's face was smooth as light, caramel ivory.

"Major?" Tears sprang to Akemi's eyes when she saw that Jean too was crying.

Jean looked back at the tumultuous sky of Nibiru. "My God," she whispered.

Akemi looked out at the planet too. "Yes. Hai."

It took them another twenty minutes of picking up speed before they hit their release point. Jean gunned the engines as the shuttlecraft, now going nearly four times faster than it could otherwise go, pulled away from Gargantuan. Half an hour later, they were well on their way toward their rendezvous with the *Fallen Star*. Jean's mind lingered darkly on the fate of her brother as, for the first time in a long day, the two of them could do nothing but wait.

Jean realized that Akemi had fallen into a deep sleep. Doing a quick calculation, the major decided they had several hours before they caught up to the *Fallen Star*.

We both need some sleep, she thought.

Jean set an alarm that would wake them shortly before they arrived and closed her eyes. But for the longest time, sleep evaded her.

She had failed to save Rafe. She knew this in her heart. He was dead. What had this all been about? What had they gained? They had no alien technology to bring back home; they had lost her brother, Danner, and possibly Mike too. How much pain could a human heart endure? she wondered. And why was hers so listless and unfeeling? She could cry over a dying world, but for her brother, why was there only a void of silence?

When she finally fell into a fitful sleep, Jean dreamed of cold rain on a craggy shore.

The *Fallen Star* was damaged. Major Joyce tried hailing the injured craft again, to no avail. She was tired and feeling irritated at being stuck for so long in the bio suit. But some of her energy had returned after she had finally faded into sleep. Akemi was up and running simulations on the computer. Jean knew the woman was terrified of taking a space walk, but there was no help for it. They could not land the shuttle on the *Fallen Star* and risk bringing Decarabia on board. The simulations kept the other woman's mind occupied.

At some point during their slumber, the Makers' attack on Nibiru had ended. From their vantage point, the planet now resembled a gaseous giant. However, the shuttlecraft's readings told a different story. The planet did not have the helium and hydrogen signature of standard gas giants. Nor did it have the heavier elements that were associated with ice giants. The twirling mass of material in Nibiru's atmosphere resembled a volcanic eruption of enormous proportions—semisolid fragments trapped in an expanding mass of toxic gasses. Silica, sulfur dioxide, carbon monoxide, and hydrogen chloride mixed with microlites and phenocrysts and kept all light from Kururumany from the planet's surface. Even with their distance from the planet, the women saw clearly visible flashes of lighting in the maelstrom. It was fascinating, but Jean had other tasks at hand.

"Matching velocity," she announced as the forward jets of the shuttle fired softly. She eyed the front of the *Fallen Star*, where a large, dark patch spread from the cockpit area along nearly half the side of the spaceship. The ship itself was tumbling head over heel, making matching its movements terribly difficult. Jean had not been trained for this type of maneuver.

"So soon?"

"We have to get ready to go," Jean answered.

The shuttlecraft was traveling in front of the *Fallen Star*. The larger ship was tumbling behind them like a saw blade. Jean was where she needed to be; the only thing left was the jump.

"Go to the hatch, Akemi. I'll be there in just a second."

"Remind me to never go on vacation with you, Major," Akemi mumbled and attempted to laugh, but the joke lacked conviction.

As Akemi Murakami shuffled to the air lock, Jean set the last part of her plan into motion. They could not let the shuttlecraft remain intact when they left. The Decarabia that were now in a listless state because of the cold, might someday find purchase and escape to some other spaceship or planet. And the moon base had not been attacked by the Makers' ring of satellites. There could be surviving Decarabia there too. The sensible thing to do was to destroy both of them. Jean would launch the shuttlecraft back toward Gargantuan with the framing bomb armed and ready to ignite. Not as precise as the Makers' weapons, the framing bomb would shred part of the moon, rearrange it, and spit it all back at the moon's surface. Not pretty, but highly effective.

Jean unbuckled and followed Akemi to the air lock.

"Are you ready for this?"

"No," Akemi admitted. "The bomb is set."

Jean smiled. The lithe woman was tougher than she looked, Jean thought. "Okay, we're going to do this thing tandem—tied together. I've done this before with new recruits on their first jump. You don't have to do anything. I'll steer us."

"Hai."

"Just watch it when we come up to the *Fallen Star*. We only have a couple chances to get ahold of the ship, and you'll get the first shot at it."

"I'm ready," Akemi replied.

"Okay, let's close the outer lock and shuffle to the main air lock."

Jean closed the inner air lock as Akemi half bounced to the outer air lock. She stood center of the doorway like the major had instructed and waited.

"Right. I'm hooking up to you now." Major Joyce hooked two tethers to the rear side of Akemi's suit and cinched them both tight so there was no space between the two of them. "Pull your arms in, Akemi. I'm going to start the rotation."

Akemi dutifully pulled her arms into her body, across her chest and closed her eyes. She didn't want to see what was coming. She could feel the shift in the shuttle's motion as the major wirelessly executed a series of thruster fire that would somewhat match the spinning of the *Fallen Star*. A wave of nausea passed through Akemi, but she managed not to throw up. Jean pushed her, and the two shuffled closer to the air-lock door. Akemi could hear the air cycle as the air lock depressurized. When the hatch suddenly opened, the sound of it startled her, and Akemi reflectively opened her eyes.

The universe spun before her. Two or three hundred feet directly in front of her, the *Fallen Star* turned in tandem. Akemi knew they were going to try to reach the front air lock, and she strained to see it, but the *Fallen Star's* lights were not active. The ship was murky, a shadow in a dark sky. The lights from the shuttle helped a little by providing a corridor of light that sparkled dimly off the *Fallen Star's* hull. Looking anywhere but at the *Fallen Star* made Akemi dizzy, so she tried to focus on the other ship and ignore the rest of the universe.

"Here we go," the major said as she pushed both of them through the door.

It took all of Akemi's willpower to not flail at the sensation. She heard the major using her suit's limited thrusters to drive the two of them farther away from the shuttle toward the slowly closing *Fallen Star*.

"Can't we hurry?" Akemi asked.

"Too fast and we'll bounce," the major replied. "And that could be really bad."

It seemed like an age before the *Fallen Star* was within fifty feet, and Jean expertly started braking. Akemi readied herself for the grab at the hull. To her right, one of the *Fallen Star's* wings seemed to beckon them. But they were aiming for the area to the front of the wing.

Akemi held her breath. Fifteen feet. She could see handholds near the *Fallen Star's* air lock. She braced for impact and was surprised when she gently kissed the side of the spacecraft. She quickly grabbed the handhold and latched a cable to it.

"I did it!" she exclaimed. "We did it!" She laughed aloud with relief.

Jean disconnected one of the tether lines to Akemi's suit and extended the other. Reaching out she grabbed ahold of the other handhold. "Let's see if we can get this to cycle open." Jean punched a code into the keypad located next to the air lock. Nothing happened. "Shit."

"What? What's wrong, Major?"

"It didn't open. Let me try again. No."

Both women stayed quiet for a moment. Neither of them wanted to try to reach the rear air lock. That would mean traversing the entire ship.

"Have you tried accessing the computer remotely?"

"What?"

"Try accessing the computer system remotely, Major. We should be close enough."

"Gods, I must be getting dull in my old age." Jean sighed. "Hold on."

Akemi waited and was rewarded when the *Fallen Star's* lights came online and, to her immense relief, the air lock began to cycle.

"Hurry, let's purge our suits one final time before we get on board—just to be safe," Jean suggested.

They both cycled through a purge sequence and then clambered aboard the *Fallen Star*. Jean closed the outer hatch, and the air in the lock began to cycle. When the light turned green, indicating it was now safe to open the inner hatch and remove the XM Flash suits, they both paused. Had they left all the Decarabia behind?

Akemi reached up and unlocked her helmet. "I'll go first, Major. I'm beginning to hate this thing anyway." The Asian woman removed her helmet and shook out her hair. For a moment she remained frozen, waiting to see if the Decarabia would attack her. When nothing happened, she smiled broadly.

"Let's get out of these things," she said, helping the major get her helmet off. The two of them then helped one another take the biohazard suits off. They just dumped them on the floor.

"There's some damage to the ship's systems—wires fused and some memory boards burned through. But the ship will run," the major announced. "Let's go find the captain."

Akemi grabbed Major Joyce by the hand. "What if he's dead?"

The blood drained from Jean's face for a moment. It was quickly replaced by a look of determination. "Let's hope he isn't. He'll be in the cockpit."

Jean led the way through the inner air lock and through the center of the ship toward the cockpit. The ship was clean and orderly. It was home. As they moved, the major tapped deeper into the ship's computer and began activating critical systems and slowing the ship's spin. The *Fallen Star* began pulling back from the abandoned shuttlecraft, and interior lights flickered to life. Jean tried to remain calm. Her heart thumped in her chest, and her breathing was shallow.

When she and Akemi entered the pilot's station, Jean stood stock-still staring at the unmoving body of Captain Mike Estury. He was lying, still buckled in his chair, half of his body a ruin of blisters and burns. Akemi's hand covered her mouth, and she emitted a squeak of shock. The smell was appalling. Jean stepped softly forward and reached her index finger toward the captain's jugular to feel for a pulse. When she touched him, his eyes opened.

He was alive.

Major Joyce stalked the busy hallway on William Bennet Station. Outside the para-glass windows, the huge gas giant of Luna Reach slowly moved in the midst of the Isa System. It seemed to her like years had passed since she had walked these halls as a flight student. Yet only a couple of months had gone by since she had led the fateful mission that had ended her brother's life—and the life of the detestable little man Danner Tomblin. As much as Jean tried, she could not feel any sympathy for the BII operative's death. They had discovered his digital journal on the long return and had come to understand he was planning to kill them all. For the robot Calliphon, Jean had mixed feelings.

She was not sad the robot had ... died? Jean was not sure the Federation, or any human being for that matter, was ready for the type of technology that the robot represented. And couldn't Calliphon have gone to the citadel at any time and destroyed the

Decarabia? Why had it taken Rafe's situation to force the robot into action? What had Calliphon been waiting for? But then again, Calliphon was not like any other robot in Jean's experiences. Was Calliphon alive? Had the robot feared death? Did Calliphon have some type of moral code? Would she, Jean wondered, readily wipe out an entire race of creatures just because they *might* be a threat? Weren't humans a threat? What required the universe to save humans over other species? Perhaps, in the end, Calliphon had chosen to support diversity of life and hope over the single-minded hunger of the Decarabia. That is what Jean suspected, and in those moments of reflection, she did not feel sad the robot had died. She felt an immense grief.

The major was on her way to the medical unit, where Captain Mike Estury was in recovery. She had no mixed feelings there. On the long return flight to William Bennet, she had hovered over the medically comatose pilot, watching as the captain struggled for each breath. Akemi had turned out to be a fair medical technician. The Asian woman had kept Mike alive and mostly out of pain. But the damage the captain had sustained was significant. It would be months to years before he was able to begin a mostly normal life. It was clear, though, that his days as a navy pilot were over. He would eventually get medically discharged. And Jean was determined to be there when that happened. She had been thinking a lot about her future. It was difficult for Jean to grasp, but she knew that her life had been irrevocably changed.

Major Joyce stepped into the lift and pushed the button for the medical unit's floor.

Her mother and father had taken the news of her brother's death in their own ways. The knowledge that Rafe had died trying to help the Federation win the peace had helped the old colonel come to some type of terms with Rafe's desertion. Her father was able to come a little out of the shell he had collapsed into, and for the first time in a long while, Jean had seen him take a more companionate approach to her mother. Their marriage had been a strain for both of them, but Rafe's death had provided them the impetus they needed to start bridging the distance between them. Her mother had wept, and her emotion had visibly moved Jean's father. Her father loved her mother, Jean was sure. But being in the marines turned you hard, distant. That tendency did not end when you hung up the uniform. Jean wondered if she and Mike would have the same issues. Could she allow herself to be vulnerable and open after a lifetime of military discipline and carnage? And being honest with herself, Jean knew she was not done with the marines. She had other things she wished to accomplish before hanging up her own uniform besides her father's.

The lift opened and Major Joyce smiled at the receptionist. The woman was from one of the inner, ringed planets that were so popular with the tourist class. The woman was friendlier than her colleagues. Jean was glad to see her. The major did not want to deal with attitude today.

Jean waved at the woman and continued past the desk. Having spent most of her time in Mike's room since her return, Major Joyce knew exactly where to go. Twenty-five steps to the right, turn left, and forty steps until the bulletin board. Mike's room was on the left.

Today was a special day for her, but Jean did not feel any particular joy or sense of accomplishment. Although she'd kept her pilot's interface, the *Fallen Star* had been reassigned to another crew and other missions. It was flying high-ranking Federation government types through the systems. She missed the way it felt when she was intertwined within its systems. The loss of the enhanced sensory stimulation was like an old ache from a distant battle wound. But true to form, the Bureau of Intelligence and Insurgency was meeting their side of the bargain with her. Paul Temple, the BII's station chief in the Isa System was bringing the orders. Jean was to be promoted to lieutenant colonel and given a strike battalion command. She was getting the Fifth Wing Group, Second Marines. The unit had a good reputation, and Jean was looking forward to leading it. The actual change of command ceremony would be held later, on her home world of Baile Mac Cathain. Her parents would attend. Today was just the promotion. Yet, it was a hard day too.

Jean would be shipping out tomorrow. She dreaded leaving Mike still in the grips of the medical unit. He had several more minor surgeries and treatments left to go, and then there would be the beginning of a long and painful rehabilitation. The captain had lost his right arm completely when the energy weapon had grazed him and cooked the right side of his body. The doctors had been able to regrow some vital organs using his own progenitor cells and transplant them back into his body. They had used the same technique to regenerate skin tissue. But his arm had been too badly damaged, as had his right eye. Luckily, the navy had ponied up for advanced cybernetic replacements from Syrch Corp. The cybernetic implants had required some delicate surgeries, but most of that was behind him now.

Jean stepped through the doorway into Mike's room, where a small group of people had gathered. She had arrived purposefully late to avoid having to spend time chitchatting with any of them. Paul Temple and Akemi Murakami stood on either side of the bed where Captain Estury held court. Admiral Alke Baumhauer and two members of her staff were there as well. The room was a bit crowded, but Jean didn't mind.

"Major Estury," Paul's anchorman-like voice cut through the conversation, and the entire group grew silent and turned to look at Jean.

"Sir," the major acknowledged. "Admiral. Akemi," she said the technician's name warmly. The two had become fast friends. "Hi, Mike."

Mike smiled warmly, his entire face alive and buoyant. "Jean," he said, "you look great."

Major Joyce tugged at the front of her battledress uniform, straightening the fabric. "Thanks." Jean pushed her way through the little gathering and gave the captain a quick kiss. "How are you feeling?"

"Good," he said, returning her kiss and reaching out with his good hand to grasp hers. "It's your day, Jean."

Jean returned the smile. She did not let go of his hand.

"Well," Paul said, "should we get this ceremony moving?"

Admiral Baumhauer moved forward, and everyone shuffled around the bed. "It is nice to finally meet you, Major," the admiral said. "I've read your file. We have great expectations for you."

"Thank you, ma'am."

One of the admiral's aides handed the admiral a blue folder with the Federation Marines' symbol embossed upon the cover. "Attention to orders," the admiral read. "Be it known to all here who bear witness that Major Jean Joyce, being found worthy and having demonstrated personal courage and leadership in the Federation Marines, is hereby promoted to the rank of lieutenant colonel with all the responsibilities and authorities thereof. Her promotion is part of the continuum of leadership and faith that we who have gone before her now so imbue her to carry, leading and developing her subordinates, setting the standard in discipline and personal conduct. The promotion is representational of the high esteem the corps and the Federation hold for her past service to our great union. All subordinate ranks are hereby charged to carry out her lawful orders, and Lieutenant Colonel Joyce is likewise charged to follow the lawful orders of her superiors to the utmost of her ability. This promotion is effective immediately, given this day by my hand, General Alexander T. Robinson, Commander Federation Ground Forces."

Jean stood stock-still but did not release Mike's hand.

"Congratulations, Colonel Joyce," the admiral said as she pinned Jean's new rank onto the upper right pocket of Jean's uniform.

"Thank you, ma'am."

The small assemblage clapped and shook the colonel's hand. Akemi Murakami gave Jean a hug and squeezed Mike's arm.

"See you on the next jump," the admiral said before she and her aides left the room.

"You did a good job, Colonel," Paul Temple said as the group was breaking up.

"We didn't accomplish anything you sent us out to do," Jean replied.

"It all depends upon how you look at it," the BII station chief said in return. "You might not have saved your brother, Colonel, but you did prove the means to his redemption. He died a hero's death."

"Not much of a consolation," Jean retorted.

"No. Perhaps not for you. But for your parents? Maybe even for your brother …" The BII chief looked down at Captain Estury. "Get well," he offered.

Then he turned to Akemi, and the two looked at one another awkwardly. Jean knew that Akemi's recent adventure had forever put a wedge between the technician and Paul Temple. "Akemi," Paul's voice was apologetic. He reached out and gave the Asian woman a hug and then, without another word, departed the room.

Akemi turned to Jean. "I feel like a disease just gave me a hug," she said.

Jean laughed. Then she leaned forward and gave the woman a warm embrace.

"Are you really quitting the BII?"

Akemi looked down uncomfortably. "Yes. I have had enough duplicity and adventure in my life. I am looking forward to doing something else."

Jean nodded her understanding.

"And you, Colonel? How are you, really?"

"Better, Akemi. Better." Jean looked at Mike. "When Mike is better, we're going to get married."

"Really? That's so wonderful!" Akemi beamed at the two of them.

"And what about you? What will you do?" Jean asked.

"I'm not sure yet. I suppose, find a job."

Mike cleared his voice and lifted his head at Jean, encouraging her to say something.

"I," Jean began, "I might have an offer for you—if you don't mind."

"An offer? What type of offer?"

"It seems that Rafe started a little computer consulting company just before we picked him up in the Tianjin System. It's not much, but I'm told there's a steady stream of business. I'm not much of a businesswoman and know next to nothing about the computer consulting business. I thought maybe," Jean said a little uncertainly. She was not sure how Akemi would respond. The beautiful woman was still healing from the emotional scars left by Rafe's death. "Maybe you would run it for me? Give it a try?"

"Rafe started a company?" Akemi's voice was suddenly raw. She paused for a moment before continuing. "I would be honored, Colonel Joyce. Thank you. Thank you for everything."

The two women embraced again, and then the technician walked out of the room.

"And you, Mike. You're happy? You've lost so much. I'm afraid …"

"Hush." He stopped her and brushed his hand across her face. "I'm happier than I imagined I would be. Maybe it was time for me to give it all up anyway. This will give me a chance to do something new. I think I am fine with it all."

"And me?"

"You're the most wonderful thing in the universe."

The battle group entered the Siradia System. Weapons fire danced between the stars. The long anticipated invasion of the Consortium home world had begun. Federation warships bore a hole through the system's defenses and advanced against the Consortium's home world of Sala. Fleet transport ships moved into orbit as covering fire rained down at the Consortium's capital of Mahenjo-daro. Return fire flashed, and ships were hit and went down. Colonel Joyce gripped a handhold as her drop ship fell through the planet's atmosphere. Her staff stood around her, their weapons glistening in the red, tactical lighting as the marines made planet fall.

The crew chief called out, "Get ready!"

Colonel Joyce's staff tensed, along with the hundred men and women of Alpha Company, Fifth Wing Group, Second Marines.

"Okay, marines!" the Colonel yelled. "This is it! Move smartly and Godspeed!"

Jean heard the marines cheer. They new this was the start of the end.

The drop ship shuddered, and the forward bay opened, a ramp scrolling with a thud to the planet's surface. Beyond the door the whiz and clash of weapons fire twirled chaotically through the air.

"Go! Go! Go!" Jean's young captain yelled as the man stepped off the transport, leading his marines into battle.

Jean followed hotly behind, her tactical net alive as massed troops descended upon Mahenjo-daro. Her personal protective unit fanned out to her sides, while her staff and robotic Dog of War followed. All around the battle raged. Jean looked back and saw the Dog of War leap forward, its guns blazing. It rotated its head at Jean, and for a moment, Jean felt its electronic eyes lock onto hers. A shiver ran through the colonel's spine, as some animal intelligence seemed to study her from behind the robot's eyes. But then the Dog of War was off, loping ahead into the fray.

Jean gathered herself and took in the situation. The Consortium was fighting with its last breath. Their imminent defeat felt good.

Through the clangor of battle, Jean called to her marines. "Bring up the jump ships! Let the Dogs of War loose! Rain fire on them and kill them all! Kill them all!"

She had had enough of war. It was time for a final peace.

Epilogue

The probe framed into the Kururumany System. The blue-white star flooded the system with a soft and forgiving light. The conical probe ignited its engines and began a slow approach to the fourth planet, a large planet roughly the size of five earths and encircled by three moons. The planet, Nibiru, rotated peacefully just outside the habitable zone. A dust ring looped off the planet's largest moon, Gargantuan. The debris was already forming a planetary ring.

The probe slowed and dropped into orbit. Besides the streaming particles from the moon, likely caused by a cosmic collision, nothing else orbited the planet except its moons. Noctilucent clouds, thin strips that defused Kururumany's light, floated high in the planet's atmosphere as, below, more robust cumulus clouds drifted with the breeze. The probe registered two large snowstorms in the north and one on the southern pole. Yet rain fell near the equator, where a vast ocean churned, throwing thirty-foot sheets of spray onto the rocky shores of a great continent. The probe registered nearly 23 percent oxygen in the atmosphere. Its sensors also recognized nitrogen, ozone, and carbon dioxide, along with many other things in minor concentrations.

The planet was ripe for life. This was a curiosity.

The probe scanned deeply. Rivers meandered over plains of native grasses and twisted through forests of great trees, with their orange and purple leaves and mighty trunks. A huge herd of some lumbering animal moved slowly over the landscape as other, smaller animals intermingled. The probe located a flock of some type of bird, large and possibly predatory, circling high above the herd. Near the coast of the great continent, a cacophony of plant life thrived, insects hummed, and an occasional flicker through the canopy indicated the abundance of animal life too. Plants flowered. The ocean teemed with life. Great beasts and small plied its warm waters. But it was the mysterious structures that caught and held the probe's attention.

Large pyramids of some unknown metal rose at regular intervals along the equator. These structures were active, spewing forth oxygen-enriched air and heat that seemed to be generated within the heart of the planet. But there was something else, scattered here and there near the base of the structures.

High-definition cameras whirled and focused as the probe turned its attention to a small tendril of smoke that rose independently from the pyramids into the soft shades of the evening. It followed the smoke trail and found a small collection of crude structures huddled together near the mouth of a river, where the river emptied in a cascade from a grand waterfall into the salt ocean below. Lined along the great bluff, these buildings were mathematically aligned in four groups of rectangles.

A shape moved unknowingly into the probe's field of vision. The creature was tall and elegant, muscular with broad shoulders. It carried a spear. As if by instinct, the creature turned its gaze upward toward the evening sky. It had three eyes and a small snout. It tilted its head slightly with curiosity at something out of the probe's narrowed field of vision. Then it looked down and moved off toward one of the structures, where a smaller creature of the same ilk rushed out and clung to the other's legs. The larger creature reached down and pulled the child into its arms and, without a look backward, entered the structure and left the coming night behind.

The probe observed and cataloged. The three moons floated like ancient benefactors, and time on the planet moved to the rhythm of life.

Afterword

The Dryden Experiment is a futuristic multiverse conceived by John Berg and Joel Stottlemire. Stymied from independently publishing stories that take place in the most popular science-fiction multiverses, and conceiving of a multiverse where fan art forms the backbone, the two writers set off on an adventure to bring the Dryden Experiment to life. Through them, I found voice for several stories that had been kicking around in my head for quite a time. They encouraged me to dust out the cobwebs and put those stories into the context of the Dryden Experiment. The only limitation they set was that the stories had to conform to the technologies that were part of the formal concordance for the multiverse.

In 2012, John Berg posted a message talking about the Dryden Experiment. I investigated and was drawn into it. With Joel Stottlemire's encouragement, I wrote a series of Dryden Experiment stories. The last of those short stories was supposed to be *The Eclipsing of Sirus C*, an old, written scene that I dug out of a box.

The writing of this novel began in the early 1990s, while I was a young lieutenant serving in the Kansas Army National Guard Infantry. I was attending basic infantry officer school at Ft. Benning, Georgia. We had just spent a couple weeks doing platoon-level, live-fire exercises. I was standing on the upper landing outside my room in the bachelor officers' quarters when a female lieutenant stepped out into the dusky evening and stopped to watch the quiet night unfold. She looked at me. I looked at her. The exchange lasted about ten seconds. Then I went inside and started preparing my uniform for the next workday. But afterward, I sat down and hastily wrote the opening scene of this novel. My protagonist became a caricature of the female lieutenant I had just seen. The opening story remained in its initial form, collecting dust, until I began rooting around for one final short story for a Dryden Experiment collection (soon to be released).

I sat down and drafted a basic, eight-point outline, which I sent to Joel for his comments. He told me he thought it had the structure of a novel, not a short story. I told him I thought I could keep the length down and began writing it in earnest. Soon, Joel's words became prophetic as the story morphed. It took me another two years to finish the novel and a few months to get it published. I have quite enjoyed the adventure.

I am grateful for John's and Joel's encouragement and vision. I am also very thankful to you for purchasing the book. Thank you for spending a few hours roaming the Dryden Experiment multiverse with me. I hope you have enjoyed it and that you take the time to seek out additional volumes in this exciting multiverse.

Daniel B. Hunt
April 2015
Baku, Azerbaijan

CORPORATIONS

Terra Corp. One of the large three corporations, Terra Corp is the oldest and most powerful. Based in the Terra (or Earth) System, it is known for its terraforming, human augmentation, shipbuilding, and its science divisions.

Lin Corp. One of the big three corporations, Lin Corp specializes in human augmentation and shipbuilding.

Kuball Arms. Kuball Arms makes solid, general-purpose weapons, including crew-served weapons and artillery.

Laymay. Vehicles (cars and combat), airships, and spaceships are Laymay's specialties. (Laymay's spaceships are mostly of the transportation and bulk shipment variety, but the corporation has the Kiln Works, which make specialty and luxury ships as well.)

Hadrellie and Killitz (H&K). H&K is a high-end manufacturer of weapons and weapon systems.

Syrch. One of the large three corporations, Syrch is particularly known for its ships and its heavy mining activities.

Syndicate. Syndicate is a corporation that specializes in high-end computer interface devices.

Huritz StarCraft. Hurtiz StarCraft is a spacecraft-building corporation that makes high-end and specialty ships.

GOVERNMENTS

The Consortium. A seven-planet rebel group vying for independence from the Federation.

Consortium Worlds (Rebel Forces)

Maxim (Little Paradise). Maxim orbits Sirus C and is a naturally virulent world and where Major Joyce fights in the Battle of Edmund's Field and is injured.

Sala. The capital planet of the Consortium, Sala orbits Siradia, an F III Class (white-burning, normal giant a hundred times more luminous than Earth's sun and much more massive). The capital city of the Consortium, Mahenjo-daro, is located here.

The Federation. The Federal Empire wants out of Earth's control, and Earth is trying to keep it in the circle.

Federation Worlds (Jean's Forces)

Ta-Braun. Located in the Epsilon System, Ta-Braun's brutish little moon, Caspian One, holds a training station for the Federation Marines.

Baile Mac Cathain. Baile Mac Cathain is the home world of the Federation and also Major Jean Joyce's home world.

Baile Mac Cuithein. The sister world of Mac Cathain, Baile Mac Cuithein is also inhabited.

Luna Reach. A gas giant located in the Isa System, Luna Reach is home to William Bennet Station, where Major Joyce meets BII station chief Paul Temple.

LAWS OF SPACE AND TIME

The Law of Life. The universe tends to life. Where energy and form meet, life emerges.

The Law of Energy Consumption. Living things consume.

MILITARY UNITS

Omega Company. Jean's company during the Battle of Edmund's Field. Omega Company is part of the Eighth Wing Group and is stationed on the moon base of Caspian One, one of the moons of the planet Ta-Braun, located in the Epsilon System.

Fifth Wing Group, 2nd Marines. The battalion that LTC. Joyce leads at the end of the novel in its attack on the Consortium world of Sala.

ORGANIZATIONS

Bureau of Intelligence and Insurgency (BII). The intelligence apparatus of the Federation planets.

The Miscreant. A loosely associated group of criminal hackers who ply the Dark Web.

the Church of Chaos. A radical religious group that believes order and stability lead to corruption and degradation. Their prophet's mantra is, "A soul without denial is a soul in rapture."

Warders of Nibiru. A group of alien, self-aware and intelligent robots specially created by the extinct Makers as prison guards for the Decarabia. The last warder is the robot Calliphon.

PEOPLE

Akemi Murakami. A Japanese medical specialist in cybernetic computer interface, Akemi is extremely beautiful and intelligent. She works for the Bureau of Intelligence and Insurgency (BII).

Alke Baumhauer. A Federation Navy admiral.

Alexander T. Robinson. The senior commanding general for all Federation ground forces.

Calliphon. The last, humanoid robot Warder of Nibiru. It has been containing the Decarabia (plague-like nanobots) to the planet of Nibiru for eons. Calliphon is tall, lanky, and silver, with three camera eyes that provide excellent depth perception. It is dinged and damaged, and its gears whirl.

Colonel William Joyce. Major Joyce's father. Colonel William Joyce is a retired marine.

Danner Tomblin. An operator for the Federation's Bureau of Intelligence and Insurgency (BII), Tomblin is also a member of the Church of Chaos, which proclaims, "A soul without denial is a soul in rapture."

Decarabia: Nanobots that are self-aware. Created by the alien Makers, the Decarabia became a plague that wiped out most of the life in the universe. (This helps explain the lack of intelligent species in the Dryden Multiverse.)

Doc Stephens. A combat medic in Omega Company.

Draiger. A platoon leader in Omega Company.

Jean Joyce. An officer in the Federation Marines. She is rapidly promoted from captain to major and then from major to lieutenant colonel.

Kross. The support platoon leader in Omega Company, Kross is the senior lieutenant.

Makers. The long-dead, mysterious alien race that designed and unleashed the Decarabia. The Makers died at the hands of their creation.

Mike Estury. A flight instructor and the pilot chosen to pilot the *Fallen Star*, Estury has the rank of captain.

Paul Temple. The station chief for the Federation's Bureau of Intelligence and Insurgency (BII) in the Isa System, Temple offers Major Jean Joyce a mission to save her brother.

Raphael Joyce. Jean's older brother, Raphael is known as Rafe. Rafe joined the Federation Marines but then deserted, devastating his military family. Rafe, a.k.a. Henry Janyar, an insurance salesman, hid out on an asteroid in the Tianjin System, where he became adept at stealing other people's money by hacking their systems.

Smiley. A platoon leader in Omega Company.

PLACES

Edmund's Field. The location of the opening battle sequence on Maxim (Little Paradise).

Cave Dweller's Mountain. A prominent mountain that hems in Edmund's Field, located on Maxim (Little Paradise) in the Sirus C system.

the citadel. The prison built by the Makers on Nibiru in the Kururumany System to hold the Decarabia. The citadel is maintained by robot warders. At its core is a Heilim-3 reactor.

William Bennet Station. The Federation's station orbiting the gas giant Luna Reach in the Bhante System.

PLANETS AND SYSTEMS

Baile Mac Cathain. A Federation world and Major Joyce's home world.

Baile Mac Cuithein. The sister world of Baile Mac Cathain, Baile Mac Cuithein is also inhabited.

Epsilon System. The home system of the Federation Marine's Eighth Wing Group, Omega Company.

> **Caspian One.** The small, brutish moon orbiting Ta-Braun in the Epsilon System that is home to Omega Company.

Isa System. A Federation system.

Bhante System. A remote Federation system.

Luna Reach. The fourth planet in the Bhante System. Luna Reach is a gas giant and is the location of the Federation's William Bennet Station. It is a small, isolated outpost, where Major Joyce is stationed to learn how to fly spacecraft.

Siradia System. The home system of the Consortium. It has an F III Class, white giant sun a hundred times more luminous than Earth's sun. The capital city of the Consortium is located here, Mahenjo-daro.

Sirus C System. A Consortium system dominated by a large, orange star.

    Maxim. A Consortium world, earthlike, with a lesser atmosphere of oxygen that gives flora the bright colors of mountain meadows. Its nickname is Little Paradise.

Terra System. The home system where Earth is located. Its star is always referred to as "the Sun."

Tianjin System. A system outside of Federation and Consortium space. The asteroid field where Rafe Joyce has taken up residence is located in the Tianjin System.

Kururumany System. A system located on the edge of known space. The star is a blue-white dwarf that is six times as bright as Earth's sun.

    Nibiru. An icy world (superearth) in the Kururumany System. Nibiru has three moons—Alauda, Caleo, and Gargantuan. Gargantuan is the location of the Makers' moon base. Outside the habitable zone, Nibiru's mean temperature is minus 150 Celsius.

SLANG

birds. Airlift assets for military personnel.

box job. A low-skilled computer hacker normally held in disdain by professional hackers.

hai. Japanese word with the meaning of "agreement with" or used as a general acknowledgment of correctness.

junking in. The narcotic effect of linking directly to a computer system with its enhanced sensors and thinking capacity.

Stim. A type of genetically modified coffee. There are many varieties of varying strength.

two-day. Days are variables in the universe so this is the way of people communicate time using twenty-four standard Earth hours. A two-day would be forty-eight Earth hours.

SHIPS

Fallen Star. Major Joyce's courier class ship. The *Fallen Star* is a dual-purpose strike ship that can operate in space and within a planet's atmosphere. It has enhanced shields, forward and aft lasers, and a sublight torpedo tube.

TECHNOLOGY

AU. Astronomical units of measurement. One AU is approximately 93 million miles (150 million kilometers).

courier drones. The drones are the backbone for the communication network between systems. They frame in and out of the system to message buoys, where data is rapidly exchanged before the drones frame to the next system.

cranial mesh. A type of interface that grows inside a human brain and allows for unparalleled interface with computer systems. However, once installed, it cannot be removed. Cranial meshes are known for side effects.

Hadrellie and Killitz multipurpose FAMP-BH23. A high-impact battle helmet.

the Dark Web. An illegal web network that runs parallel to a systems communications web. Web systems ride light waves, but they are limited to the systems in which they operate. However, hackers use message drones to launch remote attacks against other systems' web services, setting up parallel, illegal web networks collectively called the Dark Web, where they conduct illicit business.

framing drive. The device that allows for interstellar travel and is driven by the insanity crystal. It is not possible to use a framing drive in proximity to large celestial objects that "bend" the fabric of space and make framing impossibly dangerous. This is known as framing effect.

frame shearing. When the insanity crystal is out of balance, it can cause shearing, or a slicing of objects within a certain range.

Helium-3 reactor. A power reactor that uses Helium-3. An increase in the flow of aneutronic fuel can destabilize such reactors.

juice. A drink containing body-modifying nanobots. Military personnel take juice to reduce wear and tear on their bodies and improve muscle function. The best juice comes from Lin Corp, whose high-end versions can do quite a bit to enhance the human body.

metasphere. The name given to the material that comprises the spherical boundaries of the universe. The Makers "proved" that it is elastic in nature and will eventually rebound into a singularity that will ignite in an endless cycle of universal rebirth.

nanobots. Nanometer-size robotic machines used for a variety of purposes.

Syndicate implant. The Syndicate made a no-model implant with a cranial mesh that was four generations ahead of anything on the market and cost half a million credits. The implant had terabytes of memory tied seamlessly into a quad, quantum-based processor that moved at the speed of light. Akemi Murakami, on behalf of the BII, offers one to Rafe Joyce to entice him into joining the mission. The implant is completely organic, and only two other people in the known universe had the technology. Once installed, it could not be removed.

the Core. An alien-made computer system that resides in the Makers' moon base on Gargantuan in the Kururumany System.

para-glass windows. Super strong carbon fiber-based windows used aboard space platforms and ships.

Peltier effect. Heating or cooling caused by an electric current flowing across the junction of two different conductors. As the current moves from one conductor to another, it transfers energy to one side, causing it to heat and the other to cool down.

WEAPONS AND GEAR

Dog of War. A robotic, dog-like war robot used by the Federation's Marines.

framing bomb. A bomb that uses the framing technology to tear an object apart by using frame shearing and physical movement.

Hadrellie and Killitz multipurpose FAMP-BH23. Hadrellie and Killitz make high-end battle equipment and weapons. This model is a fully armored multipurpose battle helmet, with refractive armor, temperature modulation, coms and tac, air filtration, and medical status. Its faceplate can dim and amplify vision, it has night and infrared vision settings, and it is radiation and wave weapon resistant.

Hinkler IV-Alpha. A computer interface of a midrange capacity. Rafe Joyce used one of these until offered the Syndicate implant.

H&K Flechette rifle. A weapon built by H&K, the Flechette rifle fires supersonic needles.

porter. An automated, low-level robot that is used to carry heavy equipment. A porter is a wheeled vehicle.

XM Flash biohazard environmental space suits. Rugged space suits designed for exploration of planets with alien life forms. They are designed for both extreme environments and rapid bio-decontamination, self-cleansing their exterior surfaces of biological threats. In addition, they use Peltier coils to conserve energy and provide both heat and cold as required. Terra Corp makes them exclusively.

Printed in the United States
By Bookmasters